She couldn't do what he asked...could she?

Scott was laughing at her again. "If you are determined to settle down in the suburbs one day, then you shouldn't object to having a bush pilot for a lover, just as a temporary measure," he said with a mischievous look in his eyes.

Marisa tried to match his lightness, although the subject was serious to her. "I don't see how that would work," she protested with a smile.

He stood and stretched lazily. Before she guessed his intentions, he pulled her close, kissing the tip of her nose and nibbling at the corners of her lips. At first she tried to push him away, but he didn't budge.

She could feel the strength of his hand pressing against the back of her neck and felt herself mold to the lean, male hardness of his body.

The protest died within her as a wellspring of warmth flowed through her veins, and she responded to his kisses with a depth of passion she had not realized she possessed.

She's in Brazil on a secret mission for her father...

A quiet, conservative teacher who's lived in one small Virginian town all her life, Marisa Elliott plunges into a desperate adventure when she meets Scott Dunbar a devilishly handsome pilot, who is apparently down on his luck. Marisa tells him she's searching for her Confederate ancestors who fled to Brazil during the Civil War. She persuades him to take her far into the jungles of the Amazon, but she doesn't tell him her relatives have offered to give back the bank money they absconded with so long ago—money her father wants her to bring home to clear the Elliott name.

He has an agenda all his own....

Once burned in a bad marriage, Scott Dunbar hates commitment of any kind. To him, love is a four-letter word. He wants Marisa, though he knows she's not the kind of girl to settle for a one-night stand. Or is she? He's hiding something, but then, so is she. He just can't figure out what. Is she really here to find her missing relatives? Or is her mission something much more sinister?

KUDOS for *Amazon Treasure*

Our two main characters, Marisa and Scott, are an unlikely match—a small-town, conservative schoolteacher and a rough and tumble, ex-pat pilot with a penchant for archeology and a thirst for danger—and for Marisa, of course. But our girl knows what she wants, or at least what she *doesn't* want, which is a one-night stand—no matter how sexy and tempting Scott is. He thinks that's a shame, and I tended to agree with him, though I can kind of see her point. Still, given a choice between a fling with a hunk and my virtue, I confess my virtue would probably lose. When the two bicker and she goes off on her own with just a native guide who doesn't want to be there, things really get interesting. The writing's good, the story's charming, and the plot's got enough surprises to keep you happily turning pages. So grab a cup of tea, put dibs on your favorite spot on the couch, sit back, and enjoy *Amazon Treasure*! – *Taylor, Reviewer*

Amazon Treasure by Pinkie Paranya is a sweet, contemporary romantic suspense. I'd call it a romantic action/adventure, but I'm not sure that's a legitimate genre. Still, when a woman goes off to Brazil seeking lost treasure, romantic suspense seems too mild a term. This novel has more of an Indiana Jones feeling to it than a normal romantic suspense. I especially liked the way the author described Brazil. Her detailed descriptions and vivid scene settings made me feel like I'd been there. As I've always wanted to go to Brazil, but have never had the chance, this was a treat. If you're in the mood for a sweet, intriguing romance, with plenty of action, but without all the sex and violence so common in novels today, *Amazon Treasure* is a good bet. – *Regan, Reviewer*

AMAZON TREASURE

By

PINKIE PARANYA

A BLACK OPAL BOOKS PUBLICATION

GENRE: Contemporary Romantic Suspense

AMAZON TREASURE
Copyright © 2006 as Treasure of the Amazon by Pinkie Paranya
All Rights Reserved
Cover Design by Black Opal Books
Copyright © 2011 All Rights Reserved
Print ISBN: 978-1937329-17-4

First Publication: OCTOBER 2011

Published by Black Opal Books **http://www.blackopalbooks.com**

CHAPTER 1

Marisa should have found her circumstances terrifying, but anger blinded her. The stolen money, the promised inheritance, her father's constant doubts as to her ability to do anything on her own—none of these should have compelled her to come here. Impatiently, she tapped her boot on the macadam of the Brazilian airport. Why was it so difficult to hire a private plane to take her into the jungle of Mato Grosso? Here she was in Brasilia, the capital city, and she might as well have been invisible.

She'd spoken to one pilot after another. Polished, wearing suits and ties, they looked like businessmen from any American city. Most spoke varying degrees of English but could have spoken in Portuguese for all that it mattered. They looked her over with admiring stares, taking inexcusable liberties with their dark, liquid eyes, and then promptly turned away when she asked them about Mato Grosso.

What was her stubbornness costing this time? Coming here, so far from her comfortable niche, wasn't the first time she had burned her bridges. Dabbing perspiration from her forehead, she remembered the cold, raw wind of winter pushing against her back as she left Virginia. Heat was better.

In the next hangar, Marisa spied a pair of broad shoulders connected to long, brown arms, leaning over scattered parts that could once have belonged to an airplane. She eyed the untidy pile of tools with distaste as she stepped over them, edging closer to the man.

"Excuse me. Do you speak English?" she asked.

The man turned slowly to face her. Marisa saw her own reflection in his rimless, aviator sunglasses. A tall, slender young woman, with honey-blonde hair escaping from its usual prim twist at the nape of her neck, wrinkled her nose at the image just as he removed the glasses. She was completely unprepared for the cool gray eyes fringed in dark lashes that returned her stare. The slight sprinkle of silver mixed with his almost-black hair gave him a certain dignity of appearance he probably didn't deserve. His lips parted in a wide grin, and white teeth contrasted against the honey-nut tan of his face.

"Yep, I speak English."

"Is this your employer's plane?" She pointed to a shiny new craft near the rear of the hangar.

He looked puzzled for a moment, as if he didn't understand her question and then down at his grease-stained hands and clothing. A dark blue T-shirt molded his chest, and his tanned legs protruded from cutoff jeans.

"You might say that."

It took him so long to answer she wanted to walk away. She felt bedraggled, grimy, discouraged, and plain tired. Her funds were too dangerously limited to let her stay in the city any length of time, waiting for someone to take her into the jungle.

"Is there any way I could speak to your boss?" She tried to match his easy nonchalance.

He scratched his chin reflectively, rasping the short, dark stubble, and further grating against her taut nerves.

His expression reflected some secret amusement he apparently did not plan to share with her.

"Why?"

"I don't see as it's any of your business." She struggled for composure. The oaf enjoyed her discomfort. Why let him get the better of the situation? Besides, he might be a pilot. He looked like a pilot.

"I need to get to Mato Grosso."

He leaned against the workbench and folded his arms across his chest. "How many in your party?"

"Only me."

"You? Alone? Forget it!"

"But why not? I'm prepared to pay. Within reason."

The grin returned for a brief second, softening the hard planes of his jaw, and then faded. "Why the Matos, of all places? You're a tourist, aren't you? Then go take a tour."

To avoid waiting for the next expression of sarcasm to come into his eyes, she looked down at her heeled boots and kicked a small stone with savage intensity. "No, I'm not a tourist. I didn't come down here to sightsee, if that's what you mean." She wasn't going to tell him about the treasure. The man was obviously an American adventurer, probably stranded here through lack of self-discipline and common sense, and not to be trusted. It was as if she stood in the middle of an old Humphrey Bogart movie.

"If your ladyship cares to sit, I'll get a couple of cold ones out of the fridge." He motioned her toward a scruffy-looking couch.

Marisa sat gingerly on the edge, expecting any moment that some loathsome creature would crawl onto her leg. She could abide snakes if they kept their distance, but she hated bugs of any kind.

"Now. Tell me all about it." He cocked a dark eyebrow at her, stretching out his long legs as if he had all the time in the world.

Maybe he had time, but she didn't. The pressure to get to the bottom of her family's mystery money and find out what happened to Sara had become like a boulder teetering just above her head.

CHAPTER 2

Marisa swallowed her pride along with the cool drink, and tugged her beige plaid skirt down, although it already reached the calves of her legs. This rude man seemed willing to listen to her story, and she was out of options.

"I've traveled from Elliott, Virginia. Elliott's a small town, you've probably never heard of it." She took a deep breath. "Couldn't I tell this to your employer to save time? You know, cut out the middleman?"

He shook his head. "Nope. All our projects have to clear through me first."

How she despised that macho smugness. Luckily she didn't run into it much in her own circle of friends. "My father lost the use of his legs in a car accident, which left him permanently confined to a wheelchair."

He waited, not interrupting.

"In short, since I'm sure your time is very valuable..." Marisa's voice barely concealed the mockery as she glanced at the large, sensible dial on her watch.

"Oh, hey, I have time." His jaunty wave and airy disregard for sarcasm annoyed her more than any retort he might have made.

"My father's dream, obsession actually, has been to write a book about our ancestors, those who left Virginia just after the Civil War started and came to Brazil." What he really wanted to do was clear the name of their infamous bank robber ancestor, but she wouldn't tell this stranger that. "Since my father couldn't come to Brazil himself, I volunteered to help him."

"Go on."

Sure, she'd wanted to get away from Thomas long enough to think over her future. Yet she hadn't wanted to leave the familiar niche of her life. A desire for adventure had never been an incentive to alter her comfortable lifestyle. At this moment she'd never felt so alone and vulnerable, and she realized belatedly how safe and secure she'd felt with her fiancé.

The pilot ran his fingers through thick, dark hair, his expression confused, as if sensing her pain. "Are you okay? You look pale all of a sudden."

She tried for a casual shrug. "Everything's fine. I guess I'm tired, that's all." It hurt to remember her last conversation with her father.

"You don't look much like an outdoors person," the man said. "That would be the very minimum requirement if I ever took a female into the Matos."

"I teach, or used to teach school in Elliott."

"No! I'd have never guessed it."

His mocking grin engaged her in spite of the jibe, but she decided to ignore it.

"You did say 'used to teach,' didn't you?"

Marisa didn't want to get into that sore subject, but the stranger waited for an answer and her habitual politeness kept her reply civil. "I taught learning-disabled children." It might help if she could get the subject out in the open with an outsider. A different perspective could be good. On the other hand, this man seemed very judgmental, and she'd had enough of that from her father. No, she couldn't tell this pilot about her failures.

"And?" he persisted.

She shrugged. "Too many complications, too many disappointments. I just wasn't good at it." Not to mention Thomas hated to see her so stressed.

"Ah, that won't wash. You have the look of a person who'd stop at nothing to achieve what she set out to do."

She lifted her chin higher. Was that supposed to be a compliment? "You don't know anything about me." On second thought, it wasn't helping to talk about leaving the school. Knowing she'd abandoned the children left an empty hole in her middle. It had been a hard decision, but Kenny's suicide had sealed it for her.

"I know enough. So what now?" He folded his arms across his chest.

Marisa raised her palms. "Who knows? I may start teaching again at the college. It's what my father wanted for me at first. Or work full time at the newspaper instead of only summers."

"You work for a newspaper?"

If she operated an atomic waste dump, he couldn't have looked more dubious.

"Yes. I have a friend who owns a small newspaper in town. I've just started in the want ads department." Why hadn't she said the word fiancé? Perhaps because she wasn't used to the word .It wasn't official, just that in Elliott everyone knew. An unusual caution made her refrain from explaining further how she hoped to earn a cover article for the Sunday supplement. A trip from Virginia to Brazil to search into the life of one's ancestor who ran off with bank funds during the Civil War should be a great human interest story.

The mocking eyebrow barely descended. "What's all this have to do with your ancestors?"

Was he reading her mind? That made her very uncomfortable. "I'm trying to explain. Three generations of grandparents ago—in the 'eighteen-sixties—that would make me a great-great-granddaughter, or something close." Sensing his attention waning—an instinctive knowledge that came with being a teacher, she supposed—she hurried on. "A group from Virginia gathered up a large family, none of them wanting to face the idea of fighting one another. They moved to Brazil about a year after the Civil War started in The States. They settled in the Mato Grosso area."

He studied her face, as if searching for a hint of deception. "I've been all over Brazil. I know about the Yellowhairs. I've heard of settlements in Santiago and Beleaguer and I think there is one at Manaus. Of course everyone knows about Americana, near Rio. But not Mato Grosso." His tone was adamant.

"Yellowhairs?"

He nodded. "That's what they call them here. They don't mix much with the locals. Most have held onto their English, even celebrate the Fourth of July and other American holidays. If there were any in the Matos, I doubt they'd even be civilized, much less speak English anymore."

"Oh, but they do! That's why I'm here. Sara is the matriarch in Mato Grosso, she's called a *Madrinha*. She's been corresponding with my father for ages."

"*Madrinha*? That's Godmother. Spanish is *madronas*. A very powerful title and not many use it. It's earned with age or deeds, I suppose."

"In her last letter she wrote that they had trouble but she didn't say what kind, and after that we never received any more letters. We're very concerned something has happened to her."

"That's another reason why you don't need to go. It could be anything. That's wild country."

"I've done my research too. American refugees did settle in some of those places you mentioned, but after the war. Our family left during the war and stayed separate in Mato Grosso."

"I heard rumors about a tribe of light-skinned people near that area," he conceded. "Some *garimpeiros* came back from the mines talking about them."

"*Garimpeiros?*"

"Yeah, gold miners. A gold mine is a *garimpo*. I never ran into any Yellowhairs near the Matos. If they exist, they keep to themselves and don't welcome outsiders. Most assuredly, they wouldn't welcome your prying. I don't suppose you know that the Matos is roughly twice the size of Texas. You talk like it's a town. It's not a town. It's an area."

Before she could gasp out a proper rebuttal, he spoke again.

"Do you know me?" A wary skepticism showed plainly on his rugged profile.

She knew her expression must have reflected confusion. "Should I? Are you a famous movie star hiding out here to escape autograph hounds?" She laughed at the bizarre image, but he was not amused.

"I have my reasons."

"Look. I arrived here two hours ago. I'm tired, hot and..." She almost said frightened, but she could not afford to let this stranger see her weakness.

"I apologize if I was rude, but——"

"Well you should. You come on like some CIA professional. Of course I don't know you."

He jiggled coins in his pocket and gazed at the floor for a moment before he spoke. When he looked up, he appeared a little chastened.

About time you lost some of your cool, Mr. Macho Man.

"I've had a nasty episode with a female barracuda, a reporter from one of those weekly rags. I'm not looking forward to another encounter. Although I must admit, you're much prettier and it might be worth the trouble."

"I fail to see how your meeting with a reporter concerns me. I told you I'm only in advertising. I work in the office." Really, the man was insufferable.

"I hope it doesn't concern you," he agreed, unruffled by her barely-controlled hostility. "I do a bit of amateur archaeology here and the Brazilian government has certain inflexible rules. One is, no publicity about my findings."

So? Who cares? Marisa thought the words, but worked to restrain her response. Her father always told her she was too quick to react, to judge. Deep down she knew he was probably right and that hurt. Sometimes she felt as brittle and taut as a thin piece of plastic, no longer able to bend, and ready to snap in two. She waited for him to continue.

He tilted his head to swig the cold drink. She watched the clean lines of his jaw as he swallowed. He could have been a cover model for a survivalist magazine. All he'd need to complete the image would be to put a holster loaded with a gun and bullets around his shoulder. Marisa had no experience with this type, so dominant, tough, and good-looking in a rugged sort of way. His blatant masculinity made her uncomfortable. She'd known Thomas since grade school, and he was as comfortable to be with—as if he were already family.

His eyes changed to a dark smoky color when he turned away from the light. "This reporter, or whatever she called herself, appeared under the guise of someone needing a lift to a remote area. Come to find out, she had researched me up and down, interviewed my friends and the people at the museum, and put together some shoddy, half-baked article. Ninety percent of it was in her imagination. The Brazilian government gave me holy hell and nearly kicked me out." He shook his head as if he still did not believe it. "Can you blame me for not trusting you?"

"I can't blame you for feeling as you do, but I've told you why I'm here. I don't know anything about your hobby nor do I want to."

Thomas hadn't wanted her to go, but as long as she was determined, he threw in an advance toward a future article or series. If she didn't find her relatives, or what was left of them, she'd have to bring back something and a story about a soldier of fortune hunting for artifacts in the jungle might be a good alternative. Still, even if this man never read a Virginia paper or found out she'd written an article about him, it wasn't ethical, since he'd objected so strenuously. Anyway, it was irrelevant because he'd plainly brushed her off.

Marisa stood and slipped on her shoulder bag. "Thanks for the drink. I saw a couple of hangars left to try, so I'd best be on my way. It'll soon be dark."

"Not so fast!" His shoulders blocked her exit and the view of the sun beyond the door.

She felt a surge of panic before bringing it under control. She couldn't identify the expression on his face.

"I didn't refuse to go, did I? But I didn't say I would either," he added. "In the first place, it's a dumb thing to do. Few men, let alone an unescorted white female, needs to roam through that jungle. You don't even speak our language."

"Our language? You aren't Brazilian."

He scowled, his brows crashing together. If he could have changed colors under his tan, she felt he would have flushed. She must have hit a nerve under his unflappable exterior.

"Damn it, I've been here long enough. It's my home. Anyway, you get the drift. It can't be done."

Just as she'd suspected. He couldn't go back to the States for some reason. "I have to find them. There are families in that area of the swamps, the same as here in Brasilia or in Rio or those other places in the Amazon that you spoke of. Roads go through there. What's the big deal?"

The grin he gave her did not quite make it to his eyes.

"Of course, families exist out there. Generations of survivors. Hardy men and women who've eked out an existence against all odds." His gaze moved away from her face to the wide-open door of the hangar and beyond. "In spite of disease, venomous snakes, insects of every variety, and hostile natives, plus the constant threat of some mercenary wandering by and raiding them, they stuck it out. But not in the Matos. I'd bet on it. That's the worst place of the lot."

"Thought you didn't know much about the Yellowhairs."

"I don't. Only what I hear and read in the archives."

"I still don't see—"

"What I'm trying to say as politely as possible, is that if these Yellowhairs are still in the Matos, the government probably relocated them by now, up near the Amazon, where most of the Indians live. You wouldn't last a day out there. I'm not about to take on that responsibility."

"Don't you think that might be up to your employer? I take it you're a pilot. Seems to me there's a lot of competition, with all those planes out on the runway. Your boss might not be so willing to turn away a Yankee dollar."

He tilted his head and laughed, in a way that ordinarily might have charmed her. "Yankee, did you say?

You sure as hell don't sound like any Yankee I ever heard."

"That was a figure of speech," she retorted.

She shrugged off the tiredness in her shoulders and straightened her back to her full five-feet-seven inches and tried to stare him down. It didn't work. She still had to bend her neck to look up at him.

"Okay. So you aren't even going to give my offer to your boss. Surely there is another pilot you could recommend? I'm going to the Mato Grosso if I have to backpack in there alone." She no longer bothered hiding her frustration.

He eyed her for a moment without speaking and shrugged, his voice tinged with obvious misgivings. "I think you'd do that. Sure, some pilots might offer to take you."

"Good!" she said. "Point me in their direction and I'll be out of your way in a jiffy."

"You have to be the most inflexible, uncompromising woman in the world! Maybe it's true. You do descend from the Yellowhairs. That's where your eyes came from, and you sure have the same pigheaded obstinacy. Some of these pilots have about as many scruples as you do patience. It would be like setting a lamb down in a lion's den. But on second thought..." His lips turned upward in a lopsided grin. "I wouldn't describe you as a lamb exactly. More like a baby wildcat. At any rate, you'd be no match for the likes of them."

Neither of them spoke for a moment. Only the soft "blip-blip" of the ceiling fans intruded on the silence. Marisa steadied herself against sharp disappointment, seeing the quiet speculation in his eyes. She wouldn't beg.

"I'm not going in that direction for another day or so. I'll decide by then. That is, I could talk to the boss about it. No promises, mind you," he hastened to add. "I have to fly in to pick up Juan. He helps me overhaul the planes and this baby's due for one soon." He pointed toward an older, solid-looking craft, nothing like the smaller shiny one over in the corner. "I might take you."

She couldn't quite bring herself to thank him. After all, he was condescending, and hadn't said for sure he'd take her, only that he'd talk to his boss. Her shoulders drooped a little in spite of her resolve not to show her anxiety.

This was not turning out at all as she and her father had expected.

CHAPTER 3

"Got a place to stay? By the way, I'm Scott Dunbar." He clicked his heels together and made a little bow. "At your service."

Marisa smiled, in spite of her worry. "My name is Marisa Elliott, and no, I don't have a place."

At his look of surprise, she bristled. "I planned to leave right away for Mato Grosso. I'll get a cab into the city and find a hotel room."

Scott shook his head in disbelief. "I can see you had this all planned very thoroughly." Before she could flare up in her own defense, he continued. "You won't find a closet unoccupied this week. Brasilia is the host to a championship futebol playoff. That's what you'd call soccer back in the States. You won't find a hotel room available at any price."

She sat back down, letting the weariness mesh with the jet lag, her mind a blank. Now what? No way could she return home now, tail between her legs like a whipped pup. Much of her and her father's savings had gone into this trip, and Thomas would be very smug and forgiving. Not a pleasing prospect.

"I can't just turn around and go back," she said.

If she didn't stay long enough to find Sara, nothing would change. Certainly not the ridiculous farce of the Founder's Day Picnic, the Bank Holiday as some wags called it, that always put her father away with a migraine for days before and after. The Picnic had been going on for since she could remember.

Her father had complained often over the years to the mayor, but the Founder's Day Picnic was too much fun for the citizens of Elliott. The mayor always mentioned the revenue the holiday brought the town too. Her family wasn't the only one with relatives who had left for Brazil, and it didn't bother them to make fun of the bank manager and hang him in effigy each year. Still, it disturbed her father so much she had become frightened for him at times.

"The Mato Grosso is near a protected area. That's one reason you won't get a rational pilot to take you there. The government's set aside that area for natives."

"Natives? As in Indians?"

He nodded. "*Txukahamei* and *Karaja* are two that come to mind. Definitely not friendly, and the government backs them up one hundred percent. Civilization has already pushed them about as far as they'll go."

"Are you telling me that my relatives live there too? Alongside these bloodthirsty Indians?"

He laughed, only it was a humorless sound. "Honey, by now your ancestors are the bloodthirsty Indians. Anyway, I wouldn't call them that. Not like you read about the Indians in The States in the days of the settlers. They don't make a game of it. They quietly steal up behind an enemy in the jungle and zap him with a blowgun, leaving him where he falls. That type. If your kinfolk are in that area, I suppose by now they've managed to work out some mutual agreement with the natives. Or they are no longer there. Likely that's the reason I've never heard of them in that particular region."

At her look of surprise, he went on. "I hope you don't think you can drop in on some misplaced Southerners who speak with a charming drawl like yours and who will be delighted to greet someone from home. The good citizens of Belem, Manaus or Americana would no doubt welcome you with open arms. If these Yellowhairs do exist, they won't speak English. They probably interbred among themselves or the natives and are wilder than the Indians."

She hadn't thought of that, nor did she believe him. "Impossible. My father has received sporadic letters from them ever since I was a child. At first they wrote in English and lately in Portuguese, but though we don't speak the language, we've studied enough to read it. Sara has been the only one to write for a long time and we felt she was in trouble."

"Did she put an address on the envelope? She must, if you write to her."

"Not exactly. I can show you the envelopes that have postmarks from different towns, and no, she never gave us an address. Yet recently her letters have come more often and she begged us to come here to help her."

"Help her? How?"

"I don't know!"

His questions irritated her, forcing her to find logic in an illogical situation. She wasn't about to tell him that Sara offered any American family member the treasure if someone came to help her. Just what a soldier of fortune like him needed to know.

He stood waiting, arms akimbo, as if hopeful she might come up with a plausible answer he would believe.

"The leader is Jacob Elliott, the same name as my father and his father and so on down to the first man who led the people to Brazil. They named our town Elliott, after them." Some people had wanted to change that, after the bank scandal.

"As Alice would say, this is getting curiouser and curiouser."

"Look. I'm not making this up. I've pictures of Sara's home. They sent my father rolls of undeveloped film before I was born. It's like a southern mansion, with white pillars." She rifled through the small case she carried, and extended a couple of photos.

He studied them and looked at her searchingly. "I think someone's pulling your leg. They can't have taken these in the Matos. If the mansion existed, I'd have heard of it. Probably mapped it."

She let that last part pass, not wanting to ask him questions to make her feel any more foolish than she already felt. It had been her secret opinion from the first that this was a wild goose chase. Still, her father had been confined to a wheelchair for so many years. Brazil was his only interest now and she wanted to help him.

"Okay." He held up his palms in a peace gesture. "Forget this for a while. Let's get practical. We have to find you a place to stay. I suppose you could stay at—at the boss' condo. I think he has an empty apartment."

She hesitated, suspicious when she heard him fumble his words, but what choice did she have? "I don't like to be under obligation to anyone, but my funds are limited," she hurried to add before he could change his mind.

He shrugged. "Don't give it a thought. My boss is, well, he could be in his eighties. If that puts your mind at ease." He winked, and this time the grin looked real. His eyes crinkled at the corners, as if he smiled a lot. The sharpness of his cheekbones and lean jawline lost some of their uncompromising spareness when he smiled.

He excused himself and came back a few minutes later, damp hair combed back from his forehead and most of the signs of his mechanical work cleaned away.

If only she could do the same. She longed for a dash of lipstick and a chance to redo the hair that had nearly escaped from its confinement. A streak of stubbornness made her refuse to ask to use the washroom. He might assume she'd primped for him and his ego appeared healthy enough as it was.

"Would you like to splash some water on your face? You look hot and tired."

Very disconcerting, how he seemed to hone in on her thoughts. "No, I'm okay. Mind over matter or at least I try to think of it that way."

He motioned her outside to a low-slung white car.

"Nice. Is this a Ferrari?"

"Nope. Manufactured here in Brazil. Runs on alcohol. Almost sixty percent of the cars here use alcohol."

"I should think that would be more expensive than gas."

"No, the fuel is made from sugar cane. The government subsidizes farmers who want to grow sugar cane for alcohol." He lowered the top of the convertible while she slid in and rubbed her hands across the elegant deep-red upholstery.

"This car's yours?"

He nodded. "Yep. Pilots make out pretty well in these parts."

He probably hadn't bothered saving a nickel, either.

As if he'd guessed her thoughts, he said, "You only go around once. I expect to enjoy myself." He laughed at her shocked look. "You said you taught school. From the look on your face, you must still think like a teacher."

She should reprimand him for making such a sweeping generalization, but he'd probably only laugh at her. They zipped along with the wind whipping through her hair, until she finally gave up holding it in place and removed all the pins.

"Mmm. Much better," Scott said.

From time to time he slowed and pointed out places of interest. "It's hard to believe that all this was only a flat, red-earthed plain in the 'fifties. They built a city out of nowhere and nothing. Only a couple of ranchers knew anything about this area back then."

"Why build the capital here, of all places?"

"To take some of the population away from the coast. Everyone crowded into Rio and Sao Paulo. At first only about ten thousand federal employees lived here, totally isolated. Gradually the city began to take on a life of its own. Later the city fathers fought to keep the population below a quarter of a million. They didn't want crowds and slums like in Rio."

"This is one of the cleanest cities I've ever seen," she said. "It sort of reminds me of an elaborate model out of someone's imagination, not a real flesh-and-blood city. You don't see any skyscrapers."

"I know. It seemed that way to me too at first. The planning and foresight still amazes me. As for the buildings, the Brazilians call skyscrapers *brise-soleils*. That translates to sunbreakers. Sao Paulo and Rio have plenty of tall buildings, but the city fathers didn't want any here. Another thing, Brasilia rarely has traffic accidents. The streets don't cross each other, because the engineers divided them all or made them one ways."

Marisa watched him from behind her sunglasses, hoping he couldn't tell how intently she studied him. She admired how he handled the fast-moving car with easy grace. Thomas owned a silver Mercedes and never went a mile over any speed limit. Her father had sold their car after his accident and neither of them had thought of driving since. Everything back home was within walking distance. Not driving hadn't been a hardship. "You sound as if you've been here a long time."

He slanted a look at her. "This isn't an interview, is it?" His voice was half-serious and half-teasing.

She smiled back at him. "Nope. Curious is all."

He relaxed his shoulders and adjusted the rear view mirror a fraction. "I came here about ten years ago. I read about work the government had done in the 'seventies called Radam." At her questioning look, he continued. "That was a project like something out of science fiction. Way ahead of its time. Pilots mapped all Brazil by radar from planes." He concentrated a moment to swerve around a slow-moving vehicle and return to his lane.

"I've never heard of it."

"Not many people have. Radam was a brilliant idea, starting out as a huge government operation and strictly covert. The planes only flew at night from hidden jungle airstrips." He laughed. "Of course nothing is secret in this country for long and when enough gossip leaked to confuse the populace into thinking flying saucers had descended on Brazil, the government brought the project into the open. That intrigued me so I had to come here and check it out for myself. They still had work to do so I hired on as a helicopter pilot. Had a little crop dusting experience which was just what they needed."

"You flew crop dusters?" Marisa tried to picture him walking the streets of Elliott, Virginia and put her hand across her mouth to still the wild giggle that threatened to erupt. She always got silly when she was tired.

"Didn't do it for long. The high insurance rates told me something, but I wanted to try it out. It was a challenge. I also did wing-walking and parachute drops at the local airport back home for festivals. Truth is, I saw it as a way to irritate my family. My brother, sister, and I, we come from old conservative winery stock."

"You're the black sheep." It figured. "Do you go back to visit them often?"

"No. We lived in Northern California. The family still does. I was supposed to take up where my grandfather and father left off in the winery, but I didn't want that. I got in as far as the crop dusting and figured agriculture wasn't my line. It did help though, in landscaping. I enjoy that."

"Don't you miss your family? Don't they miss you?"

She noticed a slight tightening of the tanned hands on the wheel. "Family ties aren't that important as I see it. I miss mom and Alice, my sis, but the old man, he's a different story. I never could please him."

Marisa knew how that felt. Her father was a dear, but she couldn't please him either. The only time she'd made him happy was when she got her degree in teaching, and then she messed up by going into special education instead of joining him in that musty old college as he'd wanted her to. He seemed pleased about her and Thomas, although they'd never talked about it. "Family is important, or should be. In Virginia if you don't have family you don't belong anywhere." As an only child raised by a remote father, she'd clung to the idea of family.

"My younger brother inherited the family business, and I guess he loves it. I'm happy here," Scott added.

How bizarre. She'd never met anyone from California before. Was he telling the truth or making up a rambling, odd story in case she did turn out to be a reporter?

"So you stayed here to be a pilot." Somehow it didn't sound right, even for an adventurer.

"You mean is there more in my future than flying?" He shrugged. "In Elliott that's probably a logical question. I guess I want to make a little money flying, and then relax with my archaeology pursuits. Is that so hard to understand? Where did I go wrong?" He hit the palm of his hand against his forehead in mock despair.

She had to laugh. "Okay, so I'm prying and it is rude of me. It's just that—"

"They don't have eccentrics like me in Virginia? Do the words wastrel and ne'er-do-well still get bandied about there? Surely all the men you know aren't insurance salesmen or college professors," he teased.

"Of course not. But most everyone your age," she judged him to be in his thirties, "all have homes of their own and families by this time."

"How about the women?" he drawled. "I've a hunch you still live at home. Sounds real exciting,"

"Exciting?" She tried her father's most expressive supercilious look on him. He wasn't the least intimidated. How had he guessed she lived at home? He had her on the defensive now. "Yes, I live at home. It's convenient for both my father and me. My mother died when I was born, and he's been my only family. I owe him a lot and he needs me now."

He'd been doing fine until he couldn't commit to Janice, their widowed neighbor who was crazy about him, but Janice had finally given up. *At least, I'm afraid she has, and who could blame her.*

"He sent you off on this crazy chase?"

"No, of course not. He didn't want me to come," she fibbed. "But when Sara quit writing after sending him a will of sorts, he became worried."

"A will?"

Had she said too much? Marisa stuck out her chin. Her father would have recognized that stubborn look. It sounded as if this man didn't believe a word she was saying. What a waste of time. "Yes, a will. She left our family the house, and other things. Said only a few remained of the family and none of them wanted the house and land."

"Why in the world would you want it?"

"We don't! We just need to know what happened to Sara. My father and I became very worried when she suddenly stopped writing."

"I can see that, I guess. Yet somehow, this strikes me as some kind of elaborate hoax played on you and your father."

Her lips closed over a retort and then she couldn't stop herself. "What could anyone possibly have to gain by playing such a joke?"

"Oh, I don't know. Maybe they plan to hold an American cousin for ransom."

She stared at him to see if he was serious, but it didn't seem so. What didn't ring true with him, her story or the relatives from Brazil? She wasn't sure which he meant. Maybe both. He was the most suspicious person she'd ever met.

They continued in silence for a few miles until he spoke again.

"So it's all wrapped up for you with a tidy Sir Galahad back home when you decide to marry, I'll bet."

His grin didn't help stop the flush she felt ride up her face from her neck.

"Maybe so," she hedged. "I do have a beau..." The moment she said the word she felt about ten years old, but he didn't laugh. "Thomas is a very successful businessman in Elliott."

"Are you going to marry him?" The question seemed tossed off but at least he appeared to be taking her seriously all of a sudden.

"Maybe."

"Maybe? You're either in love or you're not. It's quite simple, actually."

"You might suppose so. We've known each other since grade school. Everyone in Elliot probably assumes..."

He pulled down his sunglasses for a second to peer over them at her. "Everyone in Elliott? Are they all marrying him?"

"Don't be silly. But in a small town, it's a factor." Now that she spoke about it so openly to a stranger, she realized that both Thomas and her father hadn't wanted her to stress out over her teaching career, yet they overwhelmed her with their views of how her future should be laid out. She'd never really thought of it that way before.

"What did you say your father teaches?" He changed the subject abruptly.

"I don't know as I did say. Ancient History."

"Well, if you don't want to talk about it—"

She laughed. "No, I mean he teaches ancient history."

"He didn't approve of what you teach." It was a statement, not a question.

She cleared her throat, uncomfortable at his insight. "No, as a matter of fact, he didn't. I suppose he had visions of us growing old together, playing chess and entertaining a group of fellow professors every Friday night with dinner and brilliant conversation."

"And Thomas, how does he fit in with this plan?"

Marisa sat back in the cushiony luxury of the car seat and thought about it. "He's just always been there. That notion of his would have had to change anyway. My father has a friend, Janice. She's very good for him, but he's too foolish to see it. If she waits long enough, and if I'm not there at his beck and call, he might recognize all her qualities. Then he and Janice could play chess in the evenings and entertain college professors."

"Hmm. That seems a reasonable assumption. I'm curious, why did you rebel and go your own way with teaching?"

She sighed. "First time I ever did such a thing. It's hard to explain, but I wanted to be useful."

"You don't have to go into detail if you'd rather not, but you said you weren't going to teach anymore," he reminded her.

"I don't suppose you've heard of burnout over here."

"You quit to do something easier?"

She considered this an impertinent question. Or was he uncomfortably close to the truth? Marisa still thought like a schoolteacher, so how could she blame him for reading her so easily? "No, it was more than that. I'll tell you sometime if I stay here long enough."

"Fine. That's a promise. Here we are," he said, parking in what must have been his special place. The whole parking lot next to the building was full with the exception of this one place under an awning.

A lush, landscaped lawn surrounded the Spanish-modern style apartment complex. She longed to stay inside the safety of the car as a feeling of impending disaster struck her. Here she was going home with a stranger, in a foreign land a long way from home, getting ready to look for a far distant relative who had mysteriously evaporated—as far as letters went.

Marisa had never thought of herself as a daring, adventurous person. She didn't know a soul in Elliott who fitted that description.

Returning to admit defeat and the squandering of their savings was not an agreeable alternative to consider. Just another disappointment for her father.

"Here we are," she echoed.

But where was she?

CHAPTER 4

Scott walked around to open her car door. He grinned at the little flicker of surprise in Marisa's eyes. "I don't suppose they open doors in the States anymore. Old fashioned, probably."

"It might be considered a little dated, but pleasing." In his tee shirt and grease-stained Levi's, she thought he looked out of place in the immaculate surroundings, but he seemed quite at home. The apartment complex was so different from the stark, utilitarian buildings of downtown Brasilia.

He looked at her, as if expecting a response about the landscaping or the apartments.

"The gardening is magnificent, your workers must be very talented," she said.

He appeared pleased. "I laid it out and designed most of it myself. It's the other hobby of mine when I'm not flying. It's relaxing, working with the soil and plants. Of course this tropical climate helps. I'm surprised every morning when I wake up to see the street lights haven't sprouted roots or branches." He scanned her face, his expression showing concern. "You're tired. Are you too bushed for me to show you around?"

"No, I'll be fine. I'd like to see everything."

They walked through a cool, tile-enclosed hallway leading from the front of the building to the center. Scott threw open the wrought-iron gateway with a flourish.

She caught her breath. The scene spreading out in front of her resembled a miniature jungle. Dense green plants grew all around the spacious courtyard. Exotic, colorful orchids clung to every tree, interspersed with brightly-hued birds flitting about or perched on branches. She looked up to see daylight pour down through the octagonal opening in the roof. It took a careful scrutiny to locate the nearly invisible net covering the top of the opening, keeping the birds inside.

People wandered around everywhere, singly, as couples, a crowd of them lingered by the pool, yet the profuse vegetation absorbed the sounds, and left only a soft buzzing of subdued conversation. Most of the men and women called to Scott or waved when they passed by.

"We designed it so that every apartment has its own balcony overlooking the courtyard."

Marisa closed her eyes and imagined the heady scents of the flowers and humid earth wafting gently up into the rooms. "How perfect! It's like being encapsulated in the micro world of a rainforest." Confused thoughts about Scott swirled through her head. She had labeled him a reckless adventurer without a care in the world, probably spending his money as fast as he earned it. A rough-neck, free-flying pilot lacking a grain of sensitivity. That had been her first impression, but now she wasn't sure if, as usual, she had judged too hastily.

He grinned down at her, obviously pleased at her surprised delight.

"Ah, Scotty! I wondered what happened to you. You naughty man. We had a luncheon date, remember?" A tall, slender woman emerged from the shadows and with calculated familiarity, laid an elegant hand on his arm. Her shiny black hair was styled in a graceful French twist and her skin looked the color of creamed honey, as if she lived outside in the sun. Yet that fabulous skin probably never saw a freckle, Marisa thought with a stab of envy. She tried in vain to pat down her flyaway locks that curled of their own volition in the humidity.

"This is Elaina. We're kind of partners in this enterprise," Scott said. . "She's the interior decorator. Elaina, meet Marisa Elliott."

"Partner?" Marisa asked.

He looked uncomfortable for an instant, then his eyes crinkled to create the unique grin she found fascinating. "We formed a partnership to decorate this condo for the, ah, boss, and thought we might go on to decorate and landscape other places in Brasilia. When we find the time." He turned toward Elaina. "By the way, I did not have a luncheon date with you. We invited the soccer team to the yacht club, if you remember."

Marisa put out her hand toward Elaina. The woman hesitated a moment before taking her proffered hand as if she'd been offered a dead fish. Then the three of them walked together through the gardens.

"My, such a charming accent," Elaina said, turning to look at Marisa.

"I was going to say the same about yours," Marisa returned sweetly.

"Miss Elliott is staying in the empty apartment a few days," Scott said.

Elaina's finely plucked brows rose in question. "Oh? But I assumed you were saving that for some of your buddies from Rio and Sao Paulo."

Marisa looked at Scott in time to catch the quick interchange between the two, the shake of his head and frown. It was the first time she had seen him appear so intimidating.

"Mind excusing us for a second?" He led Elaina aside. The two spoke in whispers as if in disagreement, and then the woman backed down, looking apologetic. With him standing so close to Elaina, Marisa could see how tall Scott was. Every bit of six feet and four inches, she decided.

Her father was tall, with legs that used to look like stilts to her when she was a kid. It had been so long since he had walked, she'd nearly forgotten that. She missed him and wondered if he missed her, too. He'd never say so, that would be an admission of weakness.

Marisa brought her attention back to the present when the two returned. Elaina managed a frosty smile while Marisa felt her own lips form a stiff one in return. From the first moment Elaina slithered onto the scene, Marisa did not like the self-assured sleekness of the woman.

She tried to be generous, having heard so often from her father about her glaring fault of prejudging people. Perhaps if she hadn't arrived so grimy and windblown, she wouldn't have a chip on her shoulder.

If only she could quietly disappear.

"I'm going to show Miss Elliott—" Scott turned to her. "Is it okay if I call you Marisa?" At her nod, he finished his sentence. "To her apartment. Would you like to come along?"

"Of course, Scotty. I would not miss it for the world." Elaina drawled the words out slowly, mocking Marisa's faint southern accent. "I would love to see what a, oh my, foreigner is such an ugly word, what a stranger might think of my decorating skills."

Marisa thoroughly enjoyed the ride in the glass elevator in spite of feeling a little claustrophobic standing between Scott and Elaina. As they rose slowly, she looked down upon the courtyard's lush beauty. A gracefully formed swimming pool lay like a turquoise jewel behind the thickest growth of plants. No wonder he could get away with almost anything with his boss. This man knew his landscaping.

"Well, what do you think of it?"

"It's pretty extravagant by my standards," Marisa admitted, "but it is beautifully done." In spite of the luxurious flamboyance, the landscaping and architecture had stayed within control. She recognized that immediately.

"How droll. Is it not cozy that we are all on the same floor?" Elaina barely hid her waspish humor behind a veneer of civilized politeness when they stepped out of the elevator.

Neither Scott nor Marisa spoke as they walked down the long, cool, terrazzo hallway, while Elaina spoke non-stop about people and places which left Marisa out completely.

What was she getting involved in? How could she put her faith in this brash, wild bush pilot with a very possessive partner? She only had his word that his boss would not kick her out tomorrow, or even tonight, and still no promise of getting to Mato Grosso.

By now her father's obsession had nearly become hers. She had to find Sara and her followers. It wasn't only the promised fortune that her father wanted to return to the bank to clear the Elliott name. But there was the teaching, a dead end, no-win profession that she had to get away from.

A good story might make Thomas see that she needed a new career. He had first put her in advertising and then lately offered her a start as a "Dear Abby" columnist, probably hoping to lure her away from teaching. She'd rather bring in a great story so she could be taken seriously—*if* she decided to stay with the paper. A sigh escaped and she glanced up in time to see Scott look at her with concern.

"She's tired." His voice cut rudely across Elaina's brittle patter. "Why don't you turn in now? If you want to call your father, let him know you arrived safely, the long distance operators all speak English. The safest bet to be sure of your message, though, is a fax."

"Thanks, that's considerate of you to mention calling my father." What had gotten into her? She really must be tired. For the first time since she could remember, consideration for her father hadn't come first in her thoughts. Of course he'd want to know she arrived safely. And Thomas. That thought came belatedly.

"Why don't you join us at the opening soccer game later tonight? You should be rested by then," he said.

To give Elaina credit, the woman attempted to smile graciously, although Marisa waited any minute to see her face crack from the strain. "Thanks, but if it's all the same to you, I'd rather soak my tired body in a tub for an hour. Or perhaps the pool." The relief in Elaina's expression was hard to ignore.

Scott shrugged. "Another time, then. You can't leave Brazilia without seeing at least one game. It's a thrill you'll never get anywhere else." He touched Elaina briefly on the shoulder. "Mind showing Marisa to her apartment? I just remembered something I was supposed to do hours ago."

"But of course, I wouldn't mind. I'll see you later for the soccer game then."

Scott turned and walked away, his boot heels clicking on the tile.

The women walked down the long hall, not speaking. Elaina pushed open a door at the end, motioning for Marisa to follow. "Here it is," she offered ungraciously.

Marisa felt comfortable as soon as she entered. The rooms were decorated in complementary colors of orange, beige and dark cocoa. The carpet felt ankle deep. Thick swags of gauzy material such as she had never seen before clotted in front of the wide doorway leading to the private balcony.

Back in Virginia architects would have used a more prosaic sliding screen door. But then they probably wouldn't have designed a balcony to overlook a jungle in the first place. "Very nice." An understatement if ever there was one. "I suppose Scott had a hand in decorating the apartments too?" For some reason, she wanted to hear his name again. "It appears he can do almost anything he sets his mind to."

She smiled to think of how quickly Scott and her father would have bumped heads. For the first time it came to her that her father only tolerated self-assurance in himself, seldom in others.

Elaina shook her head emphatically. "No. Scotty stays with the landscaping. He trusts my ability to enhance what he has done. Of course, he has definite ideas."

It made Marisa want to grit her teeth every time Elaina pronounced "Scotty" with such familiarity, drawing her teeth and tongue lovingly across the double t's. He didn't seem a man to suffer a nickname such as Scotty. Perhaps Elaina wished to show a claim, a privilege between old friends. Yet Scott had made it clear, even in front of Elaina, that they were partners. What did it matter? She would go home soon anyway.

"That is how we met. I am the finest interior decorator in Brasilia, perhaps in all of Brazil," Elaina lifted her chin proudly. "My first patron took me to Paris and I studied with the masters."

"What you've accomplish is splendid. Where does the owner live?" He probably had a floor all to himself, a penthouse.

Elaina gave her an odd, unfathomable look before she answered. "La! He has his own suite of rooms, far from the peasants. He is a man of many faces and personalities," she said mysteriously. "He does not like to be, as you Americans say, pinned down. Scott tells me you will be leaving in a few days, so you need not worry your sweet little head about him."

They wandered through the pristine kitchen, decorated in stark white with black appliances, and stood for a time on the balcony overlooking the scene below. Marisa wondered how close Scott and the elegant Elaina were. The depth of her curiosity surprised her.

The air breezed into the apartment from the courtyard below with a delicate, flowery scent. Did Scott plan and choose each fragrant plant so that they would balance and not overpower? What an unconventionally attractive man this Scott Dunbar was, like no one she'd ever met in her life.

No sooner had Elaina slipped out the door, closing it behind her, then Marisa kicked off her shoes and lay on the bed, falling instantly asleep with thoughts of her father, Thomas, the treasure, the children she'd taught, and Scott, all mixed together.

CHAPTER 5

Marisa slept through the late afternoon and the night, awakening with an unusual excitement bubbling inside her for what the new day might bring. She sat on the edge of the queen size bed and speculated on how long it had been since she'd felt that way about a new day. Perhaps never. Security and comfort had long ruled her life. This unexpected observation troubled her.

She made her way into the bathroom. Later, just when the longing for a cup of coffee became unbearable, someone knocked. She tightened the tie on her short robe and opened the door a crack.

"Morning." Scott entered the room carrying a tray with a pot of fragrant steaming coffee, sweet rolls, and croissants.

Her favorite breakfast. How did he know?

"You decent?" He gave her a mock leer.

She laughed and hesitated. "Not really, but..."

Lucky to have showered, combed her hair and brushed her teeth at least. She looked down at her untanned leg showing beneath the robe. How foolish. Bodies out by the swimming pool showed more than that. She wasn't used to having a strange man invade her early morning privacy though.

Marisa knew he'd noticed that she didn't close the door completely behind him.

"Afraid of me?" he taunted. He headed toward the balcony and set the tray on the small marble-topped table. They sat across from one another, sipping the brew and watching the birds flying below.

"I've never had coffee this way, half cream, half coffee, and half sugar. It's good but probably has a thousand calories."

He laughed. "I can tell you aren't a mathematician."

She waved a hand holding a croissant. "You know what I mean."

"Are you always so practical? It seems like calories are the least of your worries. For one thing, you could use a few more pounds to round you out. Brazilians like their women soft and huggable."

"I won't be here long enough to worry about what Brazilians like."

"Maybe not. You probably burn up calories by the bushel being so contrary." His grin took the sting from his words.

Marisa blushed, intercepting his frank look of appraisal. It brought back the shortness of her robe and she held the fabric together over her breasts until she noticed his amusement. She dropped her hand and took another bite of the crisp, crusty roll.

"Is this how you usually look early in the morning?" He asked.

Was he laughing at her? Fresh from the shower, she knew how she looked. Her face was shiny bright, without a touch of makeup or lipstick. Her hair curled around her face with wispy little tendrils as it always did when it was damp and fluffed around her shoulders. She hated her lack of control over her hair. It had always been that way, as if some part of her wanted to escape restrictions. She should have tied it back into the usual composed style. Was he comparing her with the sultry Elaina?

"Your eyes are the color of this coffee," he said, lifting the cup in a mocking tribute. "You don't see many blondes with amber eyes."

She didn't know how to answer. No one had ever commented on her eyes but her father. "My father thinks they're outrageous. No one in our family ever had anything but blue eyes." She squirmed, not liking the intimacy that suddenly filled the room. "Won't your friend mind you taking breakfast in my room?"

He shrugged, his irritation obvious. "No one owns me. Elaina and I go back a long way. She helped me get a start here. We enjoy each other's company, but we never made the mistake of taking our friendship too seriously. Elaina set the rules at the beginning and I agreed."

Marisa regarded him over her coffee cup. She would be willing to bet her last dollar that although Elaina once might have set the rules, she had since changed her mind. Or maybe she had used that gambit to interest him, knowing that men like Scott seldom made commitments. In spite of his cavalier impudence, she had to admit he was a charmer.

He probably drank to excess, caroused each night with his immature soccer buddies and spent every cent living from payday to payday. Why would he have to be careful, living in the lap of luxury as he was? She thought of the professors and earnest young students she and her father associated with and Thomas and his business acquaintances. No, she had never met anyone like Scott Dunbar before.

"A penny for your thoughts."

Marisa felt a flush of embarrassment, as if he could read her mind. "Oh, I was curious about what you do when you aren't flying."

He grinned. "I mentioned I'm into digging. It's always been an interest of mine. I did it before in a smaller way in the States. I—" He broke off as if he didn't want to enlarge on what he'd been saying.

"Please. Don't say anything you'll regret. I could be a spy, like a foreign agent," she said.

He probably shouldn't trust her too much. The material for an excellent article that might launch her new career lay right in front of her nose. He certainly lived a splendid life style for someone who didn't seem to care about steady employment. Maybe he was taking a kick-back on the artifacts he found. That was enough justification for doing an article about him.

He must have sensed a change in her or noticed something in her eyes. He scraped back his chair, towering above her.

She stood up in haste, not liking the sensation of his overpowering persona.

"So you did read about my find in Newsmonth, didn't you?" he accused. "You aren't looking for any long-lost relatives. That story is a lot of bull. I could spot the lie all over your pretty little face."

"Of all the colossal nerve! I don't have the slightest idea of what you're babbling about." It was eerie. How did the man tune into her thoughts?

"Go ahead, play the innocent. If you know anything at all about my story, you know the government has valid reasons for not wanting publicity on anthropology digs. The natives have been pushed back into the jungles as it is. No sooner do they begin to adjust, then someone discovers a mine, or a new road needs building or it's a good site for a hydroelectric plant. The government moves the natives again, to another so-called inaccessible location. To top it off there are the greedy treasure hunters, but what's the use in telling you anything?"

Scott picked up the wrought-iron chair as if it had been wicker. For a moment she feared he might toss it over the balcony. Frustrated, he set it back down in place.

His last words, greedy treasure hunters, stuck in the air. Here she was concerned about ethics, and he was probably out to defraud the Brazilian government out of gold or whatever it was he might find out there. And afraid someone would beat him to it.

Greed and protecting natives and government intervention—her heart beat faster. Just the stuff for a journalist! Marisa couldn't believe she'd stumbled upon such a find. Why not write a series about her adventures, of her ancestors and this man's search for forbidden plunder. Finding Sara would be the frosting on the cake.

How could she lose? It might relieve the guilt she felt for leaving her teaching career behind.

"You have got to be the most opinionated, obstinate person I have ever met," she said indignantly. How dare he accuse her of something she was only *thinking* of doing?

"If you had ancestors here, they were probably the first to put a plow to the rain forest. After they chopped down the trees."

"That's progress, isn't it?" She wasn't going to get sucked into some kind of liberal ecological conversation. In her circle, they didn't believe in all that "end of the planet" stuff.

"Do you know what else I think?" He reached to cup his big hand under her chin, tilting it gently to look into her eyes. "I think maybe you don't even work for a newspaper. You aren't the type. Maybe you read about my find and came to smuggle a few precious objects back to some obscure museum. Now that is more your speed. You could be an unscrupulous museum curator." He laughed at her outraged expression and dropped his hand.

"Give it up! You're paranoid! You're making one wild accusation after another without a basis for any of them. Just listen to yourself." Marisa was angry, near tears, and that would be the worst thing that could happen right now.

"Maybe you're right. I could be ranting a bit, but the Brazilian government doesn't surrender any of its antiquities to other countries." His voice was serious, no longer teasing.

That jibe about being a museum curator stung more than anything else he'd said to her. What did he mean, she didn't look like a newspaper person? He was impressed with his own snap judgments. Now he took her for an idiot, expecting her to think he turned over all his findings to the Brazilian museums. Ha! Fat chance! A firm resolve settled her mind.

She glared at him, curling her lip in scorn. He was only an adventurer, what did he expect from others? Before she could express her angry thoughts, he spoke again.

"I don't buy all this nonsense about your long lost ancestors. Looks like you might have come up with a more enterprising story than that. Like you work for a newspaper period, sounds more truthful." His voice was controlled, his gray eyes smudged behind the thick black lashes.

Marisa stood up, debating whether it would give her more satisfaction to show him the fragile, sepia-colored letters from long-ago writings of relatives here and the latest ones from Sara now or make him wait. No, it would

serve him right to show him up for being a suspicious
nut-case when she finally pulled them out in front of the
Yellowhairs.

Logic intruded. He might flatly refuse to take her.
She rummaged through the suitcase and pulled out the
packet of old, faded pictures and drawings that the
Brazilians and the families in Virginia had exchanged over
the generations. Lips tight with unexpressed anger, she
played the tape of her father speaking to Sara in
Portuguese.

She held back Sara's last letter, tucked inside the edge
of her suitcase. The letter telling about the fortune hidden
on her property. Her father was certain it had to be the
money from the bank embezzlement and he was usually
right.

Still, why hadn't someone spent it already? Sara's
letters gave the impression that no one but she knew of its
existence. Had someone finally heard about the treasure?
Had Sara and her family attracted trouble, possibly from
roving miners or some merciless treasure hunters? That's
what her father had feared.

Scott gently touched the photographs and traced his
fingers over the brittle paper. Then he looked at her, his
expression grim but unrepentant. "I see you came well
prepared. I'd like to believe you. I really would. The letters
are Brazilian, that's plain, some very old, but you could
have filched them from any museum. I still say the
existence of the Yellowhairs in the Matos is questionable.
Where do the letters from this Sara person come from?
You should have an address."

What kind of man was he to doubt every motive?
"That's a problem," she conceded. "Sara did most of the
writing, my father answered a few times, but we never
could be sure she received them. He just read the
postmark on the envelope and sent replies, hoping they

would reach her. Her letters never suggested that she received anything from us."

If he still chose to mistrust her, let him. She would not stoop to justify herself to this big oaf. What did she care what he thought? Obviously she was going to have to find another pilot to take her.

"If you will kindly remove your presence while I get dressed, I intend to leave here before you say another word. In fact, please don't say anything more," she managed with a quiet dignity that usually worked on her most unruly student.

Taken by surprise, Scott peered at her, his forehead tucked in a frown. "No matter what I think or suspect, there's no way I'd throw you out on the street. I told you there isn't a room available for at least a week at any price."

"I don't care. For all I know, you have probably convinced your boss I'm some kind of..." Words failed her and she felt tears of frustration and anger close to boiling over. No! She wouldn't let him see her cry under any circumstances. "You can leave now. I'd rather sleep in a taxi than stay here with a raving lunatic."

"I can't let you go." Scott spoke firmly, his manner dismissing her distress as if she had been a child and he the adult. "Not upset like you are."

"That's ridiculous! How can you stop me?" She tried to keep the lost feeling from creeping upward from her chest into her voice. Never had she run into such a wall of distrust and suspicion.

He turned away and leaned against the balcony, looking out over the scene below. In spite of her indignation, she noticed the way the dark hair on his muscular arms contrasted against the rolled sleeves of his white shirt. His hands, splayed on the edge of the balcony rim, looked strong and powerful.

He swung around to face her, his expression unreadable. "Let's call a truce. I can see we're a pair of stubborn characters. Nothing to be gained by that." His voice gentled, and distrust disappeared from his eyes. "I'm going to the jungle next week to pick up Juan. If you're that determined, you might as well come with me. But I'm not going to baby any hothouse flower," he warned.

She opened her mouth to interrupt, but he shook his head. "Once there, you'll have to fend for yourself. It's a long way, over a thousand miles, and you can't come back here until I'm ready. I have to go to the Amazon first, and while we're there we can find out about your relatives. If they are anywhere around, someone will have heard something."

She had to trust this man enough to allow her to find Sara. This obsession had colored her father's life for so long, finally seeping over into hers. Was her father right about her inability to teach disadvantaged children? If she found some of their kin and brought back the money, wouldn't that prove without a doubt that she was worthy of trust? Why did she feel she always had to prove something to him?

Marisa swallowed her pride and looked Scott square in the eye. "Deliver me where I need to go. I can take care of myself." She still felt a rankling antagonism toward his unfounded accusations. What right did he have to jump to conclusions about her without knowing her first?

"Okay, now that's settled, why don't I take you on a guided tour of our city?"

Her dislike of his bossiness warred with a grudging admiration for his casual assumption of authority. Apparently his boss gave him carte blanche in his affairs and this man had grown used to privilege.

"I don't want to be a bother. You're probably very busy."

"Not too busy. I wouldn't want you to go alone. You'd be safe, I don't mean that, but..."

"But what?"

"This place gets rowdy after dark, particularly during soccer season."

"I can take care of myself quite well, thank you. I've done it for years," she huffed. At the visible tightening of his jawline, she backtracked with as much dignity as possible. "I'd as soon stay in the room, out of everyone's way."

"Let's put it another way. I told the boss about you and he insisted I make our guest feel at home. Does that sound more genteel?"

"Maybe. Will you thank him for his generosity then? Or perhaps I should thank your employer personally. He might think me terribly ungrateful."

Scott shook his head. "Nope. The boss never sees anyone these days. I'll relay the message though. You can count on it."

When they stepped into the hallway, she could have sworn the door to Elaina's room popped shut. Had she eavesdropped on their conversation? Why that should matter was not something she felt ready to think about now.

He looked at his watch. "I'll be back in an hour."

Returning to her terrace, Marisa gazed down on the opulent scene below. Should she call her father and Thomas now? But she didn't have anything to tell them, actually, except that she'd arrived safely. Until Scott took her to the Amazon, if he did, she might as well just send a fax to them both, relating her well-being. She sat on the edge of the bed and wrote out messages to Thomas and her father. Then she took them over to the fax machine and punched in the numbers.

Afterwards, she brushed the damply curled hair back from her face while she thought it over. So many questions, not enough answers.

CHAPTER 6

Marisa dressed in haste, suddenly anxious to get out of the silent apartment. She hadn't bothered to bring many changes, but all her clothing was wash and wear. She looked at herself in the full-length mirror and stuck out her tongue. Little girl blue, her father used to call her. It was his favorite color, a color she'd always disliked.

It turned her pale skin to sallow and dimmed the color of her eyes.

Her eyes were the one feature she took pride in. They were large and honey colored, always a puzzle to her father as he tried to figure which ancestors contributed to the renegade hue.

Running a brush through her hair, she thought of how much easier it would have been to cut it short. The humidity turned her normally well-behaved waves into curls. She pulled it back carelessly with a barrette. There. Ready to go.

Downstairs, Scott waited for her by the pool. She could spot him a mile away, towering over the crowd of people clustered around him. Marisa watched for a moment as the Brazilians gestured with excitement, moving their hands with every nuance of speech. He listened attentively to each one, tilting his head in an endearing way she was coming to like.

"There you are." He excused himself politely in Portuguese and walked toward her. "My, don't you look sweet." He must have read her expression, or so she imagined, because he quickly began again. "I mean you look pretty. Pretty and sweet. Anything wrong with that?"

Sweet. That was almost the last word she wanted to hear, but he was trying. "Why thank you, sir."

She admired the way the dark brown cords fit around his legs and hips. He had discarded his white chambray shirt for an Hawaiian type with bright colors and prints. It looked good on him.

Once in the car, they zoomed along the highway with a low purr.

"I want to show you all of Brasilia at once. We'll start with the Torre de TV, that's the TV tower. From there you can see all over and get the general feel of the place."

At the tower, they took the crowded elevator up until she thought it must burst through the sky. At the top, they stood looking over the entire city. Words failed her.

"Wonderful, isn't it? The city fathers laid it out like a gigantic airplane. Over there." He pointed to the 'wings' on both sides of them. "Are the residential areas. Each is called a *Super-Quadra* and contains full public services like churches, schools, medical centers. The *Super-Quadras* are linked by the boulevards."

"It's almost like a science fiction city," she said.

"You're right. The very best minds went into the building of this city. It was to be a utopia."

"And is it?"

He shrugged. "It's better than most, but not perfect. How can it be perfect when mankind isn't?" He touched her lightly on the cheek as if brushing away a stray strand of hair. "You look nice, really nice."

Gazing into his eyes, she smiled before turning back to the scenery, disconcerted by his attention. His choices of adjectives were odd, first sweet and now nice. But this time he wasn't mocking her as she thought he'd been earlier.

"A superhighway passes through the length of what would be the fuselage of the plane. Along the edges of the highway, you see the public buildings like the theater, hotels and the Palacio de Itamarati, one of the most beautiful buildings in Brazil." He touched her elbow to turn her.

She felt an odd shock at the contact and tried hard to ignore his closeness.

"The 'tail' section contains the sports arena, the train and bus terminals, and the 'cockpit' holds the government offices, the house of representatives, the presidential palace and what we would call the supreme court."

Marisa had mixed feelings and didn't know what to say. The view was fantastic, unbelievable. How her father would have loved this magnificent concept of order and logical design. The order and logic were positive elements, but it seemed too perfect. Too pat. Maybe it would grow on her.

"Okay," he said. "Now let's go down and let you see firsthand what we've seen from up here."

Back on the ground, he led her to an outdoor restaurant where they had coffee and croissants. She felt suddenly shy and tongue-tied, alone with him in the midst of a crowd of laughing, talking people.

"Come, I want you to meet a friend of mine who owns a dress shop."

She pictured another Elaina and wondered how many friends he had in Brasilia.

"Women come up from Rio to buy the one-of-a-kind fashions."

When they pushed open the door, elegance engulfed her, with thick carpets, heavy, brocade drapes on the windows and fragile, antique furnishings.

A reed-thin man rushed them, reminding her of a darting hummingbird with his crimson vest and tight black velour trousers.

"Scott! What a pleasure to see you again. And you brought a guest this time, how delightful!"

Scott introduced her to Paolo while Marisa took a deep breath in relief that Paolo wasn't a female—another Elaina. There weren't any dresses or gowns hanging on racks like she was accustomed to seeing, which puzzled her.

"I wanted to know if you'd come up with any new art work for the coloring books," Scott said. "Meanwhile, Marisa might want to look at a few of your latest."

"Thank you, but that won't be necessary," she protested. It would probably take every cent she possessed just to buy a scarf in here.

"She's a perfect size for my latest designs," Paolo enthused. "But first allow me to show you my workroom, if it wouldn't bore you."

"My, no. Thank you." Marisa followed him to the rear of the building where he flung open a door with a dramatic flair. A computer and laser printer sat on a delicate, antique desk while a skylight let in unfiltered illumination from the clear blue sky above. Tissue patterns and swatches of fabric covered a huge oblong table in the middle of the room.

"Has Scott told you about his jungle project?" Paolo inquired.

"No, I haven't," Scott interjected before Marisa could speak. "The subject hasn't come up."

"Just like the man. He's so modest, it's pathetic." Paolo removed a carton from a stack in the corner and handed Marisa a slim, colorful book.

When she opened the book and looked inside, the jungle and rain forest leaped out at her in line drawings with animals that were perfect in proportion and design.

"It's beautiful!" She couldn't think of more adequate words to express her amazement at the workmanship. "These are coloring books? For children?" They were detailed and original enough to intrigue adults.

Scott raised his palms in the typical Brazilian gesture of question. "Who else? Paolo designs them, another friend prints them, and I deliver them."

"There he goes again. Mr. Modesty. He thought up this idea. Going into the outlands like he does with his plane, he meets a lot of the populace we barely hear about here in the city. Go on, tell her about it."

Scott looked uncomfortable. "It's hard to explain without sounding like a nut-case, but I love Brazil. I saw the collision between the forests, the animals, and the Indians with civilization and realized that the key is with the children. If they understood that we must make haste more cautiously, Brazil might save herself."

Amazing. Who was this man? She no sooner had one thought about him than it was replaced by another.

Paolo, who was about the same height as Marisa, put an arm around Scott's shoulder—or tried to. "This man is a rarity. He helped me start this business, and invested almost ninety percent of the money in the coloring books. And that is not all he does. He—"

"Enough said, my friend," Scott interrupted. "You go on like an old gossip. Let her look around."

Marisa wondered at the sudden sharp warning note in Scott's voice, but decided he just didn't like to be talked about. In spite of his obvious enjoyment of people, she sensed he was a very private person. He proved to be full of surprises.

"Back home we hear about the rain forests. I figured, as is usual with most dire predictions, the problem was greatly exaggerated." She had to speak with honesty.

"No, it isn't. Not at all, but you'll see," Scott said.

His words held a promise that included her. They exchanged a long look, which shook her. She turned away, pretending to examine the book in her hand.

Before they left the shop, Paolo tried his best to get her to pick out a dress, but she steadfastly refused.

"*Senhorita*, allow me to give you only one gown from my shop. It is created exactly for you, no need to even try it on. Please, you must do this favor for me." Paolo knelt before her on one knee, his eyes wide with exaggerated pleading. "I beg of you."

Scott grinned. "Might as well give in and accept gracefully, Marisa. He won't give up until you do. If you walk out of here without it, he'll just send it over by messenger."

"Ignore him," Paolo countered. "You will go somewhere special tonight and it will be a celebration of my design. You are perfect to wear this."

"I doubt I'll ever have an opportunity to wear a garment from your shop," she told him as kindly as she could but her words sounded stilted and formal. Couldn't she just accept something from another person without questioning it to death? Funny, she hadn't analyzed herself to see this flaw before and it made her extremely uncomfortable.

"One day you will return to visit me and when you do, the shop is yours, whatever your heart desires," Paolo promised.

"Thank you, but that isn't likely. As soon as I do what I came to Brazil to do—"

"You'll be gone? Ah, dear lady, I doubt that very much." Paolo held her hand to his lips as a goodbye salute.

"He fancies himself a psychic," Scott said.

"Not a psychic!" Paolo contradicted. "I am a visionary. I see things in the future that have come true, admit it!"

"Well, maybe," Scott admitted reluctantly. "There have been a few times."

"Then permit me to say that I will indeed see you again, many times, *senhorita*. Ignore this bear of a man who sees nothing beyond his boots squarely planted on the floor."

They laughed at Paolo's excited pronouncement, and Marisa kissed him on the cheek to thank him. Scott took the box that Paolo presented to Marisa.

Once out on the sidewalk bustling with humanity, she sighed. "I like him."

Scott smiled. "Yes, he's quite a fellow. I met him at one of the games. He's crazy about soccer. He got so excited, he began pummeling the fellow in the seat next to him, and the way I heard it later, all hell broke loose. I saw this little guy at the bottom of a pile of men and waded in to help him. From that time on, we've been friends."

On the way back to the condo, Marisa let her body sink into the plush seat of the car and relax. She longed to buy some new clothes—what a tantalizing temptation. But with no idea how much money she'd need for the journey or how long it would take, she had to be practical. Would she have to buy a tent? Supplies? Plane fare? Probably. Mosquito netting, for sure. Just thinking of all the insects and snakes living in the jungle gave her chills.

Anyway, did she suppose a few exotic garments would change her into a princess? She had no one special to show them off to, she told herself firmly. Yet she began a little fantasy about wearing something absolutely stunning to flaunt before Scott and Elaina. How great it would be to let herself go, to buy something she would never dare wear back in Elliott. She sat up straight and stared out of the window at the fleeting white apartment buildings they passed. What was the matter with her? Where was her father's prosaic, sensible daughter? What would Thomas think of his steady girl going suddenly wild on him?

When Marisa got back to the apartment, visions of a nice long bath and a nap enticed her. Jet lag still nagged at her. It seemed as if she had hardly touched her head to the couch pillow when someone knocked loudly.

"Marisa? Are you there?"

She mumbled something and Scott pushed open the door. He walked in and sat with easy familiarity on the arm of the couch.

"I want you to join me at the yacht club tonight for dinner."

Not would you, or could you, but I want. Typical of the man. "Yacht club?" She sat up, rubbing her eyes. "Are you kidding? How far are we from the ocean, would you say?"

He grinned. "I'll admit it sounds pretentious to sit in the middle of a prairie talking about yachts, but the city founders thought of everything. They built a huge lake on the edge of town."

"Does your boss have a yacht?" If she hoped for any enlightenment about that subject she was disappointed.

"Nah. He doesn't have time for one. Friends do. Maybe you'd enjoy a ride some balmy, moonlit evening."

Suddenly it came to her that she liked the casual way he spoke, as if she'd be here for a long time. "You have a luxurious life here, everything at your fingertips. Must be nice."

She had always thought of her life as normally interesting and well-rounded. Especially when she taught school. The kids were wonderful and made her feel needed, as if her job counted for something. Until poor Kenny showed her how fragile life was and how inadequate her work in the end.

Why had she never had the urge to move away from Elliott to a larger, more stimulating city? Her father would not have minded her leaving, even though she had convinced herself he needed her. What was her excuse for not striking out on her own except inertia and complacency? That might be why she clung to Thomas. He was a rock, steady and reliable. She could count on him.

"I asked if you'd like to have dinner with me tonight," Scott prompted.

That was a nicer way to invite someone. "Dinner sounds nice. What about Elaina?"

"We had the date set at the end of soccer tournament. We do the same thing every year, no big deal. I told her I'd ask you to come."

That put an immediate damper on Marisa's rising excitement. For a very brief moment she had thought he was asking her alone. She agreed to go, even though she could just imagine Elaina clinging to Scott's arm, looking down her nose at every word Marisa spoke and taking all the pleasure away from the evening.

She supposed that was what prompted her to spend the next hour getting ready. Usually she required only a dab of pale lipstick and a quick clip with a barrette to neatly hold her hair back. But tonight, a furious brushing and a bit of conditioner rubbed into her hair helped her style it into soft waves. They might tighten up into curls later, but she wouldn't worry about that now.

She had put off opening the elegant box Paolo had practically forced on her, but she couldn't wait any longer.

Lifting the gown out of the tissue, she held it up in front of her. She had never seen such a dress. It must cost a fortune. Marisa slipped it carefully over her head and fumbled for the hidden zipper at the side. She gasped at the stranger staring back at her from the mirror.

A rich gold satin, the gown was a shade of butterscotch beige, a color she would never have imagined as flattering. But it brought out the honey-flaxen blend of her hair and the amber of her eyes. It was strapless with boned princess seams and a crinoline underslip so it flared out around her feet in a way that flattered her body. Three spaghetti straps accentuated her bare back.

She held out her arms and spun in a circle, loving the way it whispered around her. On the bed lay her one passable dress, which she had planned to wear. It looked pathetic now. She wanted to go out with Scott tonight, but had dreaded the comparison between herself and Elaina and other Brazilian beauties she'd seen in the city. She hadn't wanted to look like a moth among butterflies.

She dug in the tissue in the garment box and removed a matching evening wrap. Paolo had thought of everything. How had he guessed her size so expertly?

Rummaging through her suitcase, she pulled out a pair of strappy heels. Janice had given them to her as a parting gift. Marisa had thought them totally inappropriate and almost left them behind. From the bottom of her case she took out a black velvet bag and let the single strand of pearls slide out on the dresser. The pearls were the only keepsake she had from her mother and she wouldn't have left home without them. They set off the dress to perfection.

When Marisa opened the door to Scott's knock, she soaked up his look of tribute. His mouth worked, but for once he was speechless. She smiled and sailed by him, as if this happened every day of the week.

CHAPTER 7

Since the sports car only had two bucket seats, Marisa knew Elaina wouldn't be riding with them. She must have gone ahead. This gave Marisa a flash of relief.

Once within the grounds of the yacht club, she felt as if she'd stepped into another world—a world of subdued elegance that enfolded each patron in a shadowy, protective shield against outside realities. Being entertained at places like this could easily grow to be a habit.

The headwaiter met Scott at the door and fluttered around him in an enthusiastic welcome. He ushered them to a table amidst calls and waves from people at other tables who knew Scott, including Elaina. Marisa couldn't have missed her—flitting around and greeting everyone.

Scott bowed to the room in general and then turned to give Marisa his undivided attention in a way that was very flattering.

"I never expected this," she said. "Even my father would be impressed." She didn't know what else to say—but she couldn't keep going on about how wonderful everything was.

A band played discreetly from the shadows, but not many people danced or listened. Most everyone sat or stood talking in an excitable, hand-waving manner which she now recognized as so typical of Brazilians.

"Won't your father miss you, since you are half way around the world?"

Scott hadn't asked about her father since the first time she'd mentioned him. Marisa shook her head. "I don't think so. We have a housekeeper and friend—Janice. She watches over him. My father should marry her. She's a treasure. A wonderful companion to him, or she would be if he'd let anyone get that close. He says he's too old for such nonsense."

"Nonsense?" One dark eyebrow shot up. "Do you share his views?"

"No, of course not. It would be good if they did marry, although it's not like they're in love or any such silly thing."

"Silly? You have a very curious way of describing love." He cocked his head. "Hmm, interesting."

His raised eyebrow irked her. Mr. Know-It-All—correction, Mr. Handsome-Know-It-All. His tailored, double-breasted navy jacket with gold nautical buttons fit him to perfection, molding to his shoulders and tapering down over his narrow hips. He wore a crisp white shirt with a small ruffle down the front, setting off the topaz color of his tanned skin. She cleared her throat and looked away to regain some of her composure. She probably should be talking about Thomas now, but somehow it didn't seem appropriate.

"My father claims that falling in love is a cruel fantasy perpetuated by Hollywood," she told him. "He thinks love and friendship should be synonymous." The words sounded pedantic and pompous, even to her own ears. Here she was, mouthing her father's sentiments, which in the past had always been a point of argument between them.

Scott poured the wine the waiter had left for them and offered her a glass. "I don't believe I've ever heard the subject of love expressed in such a way." The side of his mouth twitched almost imperceptibly, as if he suppressed a grin.

"It's not important," she said. "I'd like to hear more about how you came to be here. To me, that's intriguing."

A brief silence settled over their table while he swirled his drink. The waiters interrupted the uncomfortable lull when they brought the first course of cold soup and a huge tray of fresh, colorful vegetables.

"Shall I mix the salads, Dom Scott?" One of the waiters asked in barely accented English.

For a brash pilot with not much to show for his existence, the waiters certainly bowed and scraped. By now she had concluded that he was playing a game with her and there was no "boss," just him. But she decided to go along with it to see how far he would take his little joke.

"I'll prepare our salads." He motioned the waiters away. "That will be all for now, thank you."

It was as if he did not want their privacy invaded. What a strange man. He gave her his undivided attention as if she were the most important human being in the world at the moment. Yet he could be so reserved and distrusting. He seemed at home with the best of everything at his fingertips, yet wanted her to think he was satisfied in his role of a pilot and mechanic. What was his little game?

A loud burst of laughter caused Marisa and Scott to look toward a table near the center of the room where Elaina sat with several soccer players and other young women.

At Marisa's questioning look, Scott shrugged. "She loves night life and the excitement of soccer season. I come here to meet business acquaintances but it's not my idea of a relaxing place. I'd rather be in the garden or out in the jungle."

She agreed, for once. The atmosphere had a cloying seductiveness which made her uneasy.

"I told you part of it." Scott finished preparing the salads and took up the conversation where it had ended the day before. "I came here to study Radam. The government still needed pilots to fly low and under large objects such as trees, someone who knew about landing without air strips. Guess I filled the bill."

"That doesn't explain why you decided to stay."

He looked at her, appraising her and the question. "Why not? To live a few hundred miles from Rio, the playground of the world? I'm paid to fly. Something I'd almost do for nothing. I developed an interest in archaeology. I have everything I want right here. Well, almost everything." He shot her a funny look she didn't understand.

"Speaking of Rio, I'll have to take you down to see it one day. That lily-white skin of yours would sure draw the interest from the beach boys and I bet you'd look great in a *tanga*."

She shook her head in firm denial. She had seen *tangas* in the elegant store windows. They had to be the tiniest bikinis in the world, mere colorful strips of material barely sufficient to cover anything important. She laughed out loud, imagining herself in one of them. Never in this lifetime.

"I might find it amusing too, if you'd let me in on it," he said.

"Merely a passing thought." She looked at him, proud to sit near this extraordinary-looking man. His finely chiseled jawline and his sensuous mouth moved tantalizingly close when he leaned forward to speak to her above the sound of the orchestra.

If only his eyes would lose that odd, guarded look. She moved back to catch her breath. "You mentioned you and Elaina are partners."

"When I finished working with the remnants of Radam, I had a few bucks, and thought I'd invest them. But I needed a national to get me started. We, I mean the boss, hired Elaina to decorate his new condo and they've been partners ever since."

There was that boss again. She was tempted to challenge him, but right now she wanted that trip into the Amazon more than anything. His reply had left a lot more questions than what he had answered, but she let it pass.

Elaina linked arms with two husky young athletes, and with others following, walked toward Scott's table. Full of boisterous good nature, they talked and laughed until they reached it. To Marisa's surprise, they became instantly subdued, speaking respectfully to Scott while he stood to introduce everyone. As each man bent low to kiss Marisa's fingertips, she felt warmed by the frank admiration in their bold, dark eyes.

Elaina must have seen it too, since she looked peeved. Her provocative halter dress was a black-stretch fabric combined with a sheer mesh, displaying her tanned body. The material barely covered strategic areas.

"Scotty, we decided we don't like this boring club. Let's go somewhere we can really dance." She lightly caressed the back of Scott's neck, where the hair touched his collar.

He sat back down and shook his head. "No, you go have fun. Marisa is tired and I'm getting old."

They all laughed politely at his obvious joke. He was lean and tan and looked as athletically fit as any of the younger soccer players.

Marisa felt a twinge of embarrassed sympathy for her. Elaina's bluff hadn't worked. The woman must have noticed how involved she and Scott had been in conversation. Even though most of it was merely polite chatting, Elaina couldn't have known that. If she figured to make Scott jealous so he would get up and leave with her or ask her to stay with them, she had misjudged him.

Now there was nothing Elaina could do but go with the laughing, rowdy crowd.

"I have to stop by the apartments first and then we'll be off." She flounced away without a backward look.

"Will she be okay?" Marisa asked.

"Of course. I wouldn't let her go otherwise. She grew up as mascot for a soccer team. The street kids in Rio are like pesky little brothers and sisters to the teams when they winter there. She'll come dragging in at daybreak, likely as not."

Marisa paused to consider this. Why had the woman made a point to tell Scott about going back to the apartments first? Was it some kind of signal? She tried to remember what she'd left behind in her suitcase. Oh God! The hand-drawn map and the last letter from Sara, telling of the treasure! She touched the small purse on her lap, but couldn't decide if she'd folded up the items and put them back in her purse after looking at them while she waited for Scott.

"Excuse me, where is the ladies' room?" Her heart did little clip-clop steps in her chest. She couldn't have forgotten the map and letter, but if she left it lying there on the bed and Elaina checked her room, she might was well go back to Virginia. The moment Marisa stood up, Scott must have made a sign to the watching waiters. One appeared in a second to escort her. In the opulent room, the outside sounds muffled by the thick carpet and drapes, she ran to a dressing table and dumped out her purse.

"Oh! It's not here!" An attendant obsequiously slid forward from the shadows as if to help. Marisa waved her away. No, she could fumble through the contents of the small clutch bag all she wanted to, but she envisioned the papers lying sprawled across her bed, open for anyone to read.

When she returned to the table, she felt as if the evening had curdled like bad milk. One part of her hated to spoil it for Scott. He was obviously enjoying showing off for her. Did she still believe he was the treasure hunter of her earlier suspicions? Then again, how much consideration did she really owe him?

The waiter pulled her chair out and when she sat and looked into Scott's face, their eyes locked. It was as if the moment was captured inside a time bubble. Neither of them seemed able to break away. She was the first to speak.

"I wonder why Elaina had to go home first." She kept her voice steady, casual.

He shrugged impatiently. "Who knows? Probably to gather up a few things to stay overnight. I have no idea."

Marisa knew there was no way to extricate herself without making a scene. If Elaina had a mind to search her room, it had been done already. She decided to make the best of it.

"Don't you ever have any desire to make a sensible, secure life for yourself? Instead of being a fetch-it man for a millionaire?" She waved her hand in the direction of the lake. "All this is lovely, but it's cotton candy. Where is your real world? Everyone has to settle for reality sooner or later."

He tilted his head back and laughed, a rich, full sound.

She squirmed, trying not to show discomfort as the other diners looked their way with frank curiosity.

When his laughter was spent, he looked at her with speculation in his eyes, shadowy in the dim light. "Settle? What a terrible word. Why should one settle for anything? Is that really so important to you? It's been my experience that women want to be free to be what they choose, but that never slows most of them down from trying to grab the brass ring. Is that what you're looking for? A steady, suit-and-tie man with a boring job and fine income. All the right security buttons to push?"

She tried for a disdainful look. "That kind of thinking went out with hoop skirts. No one has ever accused me of being a gold digger before either," she assured him with spirit. "But I don't see anything wrong with choosing a conservative, conventional life and looking toward the future."

"How unbearably dull you make life sound." He was still grinning. "I had all that before when I was married. Fortunately, we didn't have kids. I wasn't the perfect husband, working day and night to conform with the old man's idea of inheriting the vineyards someday." He pushed the salad around on his plate as if seeing the past somewhere among the green leaves.

"What happened?" She wondered if she mistook the 'little boy lost' look in his eyes for something out of her imagination.

Scott looked away and then back, his eyes cold. "I couldn't 'settle' as you put it. My wife was only interested in my inheritance. She proved that by walking out on me as soon as I decided to give it up. My father had to finish paying her off so she would leave us alone."

Marisa could see the admission of his vulnerability still made him cringe. "Is that when you came here?"

"Yep. Soon as I'd worked long enough to pay the old man off for what Diedra got away with, I decided to change scenery and my life style. Drastically. I've never regretted it for a second."

What a shame, that one woman could twist his life around so that he obviously didn't trust any female or want any family ties.

"I still don't understand what you're doing here," he said. "Such a long way to go for a wild goose chase, and you're not at all the adventuresome sort, if I read you right." His voice was deceptively soft, and he watched her with cool contemplation.

"You're right. I am running away from something. Teaching." She finally admitted it. "You see, I loved the work. The kids were so receptive and grateful for attention."

"What happened?"

"Kenny happened. I thought I'd made an exciting breakthrough. He was emotionally crippled, an abused child with serious depression. I read volumes about new procedures and experimented. It seemed to work, he would stare at me sometimes with a look that told me I was getting through to him." Tears welled in her eyes and she brushed them away impatiently.

He reached for a handkerchief. She shook her head.

"I'll be all right. I should be over it by now. Both my father and Thomas assured me it wasn't my fault, and deep down I know that, but it's hard. Kenny's mom was single with three other small ones. She has left an abusive relationship, and couldn't afford to keep Kenny in school any longer. She was making plans to put him in a state institution when he— when he..." Oh God, it was still so hard to say the words. "When he killed himself, or at least we believe he did. He jumped or fell in front of a train passing through town."

"That's tough to face, but it couldn't have been your fault. You're not a psychologist, you're an educator. I don't see you quitting, under any circumstances. What does that solve?"

It would solve a lot, according to her father who didn't believe she had taken the right direction in her profession and never had let her forget it. Hurt and bitter, she lashed out at Scott. "How would you know? You live from day to day in a selfish vacuum. I felt so close to breaking through to the boy. Now he's lost forever. It's so unfair."

Scott watched the dancers for a long moment, and she found herself calmed by the strength of his profile, the quiet dignity in the set of his shoulders.

When he faced her again, his expression was tender, thoughtful. "I'm sorry if I seemed unsympathetic, but you give off conflicting attitudes and that confuses the hell out of me."

She waited for an explanation.

"You come on like gangbusters, all sharp edges, no nonsense, with a take-charge air about you. Then you admit to leaving your career because of a setback you had no power to influence. They don't jibe. Either you are very, very complex or something's missing here that I haven't figured out yet. Someone as stubborn as you wouldn't give up that easy."

Give up that easy? Could anyone, especially a stranger, know how much grief, how much regret went into her decision to quit teaching? Surely when you see you aren't making a difference, it's time to take a new slant on life. She willed herself to stay calm. "You've told me what you think. You have something else sticking in your throat, don't you?"

"Sure you want the truth?" he asked.

He looked so serious that her heart began to beat faster. What could be going on inside this man's head?

She nodded, her throat dry.

"I still don't buy the relatives in Brazil situation. It's too off the wall for someone like you. I think you could be taking a vacation from school and are here as a follow-up for that magazine article."

"Of all the asinine assumptions! You're paranoid, did you know that?" she demanded. "If what you're doing is so legal and upright, why are you so cautious? I thought you said you had the government's blessings. Then why do you expect them to yank it away so readily?" She stared into his eyes. "You're probably gold hunting and hiding behind archaeology," she accused. That's why you're so wary."

His eyes narrowed, the only sign of his anger. "That's bull. It wouldn't be in the government's interest to stop me. We have a working agreement, and I'm one of the few foreigners they allow to dig up artifacts."

"An agreement?"

"I show them everything I find and if it's not of significant historical value, I'm allowed to keep it. Otherwise a commission from the museum decides the value and purchases the piece outright from me. At low value, of course, but I don't mind."

"It seems like a lot of work for very little recompense."

He ignored the challenge in her words. "Corny as it sounds, I like the idea of contributing to future generations of Brazilians. No, the government would never stop me, but they sure would like to know where I disappear to."

Marisa thought that was probably the understatement of the year.

As they both turned to watch the dancers, she wondered what this intriguing man was going to say next.

CHAPTER 8

Scott tilted his chair back in place as the waiters brought out a dish and set it before them with a flourish.

Marisa's eyes widened at the display. "My, that looks impressive."

He had ordered their meal, and she didn't have a clue what he had rattled off to the waiters in his fluent Portuguese.

"This is my all-time favorite. Except for *pacu* fillets cooked over an open fire in the jungle."

Before she could ask what *pacu* fillets were, the waiter volunteered a description of the meal in flawless English. "*Senhorita*, may we offer you beef tenderloin encased in a delicate puff pastry? The chefs tuck tender juicy mushrooms inside the meat and add small mild peppers. We hope you will enjoy it as much as Dom Scott always has."

It tasted delicious. The flaky pastry crust had baked to a golden brown, the meat so tender she cut it with her fork. The waiters served it with a dark red sauce made with wine and tiny new potatoes sautéed in butter, sprinkled with what looked like chopped parsley. Probably a million calories—not to mention cholesterol—but right now, who cared?

How easy it would be to grow accustomed to the luxuries these people so casually take for granted.

After they had made inroads into the meal, she paused a moment to ask what had been on her mind all evening. "You're still going to take me to Mato Grosso, aren't you? In spite of what you think I may be up to?"

"I said I'd think about taking you to find the Yellowhairs. I'm sure they couldn't live in the Matos area."

"How do you expect to take me anywhere near your diggings if you don't trust me? Maybe you could blindfold me when we arrive so I don't get a peek at your precious work?"

"Not a bad idea, but I'd probably be better off gagging you." He grinned. "I've been going over that puzzle and haven't found a solution."

Marisa switched tactics, thinking of how she would handle an obstinate child. "I'm glad you offered to take me. I'll try not to be any trouble to you."

"That's good enough for me. I wouldn't want you on my conscience if you tried another pilot. Some you couldn't trust with the devil's mother-in-law."

She stopped eating and turned to face the dancers. Why couldn't he believe her after she showed him the pictures and letters? She could see where they could be forged, or stolen from some museum. Perhaps a real journalist might go to that length to get a good, juicy story. On the other hand, she wasn't being exactly truthful to him either, was she?

"Would you like to dance?" he asked suddenly.

She nodded.

They stood and he drew her easily within the circle of his arms, moving with an agile grace for a man of his size. She felt awkward craning her neck back to talk to him and finally gave up, resting her cheek against his broad chest. They danced to the slow, sensuous music.

"You have lovely eyes. They remind me of a jaguar's fur. Pale brown and golden." His hand touched her cheek so lightly that she might have imagined it.

She felt the steady thud of his heartbeat and the vibration of his voice against her face. The music stopped all too soon and they separated. He led her back to the table. The waiter stood nearby and pulled out her chair with an obsequious flourish.

"This isn't going to be a piece of cake, Marisa. We may walk five or six miles a day, camping out in tents and bathing in the river alongside crocs and three hundred pound boas." He shook his head. "The more I think of it, the more I don't see how I can keep my word. Impossible."

"But you must!" In her extreme agitation, she grabbed his hand and held it tightly between hers. "You must! It is so important to my father, to me, to Sara. I've come too far to turn back now."

He looked regretful, but adamant. "This only proves my point. Something's not right here. Who are you really? What do you want from me?"

"You're incredible! What are you afraid of?"

"Afraid?" One dark eyebrow arched and disappeared under the swag of hair that fell across his forehead. "I'm not afraid, but you should be. You don't have any proof those letters aren't some kind of hoax."

"As I told you, no one would have a reason to do something like that." She worried about the letter left behind. If he found out about Sara's legacy, would he turn the information over to the government or try to find the cache himself? As if Scott guessed the way her thoughts journeyed, he leaned forward, speaking softly, his warm breath brushing her cheek. "Come, let's dance again. People are mistaking our disagreement for a lover's spat."

One part of Marisa's mind heard him, but her body stirred with emotions that had never intruded into her life before. She couldn't let this man get under her skin. He was a charmer in many ways, intelligent, fun to be with when he chose to be, but also irresponsible and cynical. He'd forced her to acknowledge an instinctive need for a secure life even if it meant terminal dullness to others. This was the first time she had a basis for comparison, and she didn't like the way the differences made her yearn.

They danced slowly around the shadowy floor. Marisa had to admit she enjoyed the closeness of his body even while she struggled to control the surge of pleasure that threatened to overwhelm her senses. The man was a playboy, a person of confusing scruples who believed in saving the environment and at the same time was involved in something shady related to antiquities. She'd bet on it. The music stopped and he led her back to their table.

"You look beat. Want to leave now?"

It was as if he sensed the barrier she had built for her self-protection. While he couldn't have understood it, he respected it. For the time being.

"I am tired," she admitted. "I've enjoyed the entire day, more than you can imagine. Your boss must be a real delight to work for, to let you call your own hours, work when you choose." She waited to hear his admission of there being no boss, but it didn't come. Neither Scott nor Elaina seemed willing to discuss this elusive boss.

He folded the heavy, cream-colored napkin as if at a loss for words. "I don't know. He can be a real S.O.B. at times. Not everyone likes him."

"Have you worked for him long?"

Scott looked decidedly uneasy. "Quite a while, but why the third degree?"

"It's just that your boss sounds so absolutely charming. I would love to meet and thank him for his hospitality."

Hah! He had the grace to look momentarily disconcerted. He touched her hand, lying on the table, and gazed into her eyes with such a long, searching look that she felt penetrated to her very soul.

"I have never taken anyone to my sites before, except Juan." Scott had a way of changing the subject when she least expected it, which was disconcerting to her linear way of thinking.

"Does it mean so much to you? To stay here in Brazil?"

"It means everything. Brazil is a mistress that defies description. She is seductive and virginal simultaneously. Sort of like you."

Marisa felt herself blush and was relieved he probably couldn't see it in the dim light.

"I've carved a place here for myself I never could have in the States. If the government deported me, I don't know what I'd do."

It was the first time he had shown any vulnerability. She looked away, embarrassed. Maybe it wasn't such a good idea to talk Thomas about a story after all. When she returned home she was free to do one about her relatives if she chose to.

She felt sure Scott was playing a game with her and he would take her where she had to go. Otherwise, wouldn't he have just said a flat no?

They drove back to the apartments in silence, but in spite of their quarrel, the quiet between them felt comfortable. Brilliant street lights led the way, along the freeways. He drove by the Capitol buildings and their stark beauty astonished her. Spotlights placed strategically on the rooftops of the sparkling white buildings created a magical vista of pristine whites and deep shadows.

When they arrived at the condo, she couldn't believe it was two a.m. People ambled about the courtyard or strolled arm in arm in the hallways, shouting good-natured insults back and forth. A splash of water announced someone's dive into the pool.

Everyone smiled and spoke to Scott with an air of deference. He seemed to know them all.

"Don't these people ever sleep?"

He laughed, that deep rich baritone. "Of course. Still, you have to realize that it's the end of a soccer tournament. All rules are broken or badly bent. I suppose that goes against the grain with you."

Marisa ignored the jibe, listening to the sound of the waterfall whisper in the background. Small white lights, twisted into the net above, gave the illusion of stars twinkling overhead. Flashes of color and squawks erupted occasionally as a bird became restless or disturbed in its sleep. The ride up the elevator was breathtaking at night.

At her door, he took the key from her. She waited, afraid he might insist on coming in for the proverbial night cap, and also afraid he wouldn't. She didn't know if she could handle her feelings about this man right now.

He pushed the door open and before she could form a protest, he cupped her face between his hands and kissed her lightly on the lips. His fingers lingered underneath her chin in a gentle caress. He released her and stepped back in the hallway.

"Thank you for coming with me tonight, Marisa. Sleep well."

She took a long, deep breath and closed the door behind the sound of his retreating footsteps. Leaning against it with her eyes closed, she licked her lips, still tingly from his light kiss. She had expected him to come on strong with some macho play, and he'd surprised her with his tenderness. A strange, unfathomable man.

Hurrying to the bed, she opened the suitcase and saw Sara's last letter and the map lying on top of her nightclothes, folded just as she remembered leaving them. Did that mean Elaina hadn't snooped? How could she be sure? At this point Marisa trusted no one with the knowledge of the treasure that awaited her out there somewhere.

CHAPTER 9

Rushing so she wouldn't change her mind, Marisa put through a call to her father. At first he sounded relieved to hear from her but then he followed with the usual note of disappointment. She should have been sitting in Sara's parlor by now, according to him.

On the other hand, her call to Thomas was more positive, although she hadn't given two thoughts to him or their relationship since she met Scott. After Thomas told her how much he missed her, he enthused about her proposed story. He sounded elated. Guilt churned her stomach. Thomas had worried about her while she had been absorbed by Scott's presence.

When she finally went to bed, she tossed and turned through the night with thoughts of Scott's deep laugh, the trip ahead of her, and how much out of control her life had spun, all blending in a continual thread through restless dreams.

The next morning she met Elaina in the hallway when they both stepped out their doors simultaneously. At first Marisa thought the sultry beauty might flit by without speaking, but instead she turned to look at Marisa.

"Did you have an enjoyable time last night?" Her voice dripped with sweetness.

"Oh my, yes," Marisa answered in kind. "Too bad you left. Did you enjoy yourself also?"

"Look here, little Miss Innocent." Elaina lowered her voice to a sibilant hiss. "You are not fooling me, and you are not fooling Scotty either. You may think you have twisted him around your finger with your all-American looks, but I can tell you this. Scotty and I have a long association together, and I will not permit anyone to jeopardize that. Believe me. He may be captivated by your newness, but as soon as he conquers you, he will leave you. He does not tolerate long relationships."

Elaina's words didn't shock Marisa. This was also the picture she had of Scott. A love 'em and leave 'em kind of guy. That would explain why Elaina was content to give him space. "In that case, Scott and I might as well enjoy each other's company before he tires of me, don't you think?" she answered sweetly.

For a brief instant she thought Elaina might lose control. The woman took a deep breath and her black eyes narrowed in shrewd calculation. She looked like a dangerous jungle cat ready to spring. Marisa steeled herself and remained still. Despite Elaina's seething fury, Marisa held her ground, stubbornly and returning glare for glare.

Then Elaina gathered her control like a cloak around her shoulders and shrugged. "We are partners. Business partners. Scotty is a grown man and can do as he pleases. We have our understanding. He does not wish to be tied to one woman like a pig ready for market."

Before Marisa could turn away, Elaina moved close. Her polished nails were so long that Marisa heard them click as they came together around her arm.

"Scotty's been hurt by one of your kind before. I won't let you do it again to him. I know you are here for some reason you are not telling him."

Marisa pulled away. Did that mean Elaina snooped in her room? "I have no intention of harming anyone, Elaina. How could I? You said he was a grown man. I am hiring him for one trip out to the jungle and when I find what I need, believe me, I'm gone."

Elaina stared into her eyes for a long moment and seemed satisfied by what she saw.

Marisa turned on her heels and left the dark-haired woman standing alone in the long hallway. She needed some fresh air badly and remembered a park not far away that Scott had pointed out to her on their way home last night. How special it would be to sit alone under the cool trees and watch people. Here at the apartment complex, she felt as if the tenants all watched her, perhaps wondering who she was, and if she was Scott's latest conquest. It made her uneasy.

She walked briskly along, pretending not to notice the admiring glances of passing men. When she reached the park, she sat on a bench in the deep shade, closed her eyes, and let the quiet sink in all around her body, hugging close against her. For several minutes, only the muted sounds of people speaking in low tones in the distance and a baby fretting came to her from the background.

"So this is where you're hiding," rumbled a voice, close to her ear. "I had a notion you'd be here."

She opened her eyes. "Hi." Her silly heart thumped against her chest as she struggled for control.

Scott sat next to her, touching her folded hands lightly. "The doorman told me which direction you took, so don't give me credit for being psychic. We need to talk about our trip."

Ah, the games were over. "Good. I wondered about that. What do I need?"

"I warned you of the dangers, but if I don't take you, I'll probably never get you out of my hair."

She ignored his patronizing words. Getting to Mato Grosso was all that was important.

He took a folded sheet of paper from his shirt pocket and smoothed it on his thigh. "I have to go about five hundred miles up the river to check on one of my sites. It's near a sweet little city, civilized, and a good place to start for you, too. I'll introduce you to some third-generation American-Brazilians. I'd prefer to take you to Americana, but that's in the wrong direction, down by Rio."

Marisa watched his lips move for a moment, fascinated by the beginning of dark bristle on his jaw, and then turned away, confused.

"After we leave the city, we stay in tents and sleep in hammocks."

"Hammocks?"

"No need to go into that now. You must have camped out in your childhood, Girl Scouts, that sort of thing. About the tent, and other camping equipment, I have spares, so you don't have to buy any. That takes care of your living quarters. We can't travel too heavy. The wind currents are unpredictable over the jungle. Muscatel can set down on an ant hill and I can choose which ant to land on, but I still have to watch the load."

She knew he wasn't telling her everything. Did they use hammocks because of bugs and snakes? Marisa tossed the idea away, not wanting to pursue that train of thought. Insects and snakes had never been a part of her ordered existence, and she wasn't willing to put up with them now. She hoped she wouldn't have to.

"Let's agree on a fixed amount to fly you there and back. I'll take care of the provisions."

"I'm not asking for favors," she began stiffly.

He grinned. "Of course not."

"Well, then, it sounds perfect. I can't tell you how much I appreciate your going to all this trouble for me." She felt compelled to add, "Especially since you doubt my motives."

He touched her cheek. "No, I don't trust you," he admitted. "But it makes this jaunt even more interesting. I like a challenge. When this is over, we'll sort it out. Time enough for that."

When this is over. The words brought with them a strange sadness, a sense of loss. Marisa remained silent a moment, letting the feeling pass. "I'm sure I brought more to Brazil than I'll need on the trip. Would it be an imposition to leave some things behind, packed in a store room?"

"Nonsense," he said firmly. "Consider the apartment yours for as long as you're in Brazil. The boss doesn't need to rent it. He always keeps a couple vacant for friends who drop in from out of town."

Her sense of delight at his words seemed way out of proportion, just because her belongings could remain in the apartment and would be there on her return. She supposed it was her grasp at security in a world suddenly spinning out of her control.

"I hope you're as capable of taking care of yourself as you say you are," he continued. "I can't be with you every hour of the day. We'll pick up Juan to go with us. He's a fine young man, and you can rely on him one hundred percent. Still, there will be times when you'll be on your own."

Her pulse quickened to hear the gruff concern in his voice. It was then she decided to destroy the fax she'd prepared to send to Thomas before they left, and instead cancel the story she had been planning about her long lost relatives, the lost bank money, and the added idea of a soldier of fortune, hunting for gold and his own treasure. Scott might never find out about the articles, but it still wasn't right. All she needed to concentrate on now was Sara and the treasure.

Learning to control her fear of the unknown came easier every day. Since she had broken through her paralyzing hesitation and flown to Brazil, anything after that should come easy.

Almost. In sudden panic she thought of her safe, cozy nest back in Elliott.

She and Scott walked slowly back to the apartment. Marisa was too preoccupied to enjoy his company, and he didn't speak as they strolled along the street together.

Back in her room, alone, she was reluctant to awaken Thomas at the hour it must be in Virginia, and she didn't look forward to explaining herself. She typed up a fax canceling the story and said he'd get the details later and then dialed the number of the newspaper on the machine sitting on a desk by the bed. In spite of her worries, in spite of her lack of control in her present situation, elation sped through her body. Tomorrow the adventure would begin. She felt quite certain her life would never be the same afterward. There was no going back.

CHAPTER 10

On the way to the airport, Marisa's mood alternated between excitement and doubt. She still had time to back out. Maybe she shouldn't have allowed Scott to assume she was an experienced camper and liked the outdoors. How did she hope to get away with such a crazy bluff? She'd never camped out in her life, not even in the front yard at a slumber party.

Her father loathed anything physical, even before his accident. He'd taught her to use her mental abilities, though there had been times in school that sports looked tempting. It was never worth risking the ridicule and rejection from her father if he found out.

Scott chatted to her about this and that. She liked the soothing sound of his rumbling voice and let it pour over her without listening to each word. She had too much on her mind since sleep had evaded her most of last night. She had packed, wanting to take only what was necessary and worrying about the fax. Did Thomas receive it? Would he pay attention and not fax her back to ask about her decision? That could prove embarrassing to say the least if someone else saw the fax.

"A penny for your thoughts." Scott's words jolted her back to the present.

"I was thinking of my relatives. You said the Indians are sometimes hostile. Would Sara and her family have been allowed to live among them?" Marisa turned in the bucket seat to get a better look at his expression.

"So, you're finally beginning to have doubts. That's healthy. Up to a certain point, they might have been accepted early on. Depends on what you define as hostile. The natives are the least of your worry, pretty lady. The roughnecks who bum around searching for gold, hiding from the law, they're your worst scenarios. And you have to keep a watchful eye on anacondas, jaguars, peccaries, not to mention the caiman."

"Hold on a minute!" She laid her hand on his arm to stop the flow of words. "The Matos is very nearly a plateau, a plain. I'm sure those animals don't exist there. You're trying to scare me."

"You've done your homework, looks like. But if you want me to take you to the Matos, first we have to fly up to the Amazon. I told you about that, remember? I have to pick up Juan and check my diggings."

"Don't worry about me. I'll do what I came to do as quickly as possible and be gone."

At the airport, she helped him load their camping equipment. He ignored the shiny new plane and began loading the old one in the back of the hanger. "Have you flown this plane a lot? I mean, it looks pretty old and decrepit," she commented. Maybe he saved the newer one for more affluent customers.

He reached in his back pocket and drew out a blue kerchief which he tied around his forehead like a sweatband while he continued to load the plane.

"The Bonanza is a show piece." Scott tilted his head in the direction of the shiny new plane. "For hops to Rio or Sao Paulo, you can't beat it. That's the one I use to teach Juan to fly. He'll have his pilot's license by the end of the year, but he has a permit now to fly with a licensed pilot."

"That doesn't explain why you prefer this old wreck."

"Whoa. Hold up there, woman, Muscatel will hear you." He frowned and patted the wing of the old plane. "I can explain if you give me a chance. I thought southerners were slow talking."

She put her hands on her hips and waited.

"I learned my lesson in a V-tail break-up, a long time ago when I got caught in heavy turbulence. This one's a different Bonanza, a newer model, but still—it's not the baby my old Helio is."

He rubbed the side of the older plane with fond appreciation. Marisa feared he might rub off a layer of paint to show a hole beneath it. The buzzwords he used to describe his planes were not clear to her, but she didn't ask for an explanation. Some things were better off overlooked.

"Let me introduce you to Muscatel. I named the little lady after my pop's favorite beverage. It was his specialty at the winery. She's a 295 Helio Super Courier and the safest damn plane in the jungle. Her cabin is wraparound steel so if we do crash, which is unlikely, you could survive. The Bonanza's a tail-dragger, but I can shut off the engine and glide in this one until—"

"Okay, okay." Marisa laughed and held up her hands in front of her, palms out. "Peace. I believe you, and I am truly sorry for having offended Muscatel." She made a little bow toward what still looked like a decrepit wreck.

"Well—maybe we'll forgive you. You can't judge a plane by its looks, any more than a person. And don't forget I said that."

"Mmm. Words to live by?" She smiled, feeling suddenly good about the adventure ahead of her.

It didn't take long to become airborne and soon they soared away. He maneuvered the aircraft with the same easy grace he drove his sports car, pointing out scenery as they flew. Sometimes he swooped down lower for her to see, a courtesy she could have well done without. Below she saw a two-hundred-foot waterfall, plains without a blade of grass and then miles and miles of green with trees so close together it looked like a huge manicured lawn from above.

"This is the Pantanal Swamp. Roughly the size of your home state." He tilted the plane gently and she longed for her camera, the one she'd left at home. Her father would really tear into her about that little oversight and Thomas would "'tsk tsk."

Huge flocks of long-legged white birds floated up in the air with a graceful swoop that made them all seem attached by their wingtips.

"Five-foot storks. Natives call them tu yu yu. Many a pilot misjudged and came too close to a heavy flock like that. Boom, down goes the plane."

"Is this really a swamp then? It doesn't look like any swamp I've ever seen."

"No, it's not a traditional swamp at all. Millions of cattle roam around down there along with jaguars, all breeds of monkeys and deer and so on. Only in the rainy season could it be considered a real swamp."

She sneaked a look at him. He appeared every inch a pilot and then some. "I can't believe you're wearing that white silk scarf and leather jacket. With those goggles you look like a colorized version of an old Humphrey Bogart film."

He turned to her with a lopsided grin that made her pulse zigzag. "I know. It's crazy, but it started as a joke. My kid brother got it for me the first time I went solo. This outfit's my good luck charm."

The look fit him to a T, but she wouldn't have let him know it for the world. It didn't hurt that he was more handsome than Bogart. Marisa leaned back in her seat and watched the landscape rush by.

Hours passed before he slowed and banked the plane sharply with practiced ease. She looked down, but saw nothing unusual until he began the descent. "What are you doing? There's no airport down there!" She grabbed hold of the arms of her seat, clenching her fingers tight.

"Don't worry. I've done this plenty of times."

Oh my God, was he showing off at the expense of their safety? Her heart beat in time with the noise of the propeller, she closed her eyes and felt the sweat bead on her forehead although the cockpit had been chilly only moments before.

He set the plane down in a small clearing and taxied toward a group of huts at the edge. "See? Nothing to it." He patted her arm with clumsy grace and turned away, presumably to give her time to compose herself.

People ran from the shacks, laughing and shouting. The women wore homemade calico dresses, and bright bandanas covering their black hair. The men wore cutoff shorts or work pants with bright shirts, clean but threadbare as if washed a hundred times. Children rushed out, pushing the adults aside.

"Dom Scott! You bring my beer?" One lone voice rose above the others in understandable English.

"Sure Augusto. You bet."

It surprised her that although Scott spoke fluent Portuguese, and everyone seemed to welcome him wherever he went, no one treated him with the casual familiarity she expected. There was always that little edge of reserved respect. Because he was a foreigner? How to figure?

She looked down at the small sea of brown, smiling faces. Surely Scott exaggerated the dangers. "So this is the

infamous Mato Grosso. Doesn't look so scary to me."
She ignored his rude snort of derision.

"This isn't the true Matos. We're on the outside
perimeter."

Scott grabbed her up before she could protest and
held her close before stepping down on a box the men
had put out by the plane. He set her feet on the ground,
his arm lingering around her waist a moment longer than
necessary.

Marisa stepped away a safe distance, afraid he would
notice the throbbing at the base of her throat. "Are those
thatched houses owned by these people?" she asked,
pointing to the edge of the clearing.

Scott and others were unloading the cargo of beer
cases and boxes of tinned beef. He stopped his work and
looked down at her. An unruly shock of hair hung over
the bandana he had again tied around his head. Even
while she scorned what she considered his arrogant self-
confidence, she could not help but admire the picture he
created. Standing at the edge of the jungle, legs apart, wide
shouldered and narrow hipped, with jeans tucked into his
boots, he looked as if he could do anything he wanted to.
Powerful, uncompromising, intense, he epitomized every
super hero she'd ever seen in the movies.

Then he grinned and wiped the sweat from his neck
with his sleeve. A dark stain already crept down the center
of his T-shirt and under his arms. She returned his smile,
relieved at the slight relenting of his controlled toughness.

"Houses? You mean huts? The rubber owners built
some of them years ago. When they moved on, the people
stayed, they had nowhere to go. Those more substantial
buildings are what some might hopefully call beer joints.
They service the miners hereabouts and the planes that fly
in and out. This isn't much more than a scattering of huts
throughout the jungle. The map shows it as a little dot,

but that's about it. A camp of jerry-rigged shelters. I've seen whole families living under a plastic tablecloth strung between two trees."

The first surge of hopelessness hit her. How impossible to have imagined the size of Brazil. Maps she and her father had pored over hadn't done the country justice, nor had that little pathetic hand-drawn map of Sara's. "Where will I begin to look?" She spoke her thoughts out loud.

"Hey, don't be in such a hurry. You just got here, remember?" His thick hair was mussed from the loading and for a moment he looked like a carefree boy.

She said nothing, savoring his obvious pleasure. He seemed at home anywhere and took pleasure in everything he did. She did believe he wasn't being completely honest with her. If he wasn't his own boss, she would have been very surprised, but then it seemed a small secret that amused him so she didn't plan to question him about it again.

"There you go, not fitting my picture of a Southern belle, a proper pale-skinned, slow-talking, slow-moving lady," he said. "You haven't learned to pull back the throttle yet. Relax and smell the roses."

She smiled at the picture of smelling roses in the jungle. "I think you've got me confused with Scarlett O'Hara as a proper Southern belle. I don't have a twelve-inch waistline either."

"Still, you don't have to take life so seriously. Didn't anyone tell you we won't get out of it alive?"

"Oh sure, I know that." She pushed the unruly curls away from her cheek. "It's that I've got a job, a task to do, and..." She faltered at the guarded look that leaped into his eyes. It was as if he looked deep inside her and knew about her previous intentions. But that was impossible.

She had the copy of the fax in her purse. When she found a moment's privacy she would destroy the copy and that would be the end of that.

After Scott and the others finished unloading everything except the supplies meant for the next stops, he leaped down and stretched.

"I should think you'd let them unload the cargo for you," she said.

"They would, gladly. But I like the physical exercise after sitting in the cockpit for so many hours. When we tie down Muscatel, we'll go for a beer. If we can beat the populace to a cold one."

The kids stood silently, shyly smiling, lingering around the plane.

"What are they waiting for?"

He yawned and looked around, pretending nonchalance. He said something in Portuguese causing the children to shout and run to him, pulling on his trouser legs. Even the shyest ones on the edge of the group giggled, eyes bright with anticipation.

"They're waiting for the coloring books." He pulled out a box with a big red x on it and opened it slowly. The children went wild.

"Here, pass these out, will you? They know to take one each."

Marisa reached for the stack of books packaged in individual plastic wraps, each with a set of stubby little colored pencils. While she handed them out, Scott stood close, watching.

"Has your friend Paulo ever come with you to see this?"

Scott shook his head. "No. He's a city person. One landing like we just made and he'd probably hate me for the rest of our lives. I tell him all about it though and some kids have written thank-you notes."

She opened a book. "I can't get over how beautiful the books are. I've seen almost the same things from the plane that your friend drew in here."

"You ain't seen nothin' yet." He smiled and touched her shoulder. "The thing is to get these kids to notice their surroundings. It's too late for the adults, but the kids have to see that though their lot is hard, they live in a glorious place, an important place."

"As a teacher, I appreciate how you're doing this. You don't preach. I don't understand the words underneath the pictures, but they are probably descriptive. What do the parents think?"

"I suppose they don't understand what we're trying to do. They're just grateful someone takes an interest in their kids. These who work the rubber aren't harmful to the environment. It's the cattle and the mining. I haven't been able to do much toward that yet, but—"

"These coloring books would be good to use back home to bring awareness to children. Everywhere."

He nodded. "I suppose so, but it's important to have these kids understand that each plant and animal that becomes extinct from man's greed and arrogance might have made a serious contribution to our lives, and all are worth saving."

"I guess I've never given it much thought. People have to work, don't they? That means progress."

"Right. But showing these kids other alternatives are all we want to do." He raised his hands in mock defeat and stepped back up onto the plane. "Ah, don't get me started. Before I came to Brazil, I was a crop duster, remember?"

She watched while he taxied the plane over the bumpy jungle runway to the last shanty in line. With the help of many willing hands, he tied down the wings and tail to pegs sticking out of the earth and walked back toward her. "Sometimes we get some freaky weather," he explained.

He led the way to one of the small huts and bent his head to enter the doorway, holding aside the grimy plastic strips which served as an ineffectual insect barrier.

Marisa slipped under his arm and stopped, as she could not see for a moment, waiting for her eyes to adjust to the sudden shadowy darkness. A round man with a grimy, once-white apron peeled off a roll of bank notes to pay Scott. It surprised her that the man would carry so much money on his person until she saw the huge pistol holstered on one hip and an ugly-looking machete on the other. From the looks of him, he would have no qualms about using either.

Scott introduced her to Augusto who favored Marisa with a broad, gap-toothed grin and tugged on his earlobe as he winked at Scott.

"What was that all about?" she asked, looking dubiously at the drink the bartender shoved in her direction. After everyone looked her and Scott over, the conversation in the room broke out again.

"Any time you see a Brazilian pull on his earlobe, that means he approves. In other words, he likes you."

Before Marisa had time to consider, she turned toward the still-watching Augusto and touched her fingers to her own earlobe.

Both Scott and Augusto laughed.

What are we drinking?" She smelled it cautiously.

"It's *aguardente*, made from sugar cane. Goes by many names, some pretty raunchy. They make up songs to celebrate this 'brandy of the poor.'" He swirled the clear liquid around in his glass. "Some call it 'the little blonde' or 'the grandmother,' Juan's father calls it 'thread of gold.'"

Marisa brought the lip of the glass to her mouth. Scott put his hand on her arm to stop her. "We've a custom that goes with drinking this. Watch." He took a sip and spat out a little on the floor. "The first sip goes as an offering to the saint who provided the drink."

"Which saint?"

He grinned and tilted the glass back to finish it in one swig. "No matter. Whichever one is most convenient at the time."

She took a sip and spit it out to please him. "What happens now?" she wanted to know.

"We can rest here a while or stay all night and start in the morning."

"Do any of these people know about the ones you call the Yellowhairs?"

"Oh, yeah, almost forgot. I asked while we were unloading and a couple of men claimed to have heard about these people. They used to have a village about two day's hike from here but these fellows think the government moved them up by the Amazon several years ago, like I said before."

Was he lying to her so she would be willing to leave this area and go where he wanted to go and perhaps give up the idea of finding the Yellowhairs? Could she trust him?

"That works out fine," he was saying. "I'm going up the Amazon, anyway. You can meet some civilized ex-patriots first. Former Confederate soldiers settled Santarem. They came down here after the war."

Very convenient. "How will that help me? Isn't that too much time wasted? If we're only two days away right now—"

He shook his head. "We need to get closer to the general area, to Campo Largo or Kayapo. We go there next. You're not ready to plunge right in. You need a perspective on what you're looking for. Save us a lot of trouble in the long run. If my information is wrong, we can always come back here."

She looked at him and knew he still didn't entirely believe her. He probably thought he'd call her bluff, and she would have to admit she had no relatives here. He obviously was not looking forward to going into the jungle in search of the elusive Yellowhairs. Perhaps he knew more than he was telling her.

"Okay. Whatever you say. I can't afford too much running around in a plane, though."

Scott brushed her protests away with an impatient movement of his hand. "Don't worry about it. I have to go up the Amazon, anyway, so that trip's on me. Relax and enjoy the scenery."

"You still think I'm after your silly artifacts, or a story, don't you?"

He looked at her, speculation deep in his eyes, and shrugged. "I don't know what I think."

She swirled the warm drink and looked through to the bottom of the glass as if the answers might be there. How could she explain to a stranger exactly what this meant to her father? It was an obsession. Very definitely. As far back as she could remember she had to be the practical one in the family. Her father taught his ancient history class year after year, and, especially since the accident, lived more and more in the past. But he was family, her only family.

Maybe after all these years she just needed him to see her as a unique individual; to see her as a competent, intelligent life-form instead of this irksome person who lived in his house and begrudgingly took orders from him.

She thought of how her father never did any of the mundane things like laundry, cooking, or paying bills. He lived for the past and spent countless nights poring over maps and writing letters in his small, spidery handwriting.

"After the accident, my father knew he could never make this journey. He sort of gave up the idea, which I was grateful for. Then when the letters from Sara started coming, he recovered his enthusiasm so fast, it was uncanny. But the letters stopped."

"After the one giving you her worldly possessions?"

Marisa felt a slow flush spread up across her face as she thought how close he had come to the center of her search. In his chasing artifacts had he heard rumors of a treasure chest of money? Maybe that was the only reason he was bringing her here. Her father had to get that money back at any cost.

"The property is of no value to us. What would we do with a deed to Brazilian land?"

Sara had mentioned land in her letters. She also wrote about the mansion along with the treasure chest that she claimed was cursed and should be removed from Brazil.

"Sara obviously needed help. That's when I decided to come here." She rubbed her temples. All this thinking in the heat gave her a headache, but the small sips of the liquor had warmed her belly, mitigating some discomfort.

Why should she have to prove herself to this man? Yet he had hit a nerve when he wondered why she was doing this. Did it really go beyond her father's preoccupation with Brazil? Was she making this trip a last fling of independence before settling back to a life of quiet contentment? At least that was the way she had always pictured her life in Virginia.

Now she wasn't so sure.

CHAPTER 11

The late afternoon sunlight slanted between the trees by the time Marisa and Scott left the dark, noisy bar. Bright orchids and flowered vines entwined the tall trees lining the clearing where they'd landed. Marisa smelled the dank, humid earthy aroma of the jungle and knew the crude runway barely held it in check. Like some lurking live animal, the jungle waited to reclaim the land.

She watched Scott speak to a group of locals, leaning his head down to the shorter men to give them his full attention. After that, he took her arm and led her to a large shack standing lopsided and a little aloof from the others.

A figure bent over a two-burner camp stove, stirring something that smelled delicious.

"*Cunhado*! I brought you some tins of beef this time," Scott said, greeting the cook.

"Ah, Dom Scott. You have also brought me a guest, a lovely guest. I will prepare something especially for her."

Marisa looked at the grimy apron the man wore over even grimier, once-white trousers. "What did you call him? It didn't sound very kind."

Scott laughed. "Oh that. It's the local greeting. Roughly translates to brother-in-law. Like back in the states a man might call another man cousin, or son. Something like that."

The man, whose name was Louis, served them big plates of black beans and rice along with shredded meat that tasted like pork—she hoped it was pork, but decided not to ask. Scott sopped the juice up with chunks of *farofa*, fried bread made of manioc flour and flavored with onion.

She ate every bite and proclaimed it delicious. "I can't help notice that people look at me in an odd way, friendly but as if they're puzzled. Do you know why that is?"

"Your hair fascinates them. Most have probably never seen that color before. I heard a couple of men say you were much too skinny, so maybe that's it."

She laughed. "Oh, you!"

"We'll stay here the night. You sleep in the plane, but don't go wandering around. Lock the doors. These fellows, so far, have been on their best behavior, but they're watching you. The locals are okay, but I wouldn't trust the miners. They're a rough bunch. Have to be to survive out here."

"Where will you be?"

"I'll sit in on a hand or two of cards. I don't need much sleep. We'll leave at daybreak."

During the night Marisa heard stealthy footsteps approach the plane. Heart surging in her chest, she saw the door latch turn slightly. Thankfully, she had locked it as Scott advised. She crept on her hands and knees to the window and recognized Scott's tall form heading back toward the buildings.

He had come to check on her. How dear of him. He could be so sweet when he wasn't defensive. After that she slept soundly, not awaking until she heard his banging on the door of the plane the next morning.

Once airborne again, he seemed quiet and withdrawn. That didn't bother her. She had her own thoughts to sort out.

Finally, he broke the silence. "Marisa, look below!"

As he swooped low, she gasped. At least a dozen huge crocodiles were lying in a shallow lake. The outlines of the creatures looked like menacing shadows but even with her inexperience, she could have identified them anywhere.

"Why are they lying there like that?"

He shrugged. "Probably waiting for late afternoon when the capybaras come to drink."

Having read about Brazil, she knew he referred to the world's largest rodent. They grew to be four feet long and very plump. She tried not to imagine the fat little rodents ending as dinner for the waiting crocodiles.

Brazil bombarded her senses with so many new ideas and so many new things to see, she felt like an overloaded fuse, ready to blow out. Where was her quiet, serene life? Would she ever find it again?

Several hours later, Scott pointed out the Amazon, a crooked river larger than she could have imagined and brown as a mud pie. Instead of heading toward the city in the distance which must have been Manaus, he crossed the river and turned toward the jungle.

Marisa cringed as the tops of the trees rushed by beneath them. Finally, Scott slowed, banked, and aimed the plane toward an opening—apparently one only he could see. When she dared open her eyes, he was taxiing down a dirt area not much wider than their wings. He stopped the plane with what seemed like inches to spare before they rammed head first into the jungle.

"Good Lord, we made it!" she exclaimed.

"Of course."

As she groped her way out of the plane, her eyes widened at the two wrecked aircraft on either side of the runway. They had been there so long the vines and brush had nearly claimed them, hiding most of their metal skeletons from the world—mute testimony to less successful flights.

Scott grinned, a small schoolboy showing off his expertise, happy with her amazement. "Juan always gives this landing at least one Hail Mary. I tell him when he can set a plane down here or in Kayapo, he'll get his wings."

The children, skinny, naked boys and girls, all wearing shorts or flour sack shifts, flocked to greet them, while the elders moved up shyly, as if trying for a little more dignity. Their faces broke into smiles when a young man leaped up on the side of the plane to stand next to Scott and help him hand out the coloring books.

"This is Juan. You know, that good-for-nothing rascal I've been telling you about."

Juan's lips spread in a wide smile that contrasted with the mahogany of his skin. He was thin, but looked wiry and strong, with serious black eyes, holding respectful admiration when he looked at her.

"I'm glad to meet you, Juan," she said. "Scott has said some very good things about you, so don't let him tease you like that."

"Thank you, *senhorita.*" The boy looked pleased, even if most of those surrounding them didn't understand every word Marisa said.

"Please," She laid a hand on his arm when he jumped down off the plane. "Call me Marisa."

He looked questioningly up at Scott who nodded his permission.

They made their way toward some shanties near the runway. The air closed in around them, humid and stifling. The faint breeze only pushed the fabric of Marisa's shirt closer, melding it to the prickly heat between her shoulder blades.

One small, thin man disentangled himself from the others waiting on the side lines and made his way toward them.

"Oh, there you are, Romeo," Scott shouted. He motioned to the oncoming man. They embraced, as most men did in Brazil, and pounded each other on the back with enthusiasm.

"I want you to meet someone." Scott spoke in a curious mixture of English and Portuguese.

"Marisa Elliott, meet Romeo O'Reilly, Juan's father."

Romeo smiled broadly and touched a finger to his forehead in a type of salute. "Welcome to Campo Largo." His speech was correct, his words spoken slowly as if memorized.

"I've been teaching them, and everyone wants to learn," Juan said. The boy used carefully correct English while his father beamed proudly at his offspring's wondrous accomplishment.

Marisa shook hands formally with Romeo O'Reilly. She liked him immediately. "O'Reilly?" she asked, her curiosity overcoming her sense of politeness.

"Romeo is third generation Irish and Brazilian and now the only thing Irish about him is his name, which he's very proud of," Scott said. "It makes him different and he likes that."

"How's the family?" he asked Romeo. When the man finished speaking in Portuguese, Scott nodded and turned back to Marisa. "Juan's a bright lad and went to school in

Brasilia for some years. He'll be your guide when I'm not around. That Southern drawl, no matter how charming, won't get you very far out here."

Marisa noticed a touch of pride in Scott's voice when he spoke of Juan. Everyone looked so poor, she suspected he had a lot to do with sending Romeo's son to school.

"We'll bunk at O'Reilly's tonight," he continued. "I want you to meet the family and get to know Juan a little. Mrs. O would be horrified if I didn't bring you to meet her."

"Dom Scott, you must know something," Juan said hesitatingly. It was obvious to Marisa he wasn't sure if he should talk in front of her, yet didn't know how to avoid it.

"Go ahead, Juan. Spit it out if something's bothering you."

"I went to check your digging place like you asked me to. Last week I see signs of *garimpeiros*. I know their boot tracks."

Scott frowned. "Have they bothered anything? Dug anywhere?"

Juan shook his head vigorously. "No. They walk around, sniff like dogs. Someone might watch where you go, think you dig gold."

"Hell, that means I'd better get out there, make sure they haven't discovered the mound. I hid it, but they don't miss much."

By then Scott had led her inside a shack and ordered beers. The lukewarm brew felt good on Marisa's tongue, and she swizzled it around in her cheeks before she swallowed. She was glad it wasn't the formidable drink he called the *pinga*—she'd read about that.

Not a good idea to look around too much. The men became instantly aware of her presence, talking and laughing louder. Several men waved to Scott, but no one came over to talk, much to her relief. The men looked well worn, as if they had recently returned from the front lines of a secret war.

"Tomorrow we'll go out to the digs. You need the experience of hiking anyway. How'd it go today? Enjoy the ride?"

Cheerful bastard, Marisa thought with a decided lack of charity. She nodded, struggling to match his composure. "Beautiful scenery. Sure you trust me to go with you to your precious site?"

He grinned, but refused to take her bait. "Entertain her a second while your father and I bargain with Smiley over here, will you?" he said to Juan.

Juan nodded shyly. Scott and Romeo walked over toward a short, swarthy man with a huge bushy mustache. The man wore a perpetual frown of discontent etched in his expression so that a real smile might have cracked his skin. They argued without animosity for a short period until Scott gave him some bills and shook hands.

"Dom Scott pays for Muscatel's protection," Juan said. "This man is important here, and he will guard her well." His accent was strong. She knew from experience he'd been taught phonetics and by the book. Probably his teachers didn't speak English.

"We didn't take on any fuel at the last stop nor here," she said for lack of conversation. That seems curious to me."

"Dom Scott put an extra tank on Muscatel," he said proudly. We can fly from Brasilia to the Amazon without refilling."

Scott had mentioned that Juan had a natural bent for mechanics and helped him overhaul his planes.

"How are you coming on your flying lessons?"

"Me? I love to fly. Dom Scott says I am a natural. Soon I will get license, then maybe work full time for him."

"Do you go with Scott when he digs for his museum treasures?"

Juan frowned. "I am not supposed to talk of such things, but I guess it's okay with you." He nodded. "We dig together. Sometimes we take turns watching for *garimpeiros*. There would be much trouble if they know where he goes."

So, if he had to watch out for stray gold miners. That meant he did search for treasure. Momentarily, she regretted the impulsive change of heart about doing the story. If she were ever to get away from teaching, she must make a place for herself and the newspaper was her out.

A lot less heartache than teaching. Oh, but she had come so close with Kenny. If only his mother had shown a little more patience. As angry and frustrated as Marisa had been at the time, she still sympathized with Kenny's distraught, beleaguered mother. Kenny would have been a handful as an only child. For a single mother of three other 'normal' children, it had proved impossible.

Still, as a teacher and a friend, Marisa had sensed a breakthrough. Now that was all gone with the last shovel of sod on his casket. She renewed her vow. If she ever did go back to teaching, she would never become so emotionally involved again.

"Now we go home? Mama will be glad to see you and the pretty lady," Juan's voice broke up her reverie as he spoke to his father and Scott when they returned to stand beside him.

At the door of the O'Reilly shack, Scott paused, reached up and held the strings of plastic beads aside for Marisa. They entered a clean, bright room. The dirt floor had been swept so often it was packed as hard as tile and almost as shiny. Several small children played on the floor, leaping to their feet when they saw the visitors.

"Grandchildren," Mrs. O'Reilly explained and Scott translated. "Juan is the last of my own. A marvelous mistake!" She chortled with glee and her husband joined in as Scott relayed this last bit of information to Marisa.

Justina O'Reilly could speak no English, but strangely enough, Marisa felt right at home with the older woman as they nodded and smiled at one another from time to time. Justina occasionally broke out into a long, emotional speech and then stopped to laugh at herself when she remembered Marisa didn't understand a word.

Scott and Juan vied for the job of translating with good-natured enthusiasm while they all sat down to a meal of *caldeiradas*, a thick fish stew, with rice as a side dish. Jugs of an iced drink made from the *maracuja*, a passion fruit, sat on the ancient, white, chipped enamel table. The ice Scott brought was a special treat and since it would not last, the family used it with extravagant abandon, icing everything but the stew.

"Can you ask Juan's father about the Yellowhairs?" she prompted during a lull in the excitable speech that flew around the table.

Scott frowned but repeated something in Portuguese.

Romeo looked puzzled for a long moment and spoke with Juan. He turned back to Scott. "My son and I agree. We have heard of a tribe of strange people, maybe half-breeds, maybe Indians. Not friendly. We leave them alone. Mean boogers."

Scott laughed. "I can always tell when Juan's just come back from school. These kids love American slang."

"So do American kids," Marisa said.

"Where are these people?" Scott asked Romeo.

He sketched a direction with a wave of his hand. "In there. You go so far, don't have to look, they find you."

Marisa sat back and watched how Scott conversed—the same as the other Brazilians, with hands waving and voices filled with excitement. It seemed no Brazilian could remain calm for long, probably not even while he slept.

Conversation flew around the room and when Scott looked at her with a raised eyebrow, Marisa smiled. "Don't bother translating. I'm just enjoying the sound of their language."

After dinner the men went outside. Marisa tried to help with the clean-up, but the women shooed her over to a corner into their one comfortable chair. She sat and leaned back, suddenly weary from all the excitement. What a day it had been.

She got up and went to the open window. The men had made a little fire outdoors to keep away the worst of the insects, while Scott and Juan strung up three hammocks nearby. The women stayed inside the one room hut. Marisa leaned out the window to talk to Scott.

"Once I had diggings near the Rio Negro, not far from Manaus," he said. "It was the greatest. Not a bug in sight for miles. It's a dark river, loaded with manganese, and acidic, no mosquitoes, no birds. Eerie place."

"Why couldn't you go there now instead of here?" She slapped at a mosquito which seemed bent on ignoring the repellent she had smeared all over every exposed inch of her body.

He laughed. "Once we get inside on the trail, they'll leave us alone. Then our main worries are the pesky *capuchines*, the monkeys. They're all over everything, curious as hell. They'll tear a camp apart in ten minutes if you turn your back."

After a little more conversation, they all climbed into their hammocks. Surely, she was too keyed-up to sleep, but the last thing she remembered before dozing off was the sound of Scott's husky-voiced, "Good night, Marisa," wafting in through the window.

The next morning everyone was up at dawn to beat the heat. For breakfast Justina served a table-full of exotic fruits, the like of which Marisa had never dreamed existed, jugs of still cool fresh orange juice, and the usually strong, coffee, thick with milk and sugar.

"We're going to take a hike, skirting along the Amazon," Scott said. "The next village is Kayapo. They don't have a good landing strip and don't want one. I can manage it, but haven't for a while. It's Juan's three Hail Mary landing instead of the usual one. Besides, I'm curious to see how it works out with you before we attempt to trek into where the Yellowhairs are supposed to be. And I need to check on my digs."

Marisa thought Juan's expression seemed puzzled as he looked at Scott, but the young man didn't make any comment so she let her questions pass. Why didn't Scott take her to the city first to talk to the other descendants from The States? Could it be he still assumed she had lied and he didn't want to expose her? No. She doubted he'd have that much sensitivity for her.

Once they started hiking through the jungle, Marisa wondered if they would ever stop. It wasn't a hard trail to follow. Over the years everyone in this vicinity had probably used the same path. It was unmistakable even in the dim shadows cast by the huge trees.

The first sight of Scott's diggings was a letdown. After all the reticence and secrecy about it, it looked like nothing more than a pile of stones hidden under soil and grass.

Scott knelt and pulled some stones away. "Disappointed? Most people are first time out." He raked away the piled-up earth and vines with a gloved hand and revealed part of a crumbling wall. "I don't have to work hard at covering my tracks. The jungle does most of it for me."

She could see that. The jungle reminded her of a fastidious cat, trying to cover a soiled place in its litter box. "It's as if the forest tries to bring everything back to natural, hiding away foreign objects."

"Very perceptive," he said with approval. He walked to a topsy-turvy pile of crudely-cut stone blocks, moving them away one by one to produce an opening in the side of the little mound of earth she had taken for a hill.

"This was the site of a church. Somewhere in the seventeen hundreds according to the museum curator. He dates it from the artifacts I've brought him."

"It's so well hidden. I don't see how you found it."

"I don't either, to tell the truth. On one of my mining forays, looking for gold, there it was. Except for you and Juan, no one else knows."

"Will I have to die now?" She smiled at his grin. "Your secret is safe with me. I've no idea where we are, where I've been, or where I'll be tomorrow. But I would have thought that magazine writer came here with you, too. Didn't she do an interview?"

"Never!" His voice startled some nearby birds to flight. "That was what ticked me off most, and why the government was so up in arms about it. She took a few chance quotes, put two and two together and came up with eight and then proceeded to write that damn article."

"Without verification?"

"Yes. Thank God she had no idea of where this is, but she had treasure hunters and greedy prospectors running all over the Amazon, chasing the natives out of their villages, causing all kinds of turmoil. Luckily, the government stepped in and put a stop to it by dispatching a small army to disperse them. I got in on the fall out. If they have to call me in for questioning again on my diggings, I'm out of Brazil forever."

Marisa swallowed, thinking of the fax she'd sent before she left. What if her explanation hadn't been good enough? What if Thomas decided to call or fax back to ask why she had decided not follow through with the story? With a sinking heart, she belatedly recognized the possibility.

Scott reached into the opening and pulled out a heavy object wrapped in cloth. Though the light sifting down through the leaves was sparse, she could guess by the way he lifted it, that the object must be pure gold. He unwrapped the candelabra on the ground and touched the ornate carvings on it gently.

This was a priceless antique object. She knew that. "Will you turn it all in? This must be very rare and valuable."

Scott looked at her speculatively and then down at his dusty boots. "You might think I'm irrational. Sometimes I wonder about myself. Sure, I could fly out of here with this stuff and no one would even know."

"Why don't you?"

He tilted his head back in that endearing little mannerism she'd come to enjoy. His features were spare and lean, and the light stubble on his jaw enhanced his look of bold vitality. She watched his closed eyes for a moment and dwelled on the thick black lashes against his tanned cheek.

"I'm no goody-goody."

She got lost in the gray depths of his eyes when he opened them.

"I've found my share of gold and diamonds and never gave a thought of doing anything but keeping it all for myself. I felt I earned every bit. But this is different. This doesn't belong to me. It belongs to the people of Brazil."

Marisa watched the emotions play across his features and suddenly she had such powerful feelings for him she wanted to jump up and run away as quickly as possible. "So you wouldn't keep any of this for yourself?" She struggled to keep her voice even.

"I'm a part of Brazil now. I owe her a lot. I came to Brazil a very damaged person and I healed here. I'm still healing. It would be like cheating myself to remove the country's treasures that someone would only melt away into money. I've got all I need as it is."

She could understand his feelings about the destroyed artifacts and that they belonged here, with the people. What she couldn't understand was his empty bragging about having all he needed. He admitted mining for gold, but he must have spent it as he went along. She was torn between admiring his ideals and disliking his cavalier attitude about prosperity. Unless he was leaving something out.

What would he think if he knew she came down here primarily for the treasure Sara offered her father? The solution of how she would get the money out hadn't presented itself to her yet. Nevertheless, it shouldn't be too hard. She noticed neither border had checked suitcases very thoroughly when she crossed from one country into the next. Anyway, she'd worry about that when she found Sara and the money.

It isn't as if I'm taking anything from Brazil. Just returning the money to its rightful home. It belongs to our town. If Sara's people hadn't spent it by now, after a hundred and thirty some years, then they didn't want or need it here.

"Ah, I can see your thoughts wander. What are you thinking?" he asked.

"I think it's commendable. Your principles, I mean."

"Oh hell, do I sound that pompous? A thousand apologies. I'll try not to give that impression ever again."

She laughed, in spite of wanting to forge a dislike for him and his values to insulate herself against her susceptibility to his charms. "Isn't it dangerous, trying to get this out and back to your plane without someone seeing you. Robbing you or even killing for the take?"

He shrugged. "No more dangerous than anything else I've done in my life. When I mined, I fought my way out of the jungle with my gold and diamonds, but I managed."

He wrapped the candelabra in a special material and gently lowered it into the opening in the ground. He laid the stone blocks on top and arranged the creeping vines to cover them. When he finished, she couldn't tell where he had touched it.

"Guess we'd better head for camp. Tomorrow we'll load this batch and take it to the plane. The rest of it can stay until I return next month or the next."

"Wouldn't it be easier and less chancy for you to tell the government where this place is and let them dig it out?"

"Oh, Lord no! In the first place, it would take a knowledgeable archaeologist to do this without ruining everything. You know officials, the same all over the world. So much red tape involved that it would take years for anything to get inside a museum."

He stood and removed his gloves, slapping away the dust against his legs. He held out his hand to her. "Ready to head back?"

Hesitating only a fraction of a heartbeat, Marisa took his hand. He pulled her close then released her. Her thoughts bounced around in her head like marbles as they walked through the jungle. Somehow she felt as if he might have guessed about Sara's treasure.

Was that why he wasn't helping her more? Would he try to find Sara before she did? To take her mind off her turmoil, Marisa spoke into the silence that was building between them. "How long have you worked for the man who owns the condo? What did you say his name was?" She hadn't planned to ask again about his so-called boss, but her curiosity was getting the better of her. Would he continue to avoid the issue?

She had been walking behind him. He stopped and she nearly ran into him. "I've been meaning to talk to you about that. You see, at first I had my reasons and—"

Something huge slithered across the path between them. Instantly, he scooped her up by her waist and swung her toward him, holding her feet off the ground.

"What was that?" she managed, having only seen a blur. A very large blur.

"It's just an anaconda. They don't generally bother with anyone as big as us."

Marisa swallowed past a lump in her throat. "He *was* bigger than us!"

Scott laughed and started to let her down again. She turned her face up and their lips met in a long kiss that felt as if it melted her bones.

Feelings poured over her, feelings she'd never imagined before. A seductive warmth spread upward and downward from her middle. She hoped he wouldn't set her down yet. Her legs felt wobbly and probably wouldn't hold her. What was happening to her? Her pulse raced, her lips felt bruised by the force of his kiss and yet she wanted more.

"Marisa." He kissed her throat, his voice husky. "You're driving me crazy."

She pushed him away. Hating to separate herself from his strength, the warmth of him, she battled between emotions and common sense. He wasn't husband material and since she had waited this long, she wasn't about to go foolish now.

Reluctantly, he let her down.

His fingers gently touched the hair on her cheek, tucking it behind her ear. "Hair the color of raw honey," he said. "You're so fresh, so new. I've never met a woman like you, one who doesn't use her beauty as a tool to get what she wants. Will you let me make love to you someday soon?"

"Make love to me?" she echoed. "We barely know each other." That wasn't what she'd wanted to say exactly, but he caught her off guard.

"Of course. You need a commitment first, or some promise of tomorrow. Can't you, for once, live for today?" He turned away from her, his jaw clenched as if he struggled for composure. "Why do you have to plan everything out to the last degree?"

"Because I'm made that way." If she harbored any doubts about the depth of his feelings, his words put the cap on it. He would never trust anyone again, never allow anyone to share his inner person. A woman had damaged him, and he wasn't about to surrender that hurt. It was his protection. Yet without trust, he was only a shell. She wasn't about to yield her body and soul to anyone like that.

She moved past him to lead, knowing he had no recourse but to follow.

CHAPTER 12

Oooh! What is that?" Marisa danced away from something trailing down from a tree onto her neck.

Juan, who usually disappeared on solitary hikes ahead, now brought up the rear of their little parade into the jungle. He reached up with his walking stick and pulled aside a thick sticky spider web.

Oh lordy, where was the spider? She was afraid to look up into the tree and tripped on a root in her haste to move farther away. Scott reached out to steady her.

Marisa had second, third, and fourth thoughts about what she'd gotten herself into, and they'd only been in the jungle two days. The air, murky and close beneath the canopy of trees, sucked her breath away.

For the most part, Scott walked ahead and Juan came behind her. She dodged low hanging branches and had to watch where she put her feet, which was hard when leaves and decomposing tree limbs littered the path. Once she mistook a snake for a root and almost stepped on it. The thought that she was too tired to care made her smile. Monkeys squealed and protested their passage, throwing branches and other objects down at them as she and the others moved through their territory.

All day, the light had barely filtered through the dense forest in places while other spots remained almost pitch-dark. It was only the aching in the backs of her legs and in her arms from pushing brush aside that signaled evening had arrived.

Marisa took off the head covering Scott had given her and wiped away the perspiration from her forehead. The molded plastic helmet hadn't allowed for any air circulation. For a moment she wondered what lay ahead since the headgear included little flashlights mounted on them, reminding her of miner's hats. Scott had explained that they'd need them deeper inside the jungle. Marisa shuddered to think about darkness in the middle of day. She had imagined a jungle as a silent place, but this one teemed with life, with all kinds of strange, eerie noises. Crashes sounded in the trees above and through the brush ahead and behind them.

The straps of the backpack pulled painfully against the front of her shoulders. She carried the lightest, but that was the only accommodation Scott made in her direction as he mercilessly pushed them forward.

Several times during the day, Juan had pulled Scott off the trail to speak to him. The sound of their intense discussions drifted back to her, and she sensed she might be the subject of their arguments.

Scott had wanted her to start dragging behind, to beg for mercy. Ever since she dampened his ardor, he seemed bent on trying to impress upon her that she had no business being here. Her thoughts buzzed around in her head like angry mosquitoes, and she vowed to show him. She tilted her chin in the air and trudged along without a murmur of protest, mentally screaming at the outrage of her aching muscles.

"Okay, time to stop for the night," Scott said at last. "I needed to get us near an offshoot of a river so we'd have good water." He leaned against a tree whose trunk was three times as wide as he, looking carefully upwards into the branches first, before relaxing.

"Boas," Juan explained cheerfully.

Great. She slid her pack off and sat on it, refusing to look down in case she sat on some creature. As she watched Juan and Scott pitch the tents, Marisa felt sticky, hot and tired, as if her body might never be clean and dry again. But she would never have admitted it to him. Not in a million years. Grabbing up two buckets, she headed toward the sound of fast-moving water.

The stream looked inviting, and so clear she could see the sandy bottom. She filled the buckets and looked around. Everything seemed normal. No unusual animal noises. Only the muted sounds filtered back to her—Scott and Juan arguing good-naturedly while they made camp. Surely no one would miss her for a few minutes. She stripped off her sweaty clothing down to her panties and bra and waded into the water, gasping in delight as the coolness of it touched her overheated body.

What a shame to have to put her soiled clothing back on, but it would hardly do to walk back into camp in underwear to fetch a clean outfit. She giggled at the thought.

Marisa splashed and scrubbed her skin, willing her body to forget the discomforts of the past days and nights. The water moved swiftly in the center but near the edges it eddied and swirled with shallow ripples.

Something approached, crashing through the brush, obviously in a hurry. She sat up, alarmed. Was it a water buffalo? A cheetah looking for prey near the water? With her heart in her throat, she stood, trying to decide whether to move out into the center of the stream or make a mad dash for shore. Before she had time to consider her options, Scott appeared, anger and alarm vying in his expression.

"What the hell are you doing, Woman?" he shouted first in what sounded like Portuguese and then English.

If she had been the least bit timid, his arm-waving and the set of his mouth might have cowed her completely. As it was, it only made her angry. "Oh, shut up! You are the most insufferable, overbearing man I've ever met," she shouted back at him. "Why are you spying on me?" She sat again abruptly, forgetting for a moment that the water was clear and very shallow.

Before she guessed his intentions, Scott waded in, roughly grabbed her arm, and dragged her out. His senseless tantrum made her humiliation more intense as she realized her skimpy attire left little to anyone's imagination. When they reached the shore, she tried to break away from his iron grip, but he sat on a large fallen log and pulled her down with him.

To her everlasting horror and disgrace, he paddled her with a switch snatched hurriedly off a tree. In all truthfulness, he barely touched her legs and behind. Still, her outrage was so great she screamed and yelled as if the blood flowed in rivers.

After a moment he paused, listening, but holding her in place. She continued to yell and tried to twist away. He flipped her over and put his hand on her mouth to shush her. Satisfied by what he heard or didn't hear, he stood, dumping her unceremoniously onto the soft ground, scooped up her clothing, and handed the pile to her with a frown etched between his eyes. Then he folded his arms across his chest and turned his back.

She dressed with haste. The faster she put on her clothing, the madder she got. "It's sort of late to give my modesty a break, isn't it, Dunbar?" she managed between clenched teeth.

"Put your damn clothes on and simmer down. I'll explain. Not that you deserve it for that little stunt."

"Explain? Stunt? Are you crazy?" Her voice cracked over its squeak of protest. "Oh, for heaven's sake, turn around. I've dressed now and a fat lot of good it does me. You've seen what there is to see of me."

He turned his head and looked over his shoulder, an eyebrow raised quizzically. "You think so?" he challenged. "I've an idea there's more to you than meets the eye."

He walked toward her, though she backed up a little, and put his hands on her shoulders, pressing his fingers into her skin. Her legs wanted to buckle, but she forced herself to hold still and glared up at him.

"You must never go out alone without Juan or me," he said. "Now listen for once, without any discussion. Juan told me he could smell the *Cintas Largas*, that's the Wide Belts. Normally these Indians are fierce only with one another, but a woman alone is fair game. No matter her color, she is a chattel, someone to work for them and make babies. They wouldn't attach any importance to kidnaping you."

Her skin crawled and her mouth dried. She had a hard time swallowing as she realized she could disappear into this vast jungle without a trace. "I didn't see anyone."

"When I came through the trees, I saw patches of color behind you in the brush. They were watching."

The jungle looked so peaceful now at dusk. Marisa shivered, not only from the damp clothing clinging to her skin but at the thought of strangers watching her every move

"That still doesn't give you any excuse to assault me, to carry on like some madman."

Scott grinned. "I have to admit, that was the enjoyable part. I had to show them you belonged to me.

You, my woman." He hit his chest in a 'you Tarzan-me Jane' imitation.

She laughed—in spite of not wanting to.

"I let them know I was angry with you for not preparing my supper. You were supposed to be beaten, and you more than cooperated by yelling your head off. I'm surprised Juan didn't run to see what's going on. Of course, he might think you deserved a beating and stayed away out of politeness."

Her outrage dissolved when the remembrance of her wet body across his hard legs intruded. He released the grip on her shoulders, lifting her chin with his thumb and finger.

"You're a spunky one, all right. I didn't think you'd make it through the first day without calling 'uncle.'"

"So you *were* testing me! I thought you and Juan argued about it."

Swiftly, he bent his head and kissed her. Her body trembled, and her heart raced. She put her hand behind his head, twined her fingers in his thick hair, and kissed him back.

When they parted, he looked into her eyes for a long moment and then away, dropping his hands from her arms. "Promise me you'll be careful, okay? I can't be with you every minute, and I've never lost a client yet."

She turned from the gruffness in his voice, disappointed in herself for putting more emotion into the kiss than he apparently felt. He was worried about his reputation as a pilot and the kiss was probably an automatic instinct with him. She would have to show him he was off base, that she wasn't part of the deal. This was strictly business.

"There's more. You can't go skinny dipping in every stream you see. I'm serious now. No arguments. Some are okay but others have crocs, boas, and some have piranhas. Bet you didn't even notice that *pirarucu* over there."

Marisa stared into the dark water, but saw nothing. Suddenly the water parted and a sound she could only describe as a tremendous burp emanated from an object that was at least eight or nine feet long.

"Oh, my Lord! What is that? I could have been eaten alive!"

"I doubt it, but that's probably what brought the Indians so close to our camp, otherwise they wouldn't have come within miles of us. A *pirarucu* is an air-breathing fish. They get trapped in shallow water sometimes and from the size of him, he could feed a village of natives for a couple of days."

"Well, I'm so sorry I messed up someone's dinner plans," she said.

"It's okay," he answered as if her apology had been sincere instead of the sarcastic reply she was reaching for. "The natives will come back early in the morning. They know the fish can't go anywhere."

"Why did it make that noise? Is it dying?"

He shook his head. "I suppose it's a part of the breathing apparatus, but you can hear them a mile away some nights when it's quiet. Just because he's harmless, I still don't want you to get careless. I'm hoping you'll have a glimpse of the *piraiba*. He's a giant catfish, grows up to three hundred and fifty pounds. I've heard they can swallow small children."

"Now you're kidding me."

"No. I'd never kid about the jungle. The Amazon is nothing to joke about. Not to a stranger."

"You made your point then. I guess I'll forgo the swimming. I won't even wade in the water," she promised.

"All I'm asking is to let us be the judge of when you can swim."

She followed closely behind him when he turned and headed toward the camp.

Juan had finished cooking the usual beans and rice over the campfire, and they ate in silence. "Maybe tomorrow we have *pacu* fillets," Juan said as he rubbed his flat stomach.

"What's that? I remember you mentioning *pacu* before, at the yacht club."

"A delicacy to be sure," Scott answered. "The natives make a stew from the whole fish and the saying around these parts is that if you eat from the head, you will never leave the Amazon."

She wondered if he wanted her to eat it. No matter, it didn't sound very appetizing.

Afterwards they sat staring silently into the flames until she spoke. "How do you know where you're going? Everything looks the same."

He shrugged. "Beats me." She must have shown her dismay on her face. Both he and Juan laughed at her. "Just kidding. I've been up and down the river. In it, on it, beside it, and above it for years. That's why, when you think you can drop in on some strange people you call ancestors and—"

"If you're sure these so-called Yellowhairs are the ones I'm looking for instead of where I think they are, in the Mato Grosso, I don't foresee any problem. I know they'll be glad to talk to me."

He snorted. "No one out here is quick to trust outsiders. They'll probably think you come from the government, wanting to relocate them again. Even the people in Juan's village wouldn't talk freely to you. Most of them are squatters and will eventually move on. Some have settled and begun to till the land. Those are the ones who won't trust you. They're trying to get titles to their lands and it's a slow, bewildering process to deal with the government."

"Do they trust you?"

Scott grinned. "Touché. Not one hundred percent, no. But I've been coming in and out of here so long with supplies and mail, they're used to me."

"You sent Juan to school, didn't you?"

Scott looked uncomfortable. "You might say that. These people are obviously poor. Hopelessly poor. Juan's a bright boy. I could see that right off. I hated to see him wasted, working in rubber or trying to make a living by farming."

"That's commendable. But over time, did you do him such a favor? Here he is, back in his old surroundings but now he knows how the other half lives." She couldn't help comparing the situation to Kenny's. Had the boy come to realize that he didn't fit anywhere? God, she hoped not.

"I've thought of that. A lot. He won't always be here. Right now I could make a place for him in Brasilia, but it's a custom that no boy or girl leave home until they choose a mate. I'd like him to start at the university before he gets married. Anyway, his mother wants him home while Romeo goes out to the rubber fields. Juan's a damn good mechanic and a natural at working with plants. He would be invaluable to me—" He paused a moment as if thinking and then continued quickly. "To me and the boss in Brasilia when the time is right. He could begin his own gardening service or work on our planes."

"Does he have eyes for someone?" She turned to look at Juan, but the boy had disappeared, which seemed a normal occurrence after they ate and sat talking. She supposed he thought they wanted privacy.

"He sure does. Pretty little girl in Kayapo, our next stop. It'll all work out."

Marisa felt relieved to know Scott had a village destination. She'd feared they would traipse through the jungle forever, never seeing another human being. She stood and stretched, pacing around the campfire, but not too far from it. From time to time, loud, booming roars punctuated the darkness, coming from the direction of the river. She knew by now the sound came from crocodiles, or caiman as Scott called them. The first night out, the piercing cry of a jaguar sent shivers down her back. "Are you going to live in Brazil forever?"

He turned to look at her. "Why not? I have everything here."

Marisa had a sudden vision of the lovely Elaina. Of course, Scott had everything he wanted, and even if he wasn't really the boss, he apparently had a nifty salary by the looks of it. He had his archaeological explorations, a splendid bachelor's apartment. What more could anyone ask for?

Something made her persist. Something made her not want him to be satisfied. "Surely you have goals. Don't you ever want to be anything beside a pilot or puttering around in a jungle searching for treasures you don't get to keep?"

She'd never met any able-bodied men who didn't have ambition burning inside them, ambition to get ahead in their profession or buy a bigger home for their family. Most of the men she knew in Elliott were already committed to lifelong careers and showed every sign of contentment.

She and Scott stood by the fire. He bent his dark head down in that special way he had of giving her all his attention. "Why is it so important that I have a lot of ambition?"" His voice sounded quietly casual, but his eyes were intent, waiting for her answer.

"Important? To me? How could it make any possible difference to me? It just seems a shame, somehow, for a man to fritter his life away. Without goals, I mean." She turned away and stirred the coals on the edge of the fire with a long branch.

Juan's tuneless whistle echoed through the jungle.

"Won't he get lost or harmed out there alone?"

Scott shook his head. "Nope. Knows this jungle better than most people know their own back yard. I guess you might say this is his back yard. Anyway, don't change the subject. Seems to me, you're like most women I've known. Looking for a meal ticket, never mind what the man wants to do with his life."

The sharp barb of his speech startled her and she glared at him. "I'm not looking for anyone to support me. I can take care of myself. I had a satisfying career, and now I'm starting over."

"Still, it sounds like you want a good, steady type. Is that what this Thomas person is like? Steady as a rock? Probably about as interesting."

Marisa was surprised Scott remembered Thomas's name. She'd only mentioned him once. Why would he assume it was a bad thing for a woman to choose a trustworthy, reliable mate? Then she remembered what he'd said about his ex-wife. But surely he realized by now that every woman he met was not interested only in what he could give them financially and wouldn't strip him emotionally as his ex had obviously done. So sad that he remained inflexible and remote.

A small, furry object darted across her boots from out of nowhere and climbed up her body. She screamed and brushed at it with her hands.

Scott shooed it away, laughing. "It's only a baby monkey. Dropped off its perch as we walked under it. We startled it, most likely."

Marisa stood close to him. He pulled her tight to his chest for a moment then began rubbing his hands across her shoulders to soothe her. "Your heart's beating a mile a minute. Calm down now, sweetheart."

When she realized nothing was going to eat her, she felt foolish and struggled in his arms.

"You feel so fragile, I'm almost afraid to squeeze too hard. Don't pull away from me," he whispered, holding her head lightly against his chest where she felt the thump of his heart in her ear.

"I didn't mean to be a 'fraidy cat. Apparently the creature was harmless."

"Don't be too sure." He released her with obvious reluctance. "You can never take the jungle for granted. When you think you know all its surprises, she throws a few more at you."

Marisa peered at him closely through the encroaching blackness surrounding them, but could detect no playfulness or mischief this time in his expression. If he was trying to frighten her, he was doing a darn good job of it.

She bid him goodnight and went to her tent. Late during the night, she opened her eyes and saw Scott through her partially open tent flap. He sat wrapped in a blanket by the campfire, waiting for Juan to come in. She slept soundly the rest of the night.

The next morning brought a misty rain.

"What do you think, Juan?" Scott asked, rubbing his chin thoughtfully "Can we make it to the village before we get washed away?"

When their conversation about the rain grew serious, Marisa quickly started packing the tin cups and dishes. It looked like such an insignificant little drizzle. What was all the fuss about? Uneasiness crept up the back of her neck. She knew by now Scott was not one to become alarmed about small things. Besides, she'd read about the sudden, violent storms in Brazil.

Juan cocked his head, listening and then said, "Better go than stay."

What did that cryptic message mean? Were they in danger? Marisa caught a slight edge of urgency in Juan's voice. She didn't wait for anyone to tell her to get ready to leave.

CHAPTER 13

Once they were on the trail, the rain turned into a roar. High above their heads it pounded on the tightly-packed growth with impressive force, though very little of it sifted down on them. Yet. Marisa knew it had to be soaked up by the foliage first and then it would come through.

Scott and Juan amazed her by how easily they picked out a trail in the gloom.

From time to time Scott turned back to check her gear. His hands were gentle and unhurried when he adjusted a strap on her backpack, which felt tons heavier to her than when they started.

His voice broke into the thunderous screams of the rain, as he turned to her. "No matter what happens, Marisa, don't leave the trail. You shouldn't have to look for it much longer. Soon we'll be ankle deep in mud. If you stray even a few feet away, this mist could swallow you. You'd be lost forever."

Another one of his fairy stories to scare her? The cynical speculation came just as the mist appeared, sliding in on cat paws of silence. Panic cut off her breath for a moment as the air turned to thick, white cotton, enveloping them.

"Ah, *senhorita*, please do not be frightened." Juan stepped closer as if in protection. "We will be in the village soon." His soothing voice made her understand she had every reason to be frightened.

She put on a smile, feeling the wobble at the corners of her mouth. "How could I be scared with two strong men so close?" She kept her voice light and knew it was the right answer when Juan grinned happily and stuck out his skinny chest. In a flash he ran off ahead on the trail, disappearing in the mist.

While she and Scott journeyed on, the rain continued, unrelenting, sifting down on their heads in a fine spray. Just as Scott had predicted, gooey thick mud clung to their boots, making each step twice as hard to manage. Fear of getting off the path now vanished. It had become impossible to do anything other than trudge along, head down, thankful the rain felt warm.

In spite of her discomfort, she suddenly realized that this was the most exciting experience of her life, and one she would look back on fondly when she returned to Virginia. The thought of the safety and security back home for once didn't comfort her. Under the circumstances, it was hard to even picture Elliott, Virginia.

They moved along in stoic silence. The only sounds, the pounding rain, muffled now in the fog, and the sucking noise of their boots when they pulled them up out of the mud. They couldn't see Juan, but occasionally a loud splash and his tuneless whistle came back on a passing wind current. Gradually she noticed the trees grew sparser and the canopy of semi-protection against the rain had all but disappeared.

Without the trees overhead, sheets of rain engulfed them. Marisa had never felt so wet and miserable. She imagined her misery might continue forever, until they heard Juan's shout. Catching up to him, they emerged at a large clearing. People ran out into the storm to greet them.

After a moment, Scott and Juan's excited talking penetrated her despair. She saw them gesturing her to come closer. She managed a weak smile, which she hoped did not come off as a grimace to the surrounding crowd of strangers. Before she took another deep breath, several short, round women began to pull her along with them to a hut perched against the background of the forest.

Once inside the shack, the steady drone of a distant power generator overcame the now familiar sound of the rain. This hut didn't have the benefit of a generator, however, and homemade candles lit the room, keeping out the afternoon gloom.

Marisa flexed her wearied shoulders and looked around, her curiosity undiminished by her discomfort. The single room seemed clean but far from neat. Clothing spilled from the tops of makeshift box-chairs and tables, while the corners of the room were roped off with ragged blankets to separate the sleeping quarters.

The women surrounding her giggled and spoke rapidly to each other while one of them removed Marisa's knapsack and motioned for her to look inside. They thought she probably had dry clothes. She lifted out her one extra shirt and pair of corduroy trousers, as wet as the clothes she had on.

One woman reached down into a pile of clothing and dragged out a clean muu-muu-type garment that looked as if the hemline would be above her knees but go around her body twice. They all greeted this prospect with whoops of good-natured laughter. A young girl—lovely, with the shy, big-eyed look of a fawn—held her finger and thumb apart to signify waiting a moment then turned and fled out into the rain.

A woman pointed to the retreating figure. "Angelina."

Meanwhile the others motioned for Marisa to go behind a blanketed partitions. They handed her a worn cloth to wrap around her. When she had done that, a woman took out a ragged towel from the pile and hopped up on a chair close to Marisa. Amid much laughter and teasing, the woman adroitly spun the towel around Marisa's soaking hair and twisted it upwards in a neat turban.

Ah, that felt better than having the water drip down her back.

It couldn't have taken more than a few minutes before Angelina returned with something draped over her arm. It turned out to be a bright pink prom dress of the nineteen-fifties vintage, with yards of taffeta fabric in the skirt and rows of ruffled trim. Some traveling missionary probably had dropped it off with other clothing donations. The girl offered the dress shyly to Marisa who could see this was her pride and joy. Reluctantly accepting the dress, Marisa changed behind the blanket, dismissing the image of a warm bath with tons of bubbles. They would think her a crazy woman. Having soaked for hours in water, why would she want more of it?

She tugged the garment over her still-damp body and looked down in dismay. It was a cartoon dress, flouncing and billowing out around the calves of her legs as if it had a life of its own. They handed her a pair of sandals and she put them on knowing her toes would come over the ends. What would Scott think when he saw her? Would he laugh?

Stepping from behind the blanket, she looked at the row of serious brown eyes and twirled around on her toes like a ballerina as they laughed and clapped. Angelina smiled broadly, and the women broke out into excited speech and approving nods. At least they were happy with the results. Someone brought her a mirror, cracked with the black around the edges seeping toward the center, creating a warped image. She pretended to examine herself and then turned and thanked everyone, especially Angelina.

Marisa retrieved a comb from her pack and hastily ran it through her hair, tugging at the snarls. Then, like a group of chattering children, the women led her outside for inspection.

The rain had stopped by now and most of the men from the village stood in the center of the clearing, smoking pipes and gossiping. She could hardly miss Scott, standing head and shoulders above the short, stocky Brazilians around him. He turned as they approached and she waited for his reaction. He looked from her dress to the smiling, proud face of Angelina and must have summed up the situation immediately.

He walked over to the group of women and took Angelina's hand in his big one. He bowed low and spoke to her softly. Turning to Marisa, he grinned in approval.

A feeling of pride brought tears alarmingly close to the surface, but Marisa willed them away. She whirled around with a big smile on her face, holding the skirts out wide and then made a grand bow to her watching audience. When they all applauded, she hugged the thin girl close and lightly kissed the top of her head.

Angelina reminded Marisa of the children she had taught, how innocently enthusiastic they were to learn. It brought back the thrill of achievement when one of them opened up to her. Until poor little Kenny tore all that apart. She would have liked to learn Portuguese, but she wouldn't be here that long. When she found Sara and the family, she was free to leave.

After the fuss died away, they all drifted back to their tasks and left Scott and her alone. He took her hand and led her toward the forest where they walked along the wide path. The sun came out fiercely. Steam rose from the ground.

They strolled in comfortable silence before stopping in a second, smaller clearing. A large, still pond had been created a little to the side of a river where the women could wash their clothes. Marisa sat next to Scott on rocks dried by the sun.

"It was good of you to wear Angelina's dress," Scott said. He reached for her hand again and held it lightly.

She felt the hard calluses on his palm. "I thought it was you who showed kindness," she said. "I expected ridicule, at the very least, since all you've done since I arrived is laugh at me." She wriggled her feet below the billowing material, pushing away some kind of insect that a few days ago would have had her climbing up the rock, shrieking.

"To tell the truth, you do sort of look like a stick of pink cotton candy," he teased. "Pink flatters you, and I like you in a dress."

She flushed, glad he could not see her discomfort in the shadows of the towering trees. "My boots. Will I ever wear them again? I can't go jogging through the wilds with these." She held out her feet. Unembarrassed by the too-small sandals on her feet, she found herself thinking, *Whoa! I'm gaining a sense of the ridiculous. I'm not afraid to laugh at myself.* What an odd feeling.

"Don't worry about it. Some kind soul back in Kayapo has already cleaned and dried your boots. One thing about these people, if they like you, there's nothing they won't do to please you. Yet they can be cruel and harsh, make no mistake. It's the life they lead—not an easy one."

"Isn't that a funny name for a village, Kayapo? What does it mean?"

"They named it after the Indian people who were pushed out to build this village. The government resettled the natives in another area and by darn, didn't the Kayapos find gold where they'd been relocated. A fine irony, I'd say. Once the rubber workers move in, the two cultures can't exist as neighbors, seems like."

"You love Brazil and the people here."

"I wouldn't want to be anywhere else at this point in my life. It's heartbreaking though. These people are *seringueiros*, rubber workers. It's a dying industry and they've nothing else to replace it."

"Aren't they the ones cutting down the rain forests?"

He shook his head vehemently. "Not on your life! They harvest the rubber, but never destroy the source. Sometime, I'll show you."

"Then who is doing the burning that we read about back home? I've always assumed it's much to do about nothing, like worrying about the ozone layer. I mean, there are so many trees—"

"That's what makes the situation so frustrating. Most everyone assumes, if they even bother to think about it, that the forests here go on forever. But ranching and mining in Brazil spell the doom of the rain forests if no one stops it. Ranchers destroy the forest to plant grass for their cattle. Then the grasses gradually die away because the soil's not right for grass, leaving nothing but scrub. The rains come and wash away all the good topsoil. The mining enterprises pour chemicals into the rivers which in turn affect the trees and the animals."

"And you hope to help with your coloring books? To start with making the kids aware of the problem?"

He brushed back a lock of hair from his forehead, his eyes alight with enthusiasm. "It has to start somewhere.

Most of the adults are too set in their ways to think of alternatives."

"What about the summit meetings in Brazil. Doesn't that help?"

"To some extent, to make people more aware of the problem. The big banks aren't supplying as much inducement for the cattlemen to open up vast areas now. The government's placed any incentives on hold for this kind of expansion. I just hope the planning isn't too late. A lot's been lost already."

"My ancestors could be cattlemen. Sara never said."

"Probably they'd work in the rubber, though, if they're in this area." He tucked a stray curl behind her ear. "Say, you're getting on good with the people out here, usually they're very reserved with strangers. You'd better watch it. You may never want to leave." His voice remained light, but his eyes were serious and he regarded her with a long gaze that made her uncomfortable.

"I do like Brazil and the people, but can't let it grow on me. I belong in Virginia."

"What makes you so sure?"

She regarded him with surprise. "For one thing, this is a trip to me, an adventure you could say, but not my whole life. I can't exist for the rest of my future days in someone else's condo, using someone else's plane like some people."

He'd held onto this identity for so long with her that she was ready to assume he had a boss. The grin he tossed back at her made her angry. He didn't get it, did he?

"What's so difficult to understand about that?" he demanded. "I pay my way. The boss is happy with my work."

"I suppose that's true. Judging from the work you've done on the landscaping, he should be happy. Still, it isn't yours. Don't you see the difference?"

"No, frankly I don't. You aren't so much in command of your own life. First a teacher, now working in the office of some newspaper. What gives you the right to judge me?"

"I'm not exactly judging you." She knew better. "Okay, maybe I am, a little bit, but I'm my own person. I choose to make a change in my life when I need to. I'm not obligated to anyone for a living."

"Bravo!" He looked at her with approval behind his mocking expression. "That's the most sensible thing you've said since we met." He tweaked her nose gently. "I like a woman with fire and backbone."

"Like Elaina?" She couldn't stop the words from coming.

He frowned slightly. "Elaina? No, definitely not like Elaina. She's like a sleek, well-cared for cat, always landing on her feet. Sure, she can manage on her own if she needs to, but she never has to. You two are as different as the sun and the moon."

For once Marisa didn't stop to analyze his words. "Why would a woman want to spend her time with a bush pilot who probably has a girl in every airport?" It didn't make sense, but she could see why a woman might want to do just that.

He laughed. "You saying a bush pilot wouldn't be good enough for you?"

"I'm not saying any such thing. We're talking about Elaina."

"Are we?" His eyebrow shot up and a look of smugness crept into his grin. "She and I are friends. Anything between us was over before it started. We're strictly business and have been for ages." He studied Marisa, as if memorizing her face.

A feeling of warmth crept over her and she wanted more than anything to slide her fingers through his dark hair.

"You sure are hooked on security," he challenged.

"Not really. Well, maybe. I want a husband who will be productive, steady of purpose and constant. What he earns or how he does it isn't that important."

"Like your Thomas?"

"Well, yes, like Thomas. We have the same qualities in many ways. We both want a family and both want our kids to grow up secure and safe. What's so bad about that?"

"Not that it's bad. Just terminally dull." He was laughing at her again. "If you are determined to settle down in the suburbs one day, then you shouldn't object to a bush pilot for a lover, just as a temporary measure," he said with a mischievous look in his eyes.

She tried to match his lightness, although the subject was serious to her. "I don't see how that would work," she protested with a smile.

He stood and stretched lazily. Before she guessed his intentions, he pulled her close, kissing the tip of her nose and nibbling at the corners of her lips. At first she tried to push him away, but he didn't budge. She could feel the strength of his hand pressing against the back of her neck and felt herself mold to the lean, male hardness of his body.

The protest died within her as a wellspring of warmth flowed through her veins, and she responded to his kisses with a depth of passion she had not realized she possessed.

He pushed the filmy, gathered material away from her shoulder. His hand roamed over the back of her neck, his fingers rubbing gently up and down the ridge of her backbone. When she thought her legs wouldn't hold her another moment, he pulled away abruptly, his jaw clenching with his need for control.

It came as a shocking embarrassment to realize he was the one to break away. Marisa had no idea why he retreated. She should be grateful for his restraint, but that was not exactly the emotion uppermost in her mind right now. She felt as tawdry as the pitiful dress she wore, knowing she'd been on the brink of surrendering to him completely.

"Why are you staring at me like that?" she demanded, struggling to bring her breathing back to normal.

He seemed to be having the same problem. Behind the thick black lashes, his eyes were unfathomable. "It's as if I see you for the first time. Our values are very different."

"You're right. I told you that the first time we met."

"We'd better get back to the village. It'll be dark soon." He reached for her hand and after a moment's hesitation, she took his.

"When can I begin looking for Sara?" she asked, wanting a subject far from personal.

"It's not that simple. You'll need to talk to the villagers about it first. When I get back from my digs, I'll take you inside the jungle to the Yellowhairs. Juan can stay here to watch over you."

"I thought Juan always went with you. Does he know where these people are?" What she had really thought was that he would postpone his own work a few days to help her find the Yellowhairs and then take her on with him to his campsite. How could he be so charming one moment and so distrustful the next?

"Juan could find the Yellowhairs if anyone could, but he'll wait for me."

Maybe his little friend would, but would she?

CHAPTER 14

In the village of Kayapo, the shacks made of palm fronds and aged wood were lined up against the encroaching jungle, each with a candle burning inside—like little fireflies in the dark. Marisa fervently hoped her clothing would be dry enough now to return Angelina's dress.

When they reached a doorway, Scott slowed and motioned for her to go ahead. She smelled something delicious cooking and her stomach cried out in hunger. As her eyes adapted to the eerie glow of candles in the large room, she made out a kind of community restaurant. Against the side of the wall, a tall, exceedingly slim man fried fish over a makeshift charcoal brazier, made from half an oil drum. Marisa looked closer and then questioningly up at Scott. "Is that man—?"

"Using hub caps for a wok?" Scott grinned. "Yep. If we're lucky we get our fish cooked in the Mercedes hubs, it's by far the grandest."

They laughed and she felt better as the tension between them lightened. She watched the man expertly work over the four hubcaps of hot frying fish. In a very few minutes a tepid beer appeared in front of them, with tin plates of crispy golden fillets of fish and what looked like round slices of fried potatoes.

"Is this the famous *pacu* fish you and Juan have been going on about?" she asked, savoring her first taste.

"You'll never eat anything like it. These people don't have much, but if you could be here Saturday nights after the mines and farms have paid the workers for the week, you'd think they were rich and without a care in the world. They can have the best times with so little. It never fails to amaze me."

By the time they finished the meal, Marisa's eyelids drooped and she couldn't hold back her yawns, try as she might.

"Hey, sweet cheeks, you look beat," Scott said. "Come on and I'll show you where you bunk tonight. Tomorrow we can find someone who knows of the Yellowhairs."

"Will you leave right away? Not tonight?" She struggled to keep the edge of panic from creeping into her question.

He reached to smooth a damp curl away from the side of her cheek. "No. I'm not going yet," he assured her. "I'll stay long enough to make sure you get help to find your Sara."

Out in the center of the settlement, dogs and piglets roamed across the wide trail that looked like the main street.

"Where did the cook get his hubcaps?" As far as she could see, there had never been a car in the village; only ox carts and donkey wagons.

"They bring all sorts of goodies down the Tapajos River from Santarem. Hubcaps are a primo item. I've delivered them to Juan's village when I can find them at the flea market in Brasilia."

Children and adults wandered by, smiling and acknowledging them. One man walked up and shook

Scott's hand and bowed ceremoniously to her. "Missus, good morning," he pronounced slowly.

She returned his bow and when he left, she turned to Scott. "He called me Missus? Do they call all female strangers 'missus'?"

Scott appeared uncomfortable and she thought for a moment he wasn't going to answer. How odd. He didn't often lack of something to say. His sensuous lips, the hard line of his jaw, made her want to touch a finger to his mouth, to ease his disquiet.

"I let them know—oh hell, might as well say it straight out. I told them you're my woman." At her frown, he scratched his head as if delaying an answer. He actually looked embarrassed. "That way no one will bother you with unwanted attention. They respect that we are together."

"What if I want their attention?" she teased.

He didn't take the bait and smile. Still serious, he touched her arm lightly to make sure she was listening. "Even the women would be against you then, jealous if they thought you unattached. Like I've been telling you, single women don't wander off into the jungles in this country."

"Okay. Thanks. We're back to 'you Tarzan, me Jane,' looks like." She thumped her chest which made her cough.

He put out a restraining hand. "Damn, I thought you were going to burst out into a Tarzan yodel."

His grin warmed her from the inside out and she turned away to look at the village, wondering what it would be like to really be 'his woman.' What a strange term and how insufferably macho, yet dear. Very dear.

What was she thinking? Back home she wouldn't have allowed someone to talk to her like this for a moment.

☼ ☼ ☼

In the morning, the smell of coffee brewing and bread baking awakened her. Dawn had just slipped over and through the trees, spreading golden over the sparse center of the compound. She slipped on her clothes, careful not to wake Angelina and her mother who still slept on hammocks in a corner behind the stove.

Once outside, a few dogs sniffed her heels curiously and followed a ways behind. She walked to the outskirts of the camp in the direction Scott had taken her on their stroll the night before. The morning had already turned muggy and warm and she thought of what a delight a bath would be to start a new day. Surely Indians and crocodiles and huge fish wouldn't bother her this close to the village and Scott's stern warning shouldn't apply.

When she reached the pool, she draped her clothes on a branch and waded gingerly into the water. It felt warm, the right temperature for an early morning swim. She took several laps around the circumference of the pool and turned on her back to float. White plumed birds soared above the trees, changing to a soft rosy color as the first rays of sun melted over their path of flight.

"You are the greatest one for water I've ever seen." Scott's voice penetrated her reverie.

She jerked upright, swallowing half the water in the pond. "Must you always sneak up on a person?" she sputtered, between coughs of water. It was then she realized that her shoulders were above water, and her clothes hanging from the tree. He would know she came in nude this time.

As if reading her thoughts, he grinned down at her for a moment and then hunkered down on the bank as if time were no object.

"Well, you big overgrown oaf," she growled. "Are you planning to sit there and watch me? Surely you can't use the excuse of marauding Indians or anything else you've come up with so far." She had decided the night before that she would have to guard her feelings toward this man if she wanted to return to Virginia with any comfort and dignity left at all.

He raked his fingers through the thatch of thick, dark hair that had a penchant for falling across his forehead. "You're right, I don't know of any Indians this close to the village, but if you're still here by Saturday night, I'd strongly advise you not to do this alone. A rowdy bunch of miners show up every week to let off steam. For the most part, they're a harmless group, but I wouldn't push my luck."

"Okay, you've said your piece. Now how about leaving so I can get dressed."

He stood, brushing off his pants. "I could use a little swim myself. It was a warm night," he said and began to unbutton his shirt.

She couldn't deny the surge of pleasure, imagining his body so deliciously close to hers in the silky water. No. No use deluding herself. She wouldn't be any match for that situation. "If you want to swim with me, that's one thing, but I should warn you, I'm not looking for a one-night stand."

He stopped with his buttons and looked across the water at her. His gray eyes narrowed, and he chewed on the corner of his lip. "So. Is that your impression of my...ah...my needs?"

She saw the hurt in his eyes and defended herself against it with reflexive indignation. "I don't want to be another notch on your Ferrari wheel, that's all."

For a long moment they regarded each other until his rueful grin broke the pensive moment between them. "I told you, it isn't a Ferrari. You may think you have a point, but I fancied you enjoyed my kisses."

She made no denial, looking down at the water and waited for what hurting words might come next. Men had to defend their bruised egos, no matter what.

"I'm not ready for anything like a commitment," he warned. "Been there, done that."

Her face burned with shame. Had he read her mind? She had long guarded her innermost feelings and the privacy of her body. Then for one inexplicable moment, she had been ready to surrender it to this man who threw it back at her. "And as I told you, I'm not ready for a one-night stand."

He began to button his shirt. "Marisa, I...You are the most tantalizing, the most desirable woman, but I won't lie to you to get what I want. This isn't the time for me."

"Would you please leave? I'm very uncomfortable, talking like this." She spoke in her best schoolteacher's voice, trying to regain her dignity. Her heart was aching, physically aching. She had come so close to opening herself to him, and he didn't care. At least he was truthful about it. She hated to think what she would have surrendered had he lied about his intentions.

"You're so damned desirable, and the charm is of it is, you haven't a clue what you do to me. I naturally assumed you wanted—I mean—"

"You assumed we could have a little fling in the jungle and then go back to our lives as if it never happened? Scott, I'm not made that way."

He rubbed his temples with both hands, as if his thoughts were too heavy to be contained in his head. "I know. I knew that from the get-go. If anyone could move me to a permanent relationship, it would be you, sweetheart. But so many things have happened, so many reasons I can't be the way you want me to be."

He was right, though it hurt to admit it. She turned her head away so he wouldn't see the tears creeping out from under her eyelids. Her expectations had pushed her buttons and made her open to wanting his lovemaking.

It wasn't his fault. He was incapable of loving. No, not incapable of loving. She knew better. Just incapable of the responsibility of love. Maybe she was way off base. Maybe expecting guarantees attached to love was a distortion of the whole process.

"Anyway, you don't fit my qualifications as a husband," she said and hardened her heart to the inexplicable feelings that swept over her, feelings that wanted expression, that begged her to let go and change her mind.

He seemed to accept her blunt words with a composure that hurt her more than if he'd become angry. "So it's back to what I do. Bush pilot with no future, that sort of thing."

She didn't bother with denial. "That's part of it. Shows your lack of goals, an immature rebelling against taking life seriously. You're what now, in your thirties? So you've had a bad marriage, you think the world has dumped on you. You've turned your back on your family, content to be alone."

"You don't feel you're running away?" he countered, as if stung by her sharp words. "If I'm running away, so are you. Teaching was your life. Do you deny it? Because of an incident with one child, you throw up your hands and walk away. Maybe we're too much alike, you and I."

"Don't change the subject. We're talking about love and family values."

"No, you are."

Could her values be so wrong, she wondered? Her father never acknowledged love as a positive emotion, relegating it to teenagers, Hollywood and clouded judgment. Had he felt that way with her mother, too? Then why did they marry? For convenience? Because it was expected of him? He'd steadfastly refused to talk about their early years together.

Did that mean men were creatures driven by lust and that love was something women thought up? Why had Scott pulled away from her in the jungle when she might have surrendered in the heat of the moment?

Marisa shook her head and wiped the tears away with a furtive movement of her palms. "Let's keep this on a business level from now on. It's the only way."

It was going to try her self-discipline to traipse all over this exotic country, living side by side with this man, and forgo the strong feelings she had for him. Yet she would never humiliate herself again by letting him see she cared so much, while he apparently would have considered their lovemaking as merely entertainment.

"I'll catch up with you when I'm dressed," she said. "Juan is probably on his way to look for us." For a brief time the jungle was quiet except for the usual bird sounds. When she looked up, he had disappeared.

Marisa waited a little longer and then stepped out of the water, dressing without bothering to dry off. Somehow she expected him to be waiting on the trail back to the village. She fought against the traitorous disappointment when he wasn't there.

The morning passed without her seeing Scott, but she didn't have much time to consider that while Juan accompanied her from shack to shack, asking questions. Many villagers had caught glimpses of the Yellowhairs, or thought they had. Most had never seen one or wanted to.

As a group, the Yellowhairs kept to themselves, and it seemed as if a lot of myths and superstitious fears had built around them over the generations.

Excitement welled up in Marisa. They were close. She could feel it. Odd that no one had seen that huge mansion in the center of the jungle, though. How could they miss it? It was probably deeper inside the Mato Grosso than anyone here had ever wanted to go. She took the picture from her shirt pocket to look at it again. Since Scott hadn't returned, Juan finally admitted he must have gone on to his site alone.

"Okay, I'm ready to leave, Juan. Pack up and let's get started." So what if none of the villagers would go with them, Scott had said Juan was good at tracking.

"Oh no, *senhorita*! We must wait for Dom Scott." Juan looked stunned by her words and also worried at having to disagree with her.

"Nonsense," she answered, bristling at his placating manner. "By now he is probably on his way to another of his precious diggings. He doesn't have time to waste on my search. He told me that very plainly."

Juan's liquid black eyes widened in surprise. "He did?"

"Of course he did," she said crossly. "Now let's get our gear together and be off. He said you could get me to the Yellowhairs if anyone could."

"Dom Scott said that?"

"Yes, he did. Do you know how to find this village that they whisper about?" It might be one of those legends with no basis of truth, but she had to start somewhere.

He nodded, clearly unhappy. "Yes. But it is a bad place. No one wants to go there. People unfriendly."

"I've heard that, but the villagers have seen them. They're out there somewhere, and I've come a long way to find them, Juan. It's so very important to me."

He shrugged thin shoulders. "Not even Indians go there. No one even steals from them." Juan said this as if in a last desperate attempt to change her mind. They must have told him a great deal more than he translated back to her.

"I'm going. If you want to catch up to Scott, you're free to do so. I've come all this way, and I'm not leaving until I find Sara."

This was what Scott probably had hoped for. That she'd become discouraged, tucking her tail between her legs like some old blue tick hound and slinking back to Virginia, or out of his hair at least. Probably why they couldn't find him at the camp this morning. He hoped that would dishearten her.

Finally, reluctantly, Juan gave in.

Marisa rushed him along, packing a few necessities for the journey into the jungle. Leaving before Scott returned was important. If he saw she was still determined, he might try to stop her. That business at the pond didn't help matters either. She had deflated his ego, maybe for the first time in his life, and he obviously wasn't taking it too well.

Just by closing her eyes, it was easy to recapture the feel of his warm mouth against hers, the way he nibbled the corners of her lips, and his tenderness when he held her close. She had felt his heart beat when she leaned against his chest. Her emotions for him were more complicated than the rich, provocative passion that flowed through her body when they touched. Nevertheless, she would not be played with like a doll and then cast off when he tired of the game.

There was too much at stake here. Her father's life might be at risk. He was so wrapped up in his obsession of finding Sara and returning the money to the bank. He had lost interest in all else, even in his loyal companion, Janice.

"Time to go, Juan. No more procrastinating while you wait for Dom Scott. We'll have an adventure all our own."

She steadfastly ignored the look of gloom on Juan's face along with her own foreboding.

CHAPTER 15

In spite of Juan's delaying action, Scott hadn't shown up by the time they left Kayapo. Marisa was relieved, because she believed this was something she had to do on her own.

They entered the forest, leaving the sleeping villagers behind. Marisa looked back, remembering the dogs, pigs, and children running everywhere on the muddy paths. Everything was so quiet now. The jungle crowded around them, sucking them into a cocoon of green velvet.

They walked for a long time in silence. Juan didn't push jauntily forward, whistling as he did on their other trip. She noticed he'd fastened a large, ugly-looking machete to his belt. She hoped it was for cutting brush. They finally paused to drink tepid passion fruit juice from the bottles hanging on their belts then continued on until Juan stopped to ask if she wanted to eat. They opened the packet Angelina's mother had done up for them. The food looked tasty, but neither one of them was hungry.

What was Scott doing at just this point in time? Would he be angry when he found out she'd practically forced Juan to accompany her?

Dark descended early in the forest. Juan strung up hammocks to keep them off the ground, but Marisa still thought of creatures crawling up and down the trees where they strung the hammocks. Having Juan lie in his hammock with a large machete draped across his stomach didn't help her go to sleep easily either. She finally dozed off, listening to the swell of night noises surrounding them.

Raucous sounds of monkeys leaping and careening in the leafy overhead canopy awoke her. Juan had made coffee over a small fire and offered her a cup.

"I apologize for pushing you into bringing me here," she said. "I really do, but Dom Scott is too busy to take me. He said so." Maybe not in so many words.

Juan smiled, his white teeth a marked contrast against his dusky complexion. "Okay. We go. Dom Scott wait for us if he comes back before."

This morning of their second day out, Juan began to look over his shoulder often and walk faster. Marisa hurried to catch up.

"What's bothering you? You look as if the devil himself is behind us. "

The boy looked at her, his expression grave. "Wish we waited for Dom Scott."

"What did those people tell you back in the village?"

He stepped from one foot to another, as if he wanted to be anywhere else. It was very puzzling and succeeded in making her nervous, too.

Finally, heaving a huge sigh that lifted his slight shoulders, he began to tell her the truth. "Dom Scott, he be mad. He said take good care of you. The people say don't go in jungle. Not good."

"Is that all that's worrying you?" She felt like patting his wiry hair as she would have patted one of her students. "Bless your heart. I told you Scott hadn't planned to come with us. He told me that himself. What else did the people tell you?"

"Yellowhairs do not want outsiders. Even Indians leave them alone."

"Didn't Dom Scott tell you these are my relatives, my family?"

He looked blank.

"My family from a long time ago. That's why they are different, I suppose, why they are called Yellowhairs. Somewhere out there lives a very old lady whose name is Sara and she's in trouble. I must go for my father's sake. He requested it." Juan should understand that, at least and she had to calm him if they were to continue the trip.

Back in Kayapo, she'd had the impression Scott might have changed his mind and, not having the time to take her, would have postponed this journey. She wanted to get it over with and settled.

She slid out from under her backpack and let it fall to the ground. Rummaging around inside, she pulled out the sheaf of photographs bound with a large rubber band.

"Here, Juan. The photos will explain better than I could tell you."

She handed the photographs to him, watching him hold them gingerly in his palm as he looked, first at one then the other.

"Well, what do you think?"

"That place is not here in jungle." He stabbed a thin brown finger at the photograph of the large white pillared house.

"Why, of course it's here, pictures don't lie. See the jungle in the background? One of the original family was a photographer. Of course when he died, the picture taking stopped."

"House is not here," he insisted, his expression woebegone as if he hated to speak against her.

She put the photographs back in her pack and slung it over her shoulders, fixing the front straps in place. "We're here now, maybe close. Please?"

He dipped his head, as if ashamed of his fear, and turned to lead the way.

"Don't worry so much. You'll be old before your time. Then what will Angelina do? Maybe find a younger man," she teased at his retreating back. No one could mistake the looks exchanged between those two. When she asked Scott about it, he told her Angelina's mother refused to let her marry Juan until he had a permanent job. Her parents thought he should go into rubber harvesting, it had been good enough for his father, but Romeo O'Reilly wouldn't let Juan start in the rubber.

While they walked, her mind wandered to the task ahead. Could she communicate with these people once she found them? It was true, Sara wrote in English, an old fashioned spidery hand, barely legible, but did they all speak and understand it? Her Spanish was passable and the guide books said the Portuguese could usually understand Spanish but not vise-versa.

They ventured deeper into the swamp, and the dankness swelled to engulf them. The eerie sounds of birds and animals took their toll on her nerves. Maybe she had been a little hasty in not waiting for Scott, even if he had said he wasn't ready to take her. She scoffed at her worries. It was better this way, without his bossiness. Time seemed to stand still as they edged along through the thin jungle path.

The muted sound of barking dogs penetrated her reverie. That sounded like a village! They must be close. Juan stopped in his tracks and let her catch up to him.

Marisa shrieked when three men abruptly appeared from behind. That's why Juan had continued to turn and look around. He must have sensed someone following them.

She felt sweat trickle down her side and yet her skin felt icy and willed herself to be calm. With golden skin and sun-streaked beards and hair, they didn't seem threatening. They resembled Vikings from the pages of a book, taller than any Brazilians she'd seen, though probably not as tall as Scott.

Their expressions were neither friendly nor menacing, but it was obvious they didn't want her and Juan to continue without their accompaniment.

She mustered up courage to speak since Juan seemed struck dumb. "Do you speak English?" At their stony expressions, she turned to Juan. "Try to tell them why I'm here," she urged. "Tell them I have letters from *La Madrinha*, Sara," she broke off in confusion. How would she begin to explain her ancestry to these people when Juan didn't even understand? At the mention of Sara's name, she caught a flicker of interest in their eyes.

Faltering only slightly, Juan began to speak. The men appeared to listen and then turned to talk among themselves, their bare, broad backs signaling their scorn to the two watching them. Juan's eyes narrowed, his chin lifted in suppressed anger. She assumed he was upset at the implied insult of the men turning their backs on them.

Finally, they stopped talking and the tallest, youngest of the group took over, motioning for Juan and Marisa to follow. The camp was not far from where they stood but well hidden in the trees.

Disappointment flooded her when they entered the village. In the center of a huge clearing stood a pathetic imitation of a gracious, old southern mansion. From the looks of it, no one had tried to do any repairs over the last fifty years. The once-white paint had peeled off, showing the rough boards beneath. The roof over the veranda tilted, making the second story windows look sloped. The columns were a parody, although probably the first ancestor here, maybe even the infamous Banker Elliott, had tried very hard to reconstruct the building from memory.

Marisa glanced at Juan and almost had to laugh at his mouth, hanging open in a surprised "O." Then the letdown flooded back. If someone had no more care or ability to keep up this home, would they have harbored the treasure all these years?

The younger Yellowhair, who seemed to be the leader of the group, stepped forward and touched her hair. He didn't seem a bit shy. She stood still, not wanting to offend anyone. Not yet, anyway.

He motioned for her to follow and turned to part the brush in front of him.

"Come, Juan. Close your mouth and let's go. I told you this was here." She admitted to a sense of satisfaction. Wouldn't Scott have been surprised?

Before she had time to worry about blindly following the unfriendly men, they advanced into the settlement. Different from others she had seen in the jungle, these homes were constructed of logs, chinked against the rains, with crude shingles on the roofs. The village was posed at the edge of the trees, as if expecting any day the encroaching jungle would move back to claim its own and swallow them all.

"This is so strange," she whispered to Juan, needing the comfort of her own voice. Babies, dogs, and piglets wandered willy-nilly, but the color of the children was extraordinary. For the most part they were deeply tanned or rosy with sunburn, the incongruous tow heads and red heads mixed with the usual brunettes.

Marisa glanced up at the man standing next to her. He was so close, she stepped back in sudden alarm, which made him laugh. He was handsome, in a primitive way—a perfect book cover model for a romance novel.

For the next hour she passed around her pictures and cautiously showed them the lockets and jewelry with small, old-fashioned portraits inside. Maybe someone would recognize a duplicate owned by an ancestor. Hesitatingly, she showed them Sara's writing, wincing as they passed the delicate sheets around. It was obvious they couldn't read.

At first the women stood back, shy and hesitant, while the men examined the articles. Then, losing interest, as if in the end it was beneath their dignity, the men strolled away, talking and laughing among themselves. After that, the women pressed closer, touching the photos, their eyes big with wonder, whispering among themselves, even smelling the letters as if the writing emitted some strange odor.

She hadn't had a chance to really look at the men. They'd worn hats for the most part. But she noticed now that some of the women and children had blue or green eyes. Feeling something touching the back of her neck, Marisa turned around to see the tallest blond man standing near, now staring fixedly into space over her head.

Looking at the women in their makeshift dresses, with bare feet and tangled light hair, Marisa squirmed uneasily. There but for the grace of God, her mother's ancestors might also have taken this route and left The States. Then she would be here, a part of this village. Except for the circumstances of their birth, these people might easily have fit in Virginia. It was still hard to believe they would not suddenly begin speaking English.

"I am not able to understand these people," Juan complained. The tall man's continued interest in Marisa openly distressed him.

"Try," she urged him. "That's all I ask of you."

When he finally bogged down in the translation, a small tow-headed girl who had attached herself to Marisa from the beginning, ran into a dilapidated hut. In a moment she dragged out a protesting old man.

Marisa's first irreverent thought was that he looked ancient enough to have been the carpenter on Noah's Ark. He appeared embarrassed by the sudden attention of the women clustered about Marisa and Juan, until he stood straight and threw back his shoulders.

For a fleeting moment Marisa could have sworn he knew who she was.

Someone pulled over a woven chair and he sank down on it as if he had walked from miles away. The little girl whispered something to him, her expression one of pleading. He finally moved his thin shoulders as if to shed his impatience and patted her hand with loving tenderness.

Both Marisa and Juan listened in surprise when at last he spoke in halting English mixed with Portuguese and softened by the remnants of a Virginia drawl.

"You were foolish to come here, child, without protection. Our people are unaware of the amenities in your world. You are not safe here alone. They do not favor strangers in their midst. We have tried to keep to ourselves."

Marisa struggled not to smile at his old-fashioned way of speaking. Juan bristled at the notion that she was unprotected.

"I'm an Elliott, as I expect you are. I'm only trying to learn of my ancestors, my relatives. It is my father's dearest wish to find you and—" She couldn't trust anyone enough to tell about Sara's promise of the treasure yet. Of course she'd have to smuggle it out. No doubt there were laws against removing that much currency from a country, but she'd find a way.

Marisa gathered up the photographs and other objects, spreading them on the small, rickety table the eager women carried out of a house. The old man picked up each item, carefully one at a time as if they burned his hand.

After minutes had passed, the man whispered to the child. She ran away and returned with a moldy leather case. With trembling fingers, he struggled to open it, brushing away the girl's help.

The contents spilled on the table and Marisa gasped as he offered her a picture to look at. It was identical to one of those photos she had brought! Tears ran down her cheeks when she thought of how long her father had hoped and dreamed for something like this to happen. How wonderful it would have been if he could have seen this himself.

The little girl noticed Marisa's tears and ran to stand next to her protectively, sneaking a tiny hand to nest inside hers. Marisa smiled and knelt to touch the girl's cheek. Such a pretty child, as slight and delicate as one of the golden butterflies that clustered in giant hoards in the jungle. Her skin was tanned a pale honey color, yet she appeared sturdy in spite of the delicate bone structure and small size.

"What is your name, child?"

The little girl obviously understood part of what Marisa asked, but didn't know how to answer. She looked at the old man for assistance. Her eyes were the same golden color as Marisa's own.

"Her name is Saffron. I have taught her a little English, but she is fearful to try it with a stranger."

"Saffron? Like the spice?"

The old man smiled a toothless smile with pink gums showing. "A very uncommon spice. When she was born, an Indian tribe came through here, and we took the name from what they said about her. She has always been a golden child." He looked as if he wanted to bring the girl closer to his side, away from where she stood near Marisa, but he refrained. It clearly would have been beneath his dignity.

"Where is her family?"

"I am her family. I and Manolo, who is her uncle, and the others," he waved a thin arm toward the young man standing at the door and the crowd outside. "A mine explosion killed her mother and father."

How sad, but at least she had people who loved her.

"My name is Jacob. Jacob Elliott."

"That's my father's name!"

He nodded, eyes solemn. "Every family named a son Jacob."

He pronounced the name reluctantly, as if the words stuck on the way out. "When my mother and father died, we stopped using American names. Then I was called El Blanco, and now they call me El Viejo, the old one."

Marisa took her time, reading the folded letters he laid on the table. Her father's letters to Sara. She paused and looked up at the circle around her, the men and women clustered close, waiting. Waiting for what? She could feel the tall bronzed man, Manolo's, steady gaze, but didn't look in his direction.

"I don't understand this. If you have these letters, then where is the *Madrinha*? Where is Sara?"

The old man closed his eyes, blue veined eyelids so thin she could almost see through them into his eyes. That was one of Kenny's favorite questions, where did eyes go when you closed them. Why did Saffron remind her of Kenny and the others in her classes? Was it the complete trust and adoration she saw there? Heady stuff—impossible to live up to.

"There has never been a Sara here. You must be mistaken." El Viejo spoke slowly and carefully so she could not misunderstand.

"I can't be mistaken! What about this house? Sara wrote about the house. She—" Caution stopped her from telling about Sara's last letter where she mentioned the treasure. Although Sara said it was cursed and no one wanted it, some in the village might be unwilling to give it to a stranger.

He shrugged with bony shoulder blades that looked sharp enough to cut paper. "Perhaps she lives over there." He swung his arm toward the jungle. "Our people quarreled many years ago. Some moved away, to the other side of the Matos."

That didn't make sense. Why would he have possession of Sara's letters then? He was hiding something, but challenging him outright would not be prudent.

Manolo stepped forward and bent to whisper in the old man's ear. The tall Yellowhair's voice sounded harsh, his gestures agitated.

When El Viejo didn't respond, Manolo stepped back, an expression of cunning leaped into his eyes.

"Manolo tells me you have come a long way. He wants me to permit you to stay the night. I do not think that wise."

How did Manolo know where she and Juan had come from? How long had he followed them? Maybe Juan told him while she was occupied with Jacob. "He speaks English?"

The old man nodded. "Several of us do, imperfectly. Saffron will be the last. The others choose to let that part of our heritage die."

"It's hard to understand that you don't know where Sara is. I imagined her about your age. Surely you know her. There can't be that many of you left." Marisa recognized the straight lips and the blank look in the old man's face, something akin to that of her father when he decided to be stubborn.

He folded his arms across his skinny chest and the three men moved closer, menacing.

"I appreciate what you've shown me, but it's very important I find Sara. She has something for us that my father must have. She promised. I believe it's in there somewhere." Marisa pointed toward the house.

The ancient one summoned those closest to help him up. "We want nothing that comes from the house. Nothing. The house is cursed and none of us will go inside."

"But—" Marisa didn't know how to plead. It went against her grain. However, she'd come too far to let him turn her away with no answers to her questions.

"I regret your coming a long way in vain," he said stiffly. "I am unable to offer you respite for the night." El Viejo frowned, seeming to drag the words out from some hidden recess in his memory. "We do not wish visitors. We have worked very hard to frighten outsiders away, providing us peace and tranquility here."

He had a point. They looked very self-sufficient. Large, neat gardens filled the inside perimeter of the compound. Corn, and vegetables with lush green leaves and fruit trees grew in sedate profusion, showing evidence of seeds and plants brought from Virginia.

El Viejo spoke again, his voice a harsh whisper. Marisa had to lean forward to hear. "Keep the letters. They mean nothing to me. But then Saffron may want them one day. It has been my conviction that we must not expose the girl to the outside. We have kept her safe, here."

"Oh, but—" Marisa began to sputter in her haste to speak. The outside world held many benefits in spite of civilization's flaws. Saffron would probably live to twice the age out there as she would hidden away here. But it was plain to see the old man would never listen to her arguments. His skin had taken on a bluish pallor beneath the butternut of his tan. His face appeared drawn and he looked older than when he came out to talk only minutes before.

He knew where Sara was, or the money. She'd bet on it. But why the secrecy? Had the old woman changed her mind about the treasure and asked El Viejo to cover up for her? Or had something terrible happened to her?

Marisa looked around at the neat, shabby dwellings. The people crowding around wore clean, mended old-fashioned clothing. What an inferior existence these people's ancestors had chosen for them.

Yet Scott claimed offshoots of the southerners lived in cities across Brazil and fared very well. How odd that this group, of all the refugees, had the best start with the treasure chest of money absconded from the Elliott Bank but settled in to become primitives.

If Sara did break with this group and form her own gathering, the treasure could still be here. It was plain from Sara's letters that she didn't want any part of the money and wanted the Americans to come take it away. She had either left the letters with the old man. Or they'd been taken away from her.

"Come inside, young woman," El Viejo wheezed. "I can see you have stubborn qualities of the Elliott family. When I catch my breath, I will try to explain what is puzzling you. I cannot let you leave like this." He motioned for her to follow and, brushing away the offered support of two women, he hobbled toward a hut.

"No, *senhorita*!" Juan had never strayed far from her side, and now he pulled on her sleeve, a familiarity couched in desperation. "We do not have time! We cannot stay here tonight and the rains will come after dark."

"Nonsense. This won't take long. If the rains come before we leave we can camp in the old house." She brushed away his clutching fingers, eager to follow the old man inside before he changed his mind.

She listened to the buzz of conversation that followed them. Maybe she had been too hasty to leave without Scott. He would have been invaluable here. Juan's translation was faulty at best, and the old man's English was archaic and hard to understand.

Once inside the small room, Jacob, who she still thought of as El Viejo, motioned for her to take a stool. Someone brought them fruit drinks and since they didn't offer Juan any, she insisted he take hers. The watchers looked surprised and hastily brought her another.

"You don't stay in the big house?"

Jacob shook his head. "No, it would be too inconvenient. The people imagine it to be haunted. No one has stayed inside for years, and Saffron and I would be all alone."

"Do you think it's haunted?"

The old man laughed, a raspy sound like two dry leaves brushing together. "I don't believe in anything I don't see. Life does that to you when you are my age. Yet strange sounds have come from the house at night. I have noticed this especially with a full moon."

She waited for him to settle in his chair. Following his conversation was hard until she became used to his old fashioned way of speaking. When he grew tired, he lapsed into half Portuguese, half English, most likely to ease his strain. He didn't seem to notice when she turned on her little tape recorder. She doubted he knew what it was.

"It was a terrible journey they told me. My grandfather was the leader of this group, and when they arrived, the group split into two factions. Not all were of our kin, some were neighbors and friends. Those who stayed in this area learned to harvest the rubber and mined. My father told me my mother died when I was born. I remember starting work when I was very young."

"They could have returned to the States," Marisa said. "I'm sure your grandfather corresponded with people there and knew when the war was over."

"Child, it is never wise to dig into the past. It does not change anything. In spite of the hardships, we all grew to love this land. We are Brazilians, not Americans, something you do not seem to understand." He took several labored breaths, and then just when Marisa thought he was finished speaking, he continued.

"We own title to our land now. We grow our own food, trade for cloth sometimes, but it is a hard life. A part of me wishes better for Saffron, but the other part wants her to be left alone. I have not decided which is the selfish side."

His voice began frail and weak but garnered strength as he spoke. Juan had to translate faster and faster. Jacob had lost his English when he became caught up in his story.

"Our people made this their home. Each generation in turn vowed never to leave. Now many children of Saffron's age do not know of our beginnings." He turned to look at the people stoically sitting just outside the doorless opening, listening intently. "I have tried to pass on my gift of the language to all who would listen. I am the last teacher."

He regarded Saffron with a fond look, and Marisa knew she would have been his choice had he decided to pass on his knowledge.

It didn't appear that he had much time left.

"That still doesn't tell me about Sara. She has something for me, and my father needs it." If they suspected it was a treasure, they would think that was all she wanted from them. It could turn ugly. Manolo, who was never far from her, made a throat-clearing noise in the background which she ignored.

Jacob sighed, a rattle deep in his chest. "You are a very persistent young woman. I admire that."

Marisa nodded at the compliment and waited.

"Very well, stay here the night and study the letters. You are welcome to search through the house if you like, for what you imagine Sara left for you. As an American, I am certain Brazilian spirits will have no dominion over you."

"I'm not frightened of ghosts, if that's what you mean."

The old man's thin lips turned up in what could have passed for a smile. "No, I don't imagine you are, but you must be careful. Accidents have happened to people, odd noises come at night inside, and we have seen candlelight in the darkened windows. Not even the children play near the house. Perhaps this Sara person could be a ghost, since we know nothing of her."

Ghosts didn't write letters. The old man's story didn't ring true in what he said about Sara. Why would Sara use the closest town as a mailing place if she didn't live nearby?

The answers might be found in the house.

Jacob looked as if he wanted to say more, but the watching, listening crowd in his doorway stopped him.

What was he hiding? What truths did he hold back? And why?

"I have instructed Manolo to see to your needs while you are here," he said plainly, without Juan needing to translate.

Marisa looked at the tall man standing close, but not too close. Cleaned up with his beard trimmed and his long, blond hair washed and combed, he would be good to look at. "Can he understand us?"

Jacob nodded. "Most of us comprehend some English. Manolo speaks a little, although you should not expect a conversation from him. He is a man of few words. In any language."

"Yes, I noticed. He resembles Saffron."

"He's her half-uncle. His father was a Brazilian, a rubber worker, killed in a bar fight years ago. His mother was one of us. That is all I wish to say. I am weary," he waved his hand, dismissing them.

Juan looked relieved and headed toward the door. What else could she do? El Viejo did look exhausted, and she didn't want to be responsible for bringing harm to him.

Outside, the sunlight in the clearing had dimmed and clouds hovered above while thunder sounded in the distance. Juan's anxious looks began to rub off on her. To make matters worse, Manolo still watched, leaning against a nearby tree.

"Juan, I have to stay here tonight. We'll leave in the morning. Please tell the little girl that I am staying."

"But *senhorita*—" His face openly showed alarm.

"There's something wrong here. Someone knows where Sara is. I feel it."

Juan bent and whispered to Saffron, gently touching the fine white-gold hair with wonder in his eyes.

The child ran to Marisa and taking her hand, began rattling off Portuguese so fast that even Juan puzzled how to translate it.

Finally he simply said, "She says she has waited for you all her life and knew you were coming." He shivered and stepped back from the little girl. "She says she will stay near you to protect you."

Strange little creature. Did she know her grandfather might die soon? It was sad to think she would have no one then, but that wasn't true exactly. The whole village would adopt her. Had adopted her. The tawny eyes and honey-tanned skin didn't go with the flaxen hair framing her face. Saffron didn't seem to fit in with the others. Maybe that was what worried her grandfather. He could have done more harm than good by instilling a desire for something beyond her lot in life.

Yet, it was a shame he hadn't given any of them a sense of their roots. They had to know they were different from other Brazilians.

Several women gave Marisa and Juan lamps, crossing themselves in the process and muttering prayers for their safety, she supposed.

She couldn't wait to get started rummaging through the house, but even now she felt someone watching her. Although Marisa turned quickly, everyone had walked away, leaving her and Juan alone.

CHAPTER 16

Inside, the house smelled of stale mildew. Marisa opened the windows first, choosing to worry about the night insects later.

"You're not much help, Juan. Aren't you going to look through the house with me?"

Juan's wide eyes and thin lips showed his fear. He backed out of the shadowy room toward the open doorway.

Eerie splashes of light flung up against the walls and the lit lamps trembled in their hands. Marisa set her lamp down on a nearby table and reached for Juan's. He wasn't about to surrender it, but she figured even though he was scared, maybe if he found something to do, he would forget his surroundings.

"I am regretful, *senhorita*. I do not move from this door. Dom Scott told me to watch you, but—"

She touched his shoulder. "You're very brave to come this far. Why don't you set your backpack down next to the door and go outside?" She almost said outside in the sunlight, but the usual afternoon rain had begun, adding to the gloom.

"Go ahead and wait for me on the veranda. You can watch out from there if you want to."

What was Scott doing at this very moment? In spite of not trusting him with a fortune, she would have trusted him with her life. He had a take-charge attitude that was both annoying and admirable. He would have been an even match for Jacob and Manolo too. The thought of him chased away some of the panic that threatened when she looked upstairs at the curving, dark staircase.

It didn't take long to forget Juan, and everything else outside the house, when she walked slowly through the rooms. The first settlers must have brought down many pieces of furniture. She touched her hand to a mahogany console table in the dining room, a rare Duncan Phyfe worth a lot of money, and now, sadly, so eaten by insects a big wind would have collapsed it.

Some furniture looked handmade, with loving care and attention to detail. The relatives who built the house must have been desperate to remember an earlier time, a gentler life.

When had the ghostly rumors started? It had to have been many years ago, because everything in the house seemed untouched, resembling a museum fallen to disuse. A fine patina of dust covered every surface.

Marisa had wished for Scott before, and as much as she still wished it, she could see that wouldn't have worked. A gold miner and adventurer such as Scott Dunbar would not miss a chance to grab up a buried trunk of money, no matter what morals he espoused. One part of her scolded that she could trust him, another part scoffed and said no.

Anyway, he wasn't here, so she must get on with this alone. It was hard to tell how long Juan would wait for her. At night, with the house shrouded in darkness, he might disappear into the forest to return to Kayapo, leaving her behind. She shivered at the prospect and couldn't decide which terrified her more, being outside with Manolo hanging over her or inside in the dark house.

She didn't blame Juan. The house did emit an atmosphere of foreboding. It was chilly inside in spite of the warm, muggy day. She pulled a sweater out of her knapsack and put it around her shoulders as she walked toward the kitchen. The floor squeaked in protest at every step.

Marisa's father had insisted the letters implied someone had buried the trunk. But under what and where? Why hadn't the old woman been more specific about where they buried the treasure, since she had been generous enough to offer it to them?

That was another point. Didn't anyone here want the money? She suspected that Jacob knew about the chest full of money and had decided many years ago that it would do more harm than good. Perhaps he was right. She couldn't take something away that these people wanted to keep, but surely Sara wouldn't have offered the money if they'd wanted to keep it here.

A noise from upstairs suddenly interrupted her troubled thoughts. It sounded as if someone had bumped into something in the dark. She paused in mid-stride to listen. The floor squeaked above her head and then immediately, oppressive silence followed with no sounds but the drumming of rain on the roof.

She felt another presence in the house.

She sat down in the closest chair, unmindful of the cloud of dust that wafted up around her. Her idea had been to go upstairs and check the bedrooms and the closets. There had to be something in this house to give her a clue. She sat listening for a long time but heard nothing else.

"I'd better get upstairs and back down before dark," she spoke out loud, wanting anyone up stairs to hear and leave. Of course that would hardly work with ghosts, but since when were ghosts so clumsy? Juan's tuneless whistle sounded from out on the front porch, giving her a little shot of extra courage.

The lantern trembled in her hand and she steadied herself against the banister. The wood felt smooth under her fingers, as if well worn by use, as were the steps. The edges were scraped off, and they were splintered in many places.

On the second to the last step, she glanced down at her feet. One step was cracked nearly through. She could have suffered a nasty fall on that one. She stretched her leg and stepped over it.

At the first landing, she looked above her and saw more stairs, a smaller set, near the rear of the house which probably lead to the gabled rooms she noticed from outside. Something told her to walk toward the steps, to see if footprints in the dust led upstairs, but a sound made her turn toward a bedroom.

With only one lamp, the second floor was much darker than the main floor. She stepped forward cautiously, fearing broken boards beneath her feet.

The first bedroom was empty save for a handmade bed with a huge fluffy mattress. She tried to imagine how wonderful the fireplace must have seemed to whoever lived in this house many years ago.

The closet door was ajar, but nothing would have made her open it and look inside. Marisa sat on the bed and dust billowed up around her, the motes dancing in the light of the lamp. The people living here had to have made their own mattresses from the feathers and down of birds.

She stood and walked to the dresser, opening the drawers one by one. In the third drawer her fingers touched a paper way in the back. She knelt and pulled out a newspaper clipping, crisp and fragile around the edges, and held the lantern close to look.

The clipping was dated thirty years ago from The Elliott Times, their local Virginia paper. Had her father sent it? Other relatives scattered about in The States might have written to these ancestors too, but not from Elliott, Virginia. The clipping was about the annual Founder's Day picnic, a farcical local holiday in which locals and visitors alike, re-enacted the beginning of the Civil War and the bank president's role of absconding with all the town's funds.

Oh, how her father hated that day. He hid away nearly the entire week, only going to teach then coming right home. Why did he think lugging home a trunk full of money to repay the theft would change things? The townspeople were having too much fun with things as they were and the special day brought a lot of extra money into town.

She smoothed out the clipping and put it in her pocket. Nothing else turned up in the room, so she moved to the next one.

A large window overlooked the back yard. Marisa stood a while looking out, watching the rain coming straight down, like a curtain between the big house and the row of cabins where Jacob, Saffron and the others lived. She'd better hurry, it would soon be dark and she'd decided not to spend a night in the house. Not even a treasure trunk would make her do that.

Marisa opened the first drawer as she had in the previous room. The drawer felt dry and dusty, yet parts of the house were damp with a mildew smell. It wasn't hard to imagine nests of spiders or snakes hiding in the drawers and she opened each carefully.

The third drawer dragged, as if something held it in place. Kneeling, she twisted back and forth sideways to pull it out, but the wood must have swelled. Finally it let loose with a loud protesting squeal that reverberated through the entire house. She removed the offending drawer and set it on the bed.

Upon examining it, she noticed the bottom was different from the other drawers, as if someone had replaced it at one time. She looked around the room for a tool and spied a poker lying near the fireplace. Prying up the delicate wood only took seconds and when it snapped apart to reveal another layer of wood, a small book, like a diary, fell out from between.

Marisa held the book to the lamp but the light was too weak. It was then she realized dusk had gone and night closed in fast. She hid the shredded wood under the bed and set the poker down again near the fireplace, trying not to think of what an ugly weapon it would make.

Before she had a chance to replace the drawer, Juan's voice floated upstairs. She recognized the panic lying beneath the words. At the head of the balcony, she looked down but no one stood inside the foyer, although she couldn't see to the front door from her vantage point. She stepped carefully over the cracked step and hurried toward her backpack leaning against the wall. She wrapped the diary in clothing and stashed it inside.

Outdoors, Marisa breathed a sigh of relief, smelling the fresh, heavy air of the storm. The rain had slowed, and soon it would be over for the day.

"*Senhorita*, I have worried." Juan rushed up to her, his look reproachful for leaving him alone. Saffron wasn't far behind.

"Eat. Grandfather say, come eat." Saffron's voice was high pitched as if the English was so unfamiliar she had to use a different level of sound than her usual speech.

"Thank you, Saffron. Call me Marisa, please."

The little girl smiled, her white teeth brilliant against the honey tan of her skin.

"We can still make it through the jungle to our halfway camp place if we leave now," Juan urged.

Marisa looked at the two standing, waiting, and her heart went out to them, so alert, so teachable, so wasted. She put her arms around them for a brief moment, until Juan moved away, self-consciously.

"We can't leave now, Juan. I may not get another chance to come here. You heard the old man. They don't welcome visitors here and—" She wanted to say how uncomfortable Manolo made her, always at her elbow, not touching her, though she could feel his warm breath on her skin. However, she didn't speak of it, knowing Juan must have noticed and it had to make him nervous too.

Thank goodness no one could know about the diary, but she'd need time away from everyone to read it. It had to hold a clue where they'd buried the Elliott Bank money. She couldn't leave until she read it.

They stepped through mud puddles and soft mud all the way to the hut at the edge of the forest. Marisa turned around, just before she ducked her head to enter, and stared back at the house. It looked so inappropriate, looming against the jungle landscape, its windows staring darkly as if it held a pathetic dominion over everything, and yet it looked helplessly isolated.

Inside, the little hut was dry and filled with lamplight. Jacob sat near the table. He looked up when the three entered. "You are safe. I feared—"

"I told you I didn't believe in ghosts," Marisa said, although there were a few times wandering around in the old house that she had begun to wonder.

"Sometimes ignorance is more dangerous than fear," he responded. "Where are my manners? Please sit. We will eat soon. It is too late for you to leave now."

"I can find our way, easy," Juan spoke up, his voice too loud in the quiet room.

"Perhaps. Where is Manolo?" The old man sounded testy, as if he expected the man at his elbow constantly.

"Not that I wanted him around, but didn't you ask him to watch over us while we are here? I didn't see him anywhere around."

The dry rasping laugh ended in a coughing spell. When it was over, Jacob looked serious. "Manolo is an unusual young man. He is very obedient, but curious in his habits. He goes away for days at a time, no one knows where, and he does not answer any questions. I believe Saffron is the only person he cares for." Jacob touched a trembling hand to the little girl's shoulder. "He guards her fiercely."

Marisa swallowed hard when Saffron leaned her head down to lay her cheek against his bony hand. They had such a love for each other, and it was beautiful. Would the girl be all right when the old man died? If Manolo's protectiveness didn't become obsessive, she would be secure.

"Juan, I told you I have to stay another day. We'll try to get an early start tomorrow, I promise." She felt a new presence in the room and looked back toward the door. Manolo filled the doorway, holding a tray of food. How long had he stood there without speaking? Why did he insist on sneaking about so quietly? It was unnerving.

"Come inside. Did you bring our food?" the old man asked querulously.

It smelled really good to Marisa and even Juan looked at the tray hungrily. "Do the women cook for you and Saffron and Manolo?"

Jacob nodded and motioned for Saffron to get dishes from the box that served as a cupboard.

Their stew was tasty and, served with the usual manioc bread, it made a filling meal. Manolo didn't eat with them, but stood in the rear of the hut watching. Marisa had left her backpack near the door which made her uneasy. She changed positions slightly to enable her to watch him. His stare was penetrating, his expression guarded and furtive, as if he waited or expected something from her.

What would he wait for? Suddenly it came to her that if Jacob knew about the treasure, not its location, but its existence, then others might know too. Did Manolo know? Even if Jacob thought it harmful to his people, it stood to reason that a younger man might not agree. Did Manolo expect her to locate the treasure?

That was another puzzle she hadn't figured out yet. It didn't sound reasonable that Jacob would be covering for Sara, hiding her existence. The old man seemed truly bewildered when Marisa showed up in the village, and his surprise at the letters and photographs she'd brought didn't appear fake. Yet how else would the letters from her father be in his possession if he didn't know about Sara?

After they ate, Manolo strung hammocks for her and Juan using pegs in the walls. Saffron moved hers closer to Marisa. Deciding not to take any chances, Marisa slept with her backpack beneath her head.

Once during the night she awoke to feel her pack slightly move under her cheek. She battled the hammock to sit up, and saw a shadow flit out of the room. No one else in the room awoke but sleeping after that proved impossible. Tomorrow she must find the answers to her questions. She had a persistent feeling that time was running out.

CHAPTER 17

W e're leaving today, Jacob. I know you'll be glad." Marisa spoke to the old man as they sat eating fruit for breakfast. Juan nodded his head vigorously, his face breaking into a smile, the first she'd seen since they arrived.

She had wanted to read the diary. This would have been a good place for privacy. How could she leave before she read it? Yet it might take days to decipher the cramped, old fashioned handwriting.

"No!" Manolo walked forward from his watching position near the door.

Everyone turned to look at him in stunned surprise. Jacob's sharp features arranged themselves into a stern frown. "These are guests in our village," he admonished the younger man. "They may go when they please." He reached for his cane and stood to face Manolo.

The tall blond man could have broken him in two like a twig, and for a moment Marisa tensed, ready to intercede for Jacob.

It wasn't necessary. When the elder arose to his full height, he was still only half the stature of Manolo, but the chilling disapproval in his eyes, the severe line of his mouth was enough to make the taller man back off. Humiliated, Manolo turned and rushed outside.

"I think he has a school boy crush on me," Marisa offered with a tentative laugh. At some point in her life this would have been flattering, but now it was just plain inconvenient.

"Is that your opinion?" Jacob turned his look upon her, and it was all she could do to not run out the doorway behind Manolo.

"What else? He never lets me out of his sight. Every time I turn around he's there. Now he doesn't want me to leave."

Jacob motioned for her to come closer, to prevent others in the room from hearing. "I am not so certain. Manolo is too selfish to show such interest in a stranger's physical attributes. The only person we have ever known him to love is Saffron, and he treats her like a slave."

"Then what?"

"I do not know. It is very puzzling. Perhaps you should go. As soon as possible. I feel danger for you."

Marisa shivered and walked to the door. It felt cold outside in the open, in spite of the sunlight blazing down into the clearing. She heard the monkeys and birds making weird noises in the distance. Pigs, dogs and children played in the dirt, since most of the mud had dried from the downpour the afternoon before.

"Ssst!" The sharp noise came across the clearing.

"It is the tall Yellowhair who wishes to gain your attention." Juan pointed toward the porch of the big house. "*Senhorita*, do not go."

Manolo stood at the railing, watching them. He lifted a hand to beckon, which offended her, but his look was so mysterious she decided to see what he wanted. "Hold on to this backpack, Juan, and don't let it out of your sight."

He accepted it and then tagged reluctantly behind, muttering under his breath all the while.

At the edge of the porch Marisa stared up into Manolo's eyes, dark brown and fathomless. She couldn't read anything in them. "Why did you call me?"

His lips opened in a smile that sat uneasily on his face, not reaching those dark eyes. "I wish to show you something."

"Do not go into that house again, please." Juan pleaded.

"I have to see what he wants. I'll be okay. It's daylight and it looks like everyone is watching. He wouldn't dare harm me."

Juan and Saffron sat on the porch, their faces filled with concern. From the doorways of the surrounding huts, she made out shadows of people—staring.

The thought of her ancestors, standing on this same porch more than a hundred years ago, sent chills down her spine. What did they suppose building this huge monstrosity would do for them? It must have taken all the stubborn determination, for which their family was known, to complete the task. How long had it taken? Surely Jacob knew many of these answers. Yet he refused to talk about the house or the early settlers.

Had something ominous happened to them? Or was he ashamed of his heritage now, wanting to be a true Brazilian? Sara could tell her everything—if she could find Sara.

Shadows flitted across the walls inside the house. A heavy feeling of gloom seemed to hang from the ceiling. She had forgotten to close the windows yesterday, but someone had done it for her, and pulled the heavy tattered drapes tight together again.

Manolo cleared his throat. Marisa looked up to see him standing on the staircase beckoning to her. Curiosity overcame her hesitation and she followed. His bulk blocked out the sparse light from above, and she remembered the cracked step too late. Stepping on the center, her foot sank into empty space. She felt herself plummeting over backward, after which she blacked out.

"*Senhorita*, please wake up."

As she gradually awoke, Marisa focused her eyes on Juan's worried face. Oh, but she'd had a delicious dream. She and Scott were swimming in the river. Pain flooded back into her consciousness, centered nowhere and everywhere in her body.

"I'm awake now. It's okay."

"Sit up. Careful," Jacob cautioned. The old man, Saffron, and most of the villagers clustered around the porch of the big house where Manolo must have carried her.

"I should get up, see if anything's broken." She couldn't stay here another day. This was too dangerous. Just before she tumbled over backward, she had looked up into Manolo's face and could have sworn she saw his remorseless smile.

The missing step couldn't have been an accident. Yesterday it had been barely cracked and as far as she knew, Manolo was the only one beside herself to come inside.

If Manolo finished off the step, he didn't do it to kill, but to incapacitate her. Why did he want her to stay here so badly? She believed Jacob when he insisted Manolo wasn't attracted to her. The money. Her heart leaped in her throat. She closed her eyes to prevent anyone recognizing her sudden awareness. If Jacob knew about the money, and she felt certain he did, then others might know too.

Manolo knew.

Did he know about the diary, or did he guess that she'd found something? Of course, that was it. She'd left in a hurry with the bureau drawer sitting on the bed. Long before she arrived, Manolo must have searched the house thoroughly. He was the only one unafraid to go inside. Unworldly and inexperienced as he must be, he probably never thought of the drawer having a false bottom.

"I've got to see if I can stand," she insisted. She cried out in pain, and her head felt as if it might pop off her neck and roll down the steps. Chills alternated with heat as she wavered, holding on to Juan and a chair. When the spasm passed, she asked, "Where is Manolo?"

Jacob's expression was strained. He shrugged thin shoulders. "Manolo comes and goes. Always it has been the same." The old man turned to Juan. "Go bring a stout limb. You'll find some cut for firewood in the back of the houses. We will make her a crutch. She must go. Now."

Without waiting for more instructions, Juan ran toward the back of the cabins. Jacob motioned to several men standing by and between them, they lifted Marisa and carried her, and the backpack she clung to, back to Jacob's. After they deposited her inside, the old man motioned for them to leave.

"Child, you are a nuisance," Joseph scolded Saffron. "This woman does not wish you to hang on her like a leech." Marisa discerned some jealousy and didn't blame him.

"I'm not 'this woman,' and she isn't bothering me," Marisa reprimanded gently. "Why do you try so hard to make me feel unwelcome? I would think a short visit of a distant relative from another place would be of interest to you and your people, and yet you've told them nothing about me. Anyone can see that."

He looked at the ground for a long moment until she wasn't sure if he planned to answer.

"I know what you say is true. And part of me is ashamed. I have this knowledge of the language and of our background. A few of us have it. The others elected not to learn. It is their decision, and mine, that the big house has brought only misery to our ancestors and caring about our past is futile. Worse than futile, it undermines our existence."

"But so much is out there, for Saffron and for the other children. Even if you're no longer interested in the world."

Jacob leaned his head on his palms, elbows on the table. Marisa's heart went out to him. He looked so forlorn. She longed to touch him, to comfort him, but didn't dare.

When he raised his head to look at her, his eyes held a mixture of despair and anger. "Look what civilization, as you call it, did for Manolo! He and his family moved away to Sao Paulo when he was not as old as Saffron." Jacob pounded the table in his agitation. The little girl jumped back but returned immediately to kneel close to Marisa.

"They did not find riches. They did not even find work. Years later they came dragging back here like whipped dogs, with their sons wild and violent. They lost two of Manolo's older brothers in cantina brawls."

"Sao Paulo might have not been such a good idea. Still, several schooled youngsters like Saffron could make a great deal of difference in your village. When you are sick, when a catastrophe happens, what then?"

"The children would not return! Once they know about the outside, why would they come back to us? Are you so blind that you cannot see that? We would lose our youth, and then we all die."

Marisa understood Jacob and sympathized with him. He was right and wrong also.

Listening to him, she struggled to sit still, without the pain taking over her body. She didn't think anything was broken, but she'd be black and blue in a lot of places for a while.

"*Senhorita*, I have a stick for walking, but I do not think—" Juan burst into the room as if the devils were behind him.

"Calm down. Sit here beside me." Marisa made room while Saffron gave Juan a dark look All Marisa could think of to do now was to find Scott. She missed him in so many ways, his rough humor, his generous enjoyment of life, his carefree attitude. All these qualities she had thought outrageous at first but alone, without his commanding presence, she'd had time to sort out her thoughts. In the midst of danger, she began to think that life could and should be enjoyed rather than merely something to move through with comfort and dignity.

"Marisa Elliott, you must go." Jacob's expression was one of pleading. "Every hour you stay brings danger closer."

"Why? All I wanted was to find Sara and the—" She put her hand over her mouth, having almost blurted out "treasure."

"Yes, I know. Do not say the word out loud."

So. He did know about the treasure. "I didn't come to take anything that doesn't belong to us." How could she explain without saying the words he didn't want to hear?

Jacob held up his hands to silence her. "I know our history from the beginning and understand why you are here, although I do not know how you found us. It makes no difference. Everything would be changed. What do you think an invasion of adventurers would do to Saffron and young girls like her? Have you given that any thought?"

"No, I haven't," Marisa admitted. "A friend, Scott Dunbar, is a pilot in Brasilia. I need to talk to him about it." Just saying Scott's name gave her a warm feeling and some aches disappeared for a moment. "Juan, maybe you should go after Dom Scott, bring him here."

"Ah, no, *senhorita*. I have already bent to your will much more than a man should. I cannot leave you here alone."

"Nonsense. I have Jacob and the others. No one will harm me."

"No!" The sharp outcry from Jacob startled them all. "It is not safe! Not safe for you or for my people. I do not want us involved." Still, he wouldn't speak of the words treasure or money, as if he needed to deny its existence.

She knew now that he and also Manolo suspected she had found something in the big house. Maybe the old man was right. It was time to leave.

"Juan, I must practice walking to get my ankle working properly. Then we will leave," she promised.

He walked with her back and forth in the clearing while the villagers sat in front of their cabins, watching curiously. Saffron stood close to her grandfather, with a sad look of resignation in her eyes.

When Marisa was tired, but walking with little pain, she approached the old man. "Jacob, it is time. I feel stronger. Where is Manolo?"

Jacob shrugged. "Gone. For now. Perhaps he goes to the next village. I regret you may think he is accountable for your accident."

What made him think that Manolo was to blame? She knew it was no accident and she also knew Manolo was responsible, but she hadn't made any accusations. It would have served no purpose. Jacob had enough crosses to bear. The one burning thought in her mind was to get out of here before the tall blond returned.

She sat on the proffered chair and beckoned Saffron to come closer. Taking the child's hands in hers, she felt the fragile bones in her wrists and arm. Such a delicate little person, and yet sturdy and tenacious. She sensed the resilience, the spirit that shone through the child's eyes.

"Saffron, I must go now, but I will come back. This is my promise to you." Tears edged from her eyes in the face of Saffron's bleak look. Mercifully, the little girl did not cry. That would have been unbearable.

Juan cleared his throat, a disapproving sound. He probably thought she was lying to the child to pacify her.

Her ankle had started to throb now, and Marisa felt the swelling inside her boot. Soon she would be unable to leave and Manolo would return. They must go now.

The entire population stood at the edge of the clearing, silently watching them leave.

After they had hiked a while in the deep gloom of the forest, Marisa turned to Juan, who walked at her side now instead of his usual dozen steps ahead or behind.

"What's the matter? Is something making you nervous? This is as fast as I can walk. I'm really trying." She was frightened and she feared every sound in the jungle was Manolo coming back to finish the job. The diary had to be the clue he wanted, and if he took it from her, he wouldn't leave either her or Juan behind as witnesses.

Had he done away with Sara? Maybe after she wrote the letters, he had killed her. The hair on her arms raised, and she briskly rubbed the chill away.

Juan urged her to hurry. Her backpack didn't feel right due to his rushing her and finally she insisted on stopping to fix it.

She had no more than set it down on the ground when the greenery parted in front of them. Manolo stepped out, staring at her in a brazen way he wouldn't have dared to do in front of Jacob.

Juan bristled, touched a hand to his machete, and said something to him. The blond man frowned, his light brows drawing together as his face tightened in anger. He motioned for Juan to leave.

Juan stepped in front of Marisa. She felt a tremor go from the back of her neck down to the soles of her feet, but she willed herself to show no fear. "What do you want?"

Juan stared back at the man, unwilling to take his eyes from him while he listened to him talk "He tells me he wants you, *senhorita*. The Yellowhair says you are alone. Need a man to take care of you. He wants to be your man, and you stay with him."

She shook her head. "I know you speak English when it suits you, Manolo. I have a man, and wish no other." She knew he wasn't interested in her, but wanted to get his hands on her backpack.

Thunder rumbled, ominous in the distance. It wouldn't be long before what little light that seeping downward through the canopy of trees would be gone. Even if they could get rid of Manolo, they would have to find a large tree to stay under for the night. She shivered at the thought of climbing snakes and spiders bigger than her hand.

Juan spoke again, but Manolo stood in front of them, not moving, legs apart and plainly bored with Juan's impassioned speech.

Caught up as they were in the quiet drama taking place, a sudden loud bird call startled them all. Marisa looked at Juan in time to catch his dark face crease into a wide smile. He circled his mouth with cupped hands and echoed the strange, wild call.

Her legs went weak. She had to lean on the staff and take a deep breath when Scott strode into their midst, bigger than life.

A fire warmed her blood and sang through her veins at the sight of him. His keen intuition must have told him the situation even before he reached them. Out of the corner of her eye she saw the blond man reach for the large knife in his belt. Without waiting, she hobbled toward Scott.

"Oh, I'm so glad to see you!" She threw herself against his hard chest and pulled his head down for a long kiss. Between them, she could feel his heart racing to match her own. If she could convince Manolo she and Scott were together, at least he probably could not use that excuse for following them.

Scott took full advantage of the situation in spite of any danger to himself. He lifted her up with two hands spanning her waist and swung her around in a dizzying circle of greeting. Then he kissed her again, a long, lingering one, but his eyes stayed open, watching the Yellowhair.

She caught a glimpse of the blond's angry face. Scott untwined her arms from his waist and stepped away from her toward the Yellowhair. He held his hands out, showing he hid no weapon and began speaking in Portuguese.

Manolo didn't want to give up. His voice rose in righteous anger as he gestured with wild abandon. Scott listened politely, his speech deadly calm, almost amicable.

But the controlled authority was there, and the blond man finally yielded to it.

Scott touched Marisa's shoulder and when she pulled closer, he tucked her under his arm possessively. It felt so good to be close to him. When she looked up at Scott to say something to him, the Yellowhair disappeared into the jungle.

Juan let loose a whistle of relief. "Maybe we better go. Maybe he will come back."

"Juan, I'm ashamed of you. I know Marisa doesn't know any better, but do you realize the danger you put her in?"

Marisa felt a tremor of anger at what she considered an unjust treatment of Juan. She had forced him to accompany her. She started to sputter an argument.

Scott interrupted her. "You will listen to what I have to say later. I never gave you two permission to wander off on your own like this." He scowled down at her in such a no-nonsense manner it might have daunted her if he hadn't spoken in such an authoritative way he angered her instead of intimidating her.

"Give me permission! Who do you think you are? I was only trying to stay out of your way so you could continue with your precious digging. You as much as told me you didn't trust me to go with you. You weren't going with me so what else was I to think, but that you wanted me to go on alone?"

"You see how much you've stayed out of my way, then. You've caused me extra trouble and wasted time. I don't even get a gracious thanks for saving your life."

"Oh, come on. I doubt you actually saved my life," she scoffed. "Saved me from becoming a wife to an exceedingly fit and handsome savage, maybe," she teased. She had to tell him about the treasure chest, but she wasn't going to take the chance and tell him about the diary. Not yet.

"Woman, you beat all I've ever seen. I don't believe you've enough sense to be afraid of anything. God protect me from fearless idiots, the most dangerous species on earth." He looked skyward in exaggerated supplication then touched the staff she leaned against. "What happened here? Are you hurt?"

His expression showed concern which warmed her. She sighed. It was so hard to explain. "I fell on the stairs of the old house you said didn't exist." She had to get that said at all costs.

"Oh yes, Dom Scott, there was a very big house with..." His eyes were wide and he held his hands out to try and explain the pillars.

"Pillars, actual white pillars like in the photos," she said. "It was so odd. And no one would come near it. They thought it was haunted."

"Well, I'll be. That's a hard one to swallow. And your relatives built it?"

She nodded. "When they first arrived or soon after. It was beginning to deteriorate but held together all these years."

"Can you walk ok? I could carry you," he teased.

Now that someone else took over his responsibility, Juan relaxed, sitting on his backpack, watching them argue. His neck swiveled back and forth as if he were at a tennis match. Suddenly both she and Scott noticed and burst out laughing.

"We are glad to see you, Scott. And I barely twisted the ankle. I can walk fine. Right now, we just need to get away from here as quickly as we can."

"I know." He held onto her shoulders, looking deep into her eyes. "Marisa, did it ever occur to you that having to prove yourself over and over isn't necessary?"

"What do you mean?" Her defensive anger fired up, but she revved it back a notch, knowing he had a point.

"You know what I mean. You came all the way across the world to prove something to your father. And maybe yourself, I'll give you that. I think you left Kayapo with Juan just to show me that you could. Don't you think it's time you convinced yourself you don't have to do that?"

She swallowed the retort that wanted to spill out of her mouth. Was he right? Had she spent most of her life trying to prove herself?

"Come on, you two," he said. "Let's head for home. Juan's mother will probably give him a big swat on his behind, even if he thinks he's an adult. Everyone's been worried about you, especially Angelina." He winked at Juan and shook his shoulder lightly, but strongly enough the boy winced. Marisa figured it was a gentle reminder he shouldn't have listened to anyone but Scott.

She shouldered her pack and took the center place in their single file trek back through the jungle. The thunder rolled across the sky above the trees, and worse, Marisa felt as if eyes bored into her back while they walked. Was Manolo following them?

It seemed like an awful long way to Kayapo and a hundred light years back to Virginia.

CHAPTER 18

They trudged through the steamy rain a long way in silence. Marisa knew, by the set of Scott's shoulders and his straight back, that he was perturbed with both her and Juan. In a way, she didn't blame him. She had promised to abide by his rules, and he did feel responsible for her. Still, she had come here for this one purpose, hadn't she? What right had he to dictate all the terms?

At first she hardly noticed her swollen ankle, and the pain didn't quite register, as she had been so anxious to get away from Manolo. Now, she had to grit her teeth with every step, leaning often on the cane Juan had made for her. By the time she ceased feeling watched, the pain and throbbing had struck her full force. She broke out into a cold sweat, slowing her pace even more.

"Dom Scott!" Juan's voice came from behind her, but she dare not stop to see what he wanted or she would never put another foot on the ground again.

Scott turned and came back. By then Juan had caught up. "Her foot. She cannot walk so good."

"I'm all right," she protested. "I just can't walk as fast as you two."

"What's going on here?" Scott demanded. "You said it was nothing. Again, I believed you and assumed the walking stick was just that."

The rain had finally stopped and a sparse light again sifted down through the canopy of trees. It must be getting toward dusk. The night air dried the perspiration on her arms and neck.

Scott knelt in front of her, shining his flashlight on her legs. She winced when he put his big hand gently on her sprained ankle. He turned the light up in her face, blocking her vision for an instant. "This ankle is swollen. If it's sprained, you could have done some serious damage. Why didn't you say something? What are these bruises on your cheek? Did someone hurt you?"

The protective outrage in his voice sent a jolt of pleasure through her body, nearly causing her to forget the pain. She shook her head, tears threatening to spill over unless she held a tight control. "No. I told you, I fell."

"We're almost to the place where I stashed the tent. I'll bind your ankle, but I can't let you walk until I make sure it's not broken." He pulled his white silk scarf out of his backpack.

"Oh no! I can't let you use your lucky scarf."

"If anyone needs luck, seems like you do," he said, ignoring her protests. "Hold her shoulders, Juan, while I pull off her boot. Otherwise, we might not get it off later, and I'll have to cut it off."

She cried out once, as the boot let go. Scott held her close, comforting as one would a child. She closed her eyes, wanting to stay there forever.

"It doesn't feel like a break. We'll have to see in the daylight. I'll carry you."

Again, ignoring her objections, he wrapped the long white material around her ankle securely. "Now if this begins to feel too tight, for God's sakes, tell me. I never saw a woman so controlled. Don't you ever let go?"

Self-pity battled with indignation at what she considered his unfair comment. He touched a finger to her chin, lifting it so he could look into her eyes. She didn't see any of the mockery his words expressed, only admiration.

"You're tougher than you look, Marisa. I'll give you that. How long were you going to go on hurting without telling anyone?"

His mouth was so close to hers, the warmth of his breath so tantalizing close, the throbbing left her ankle and crept up her legs toward her heart. What was happening to her? She had never felt this dizzying awareness that tingled every nerve of her body.

Scott brushed his lips over her hair in a comforting gesture. He must have supposed the need reflected in her eyes to be only the pain. Thank God for that. She didn't want him thinking in old, out-of-date stereotypical terms of a single schoolteacher ga-ga over the first man who held her in his arms.

"Juan, when you find the tent and set it up, I want you to go on to the village. Get the men to help you make a stretcher and bring it back in the morning."

The young man nodded, taking a drink of water from the canteen Scott offered.

"That isn't necessary. I'll walk," she said.

"Not on your life. Not until I can assess the damage, and I'll want space and light for that. We need a stretcher because the path is so narrow in places we can't carry you in a jerry-rigged chair." He touched a finger to her lips to silence her next protest. "As much as I'd enjoy carrying you, and as light as you'd feel in my arms, you'd weigh a ton by nightfall." Both he and Juan laughed at her pretended indignation.

The throbbing grew worse with the pressure of her feet off the ground and the boot removed, but leaning against his broad chest, Marisa was lulled to semi-comfort. He smelled of leaves and earth, a good smell that made her comfortable. Curious. It was the first time she had actually smelled a man, not counting the usual aftershave Thomas used.

A flood of guilt washed over her when she thought of Thomas. He had completely left her mind for days. She was saddened by the thought that he was so forgettable after all their years of friendship. But in the end, that's what it had been, friendship. The realization shocked her, and she gasped at the sudden insight. No matter if she never found another person she could love who would love her, she knew she couldn't settle just for the sake of security.

"How did this happen?" Scott asked. "How did you fall?"

They were so close, she could hear his breathing, feel the warmth of his body through his shirt. She tried to ignore that and concentrate on her painful ankle.

"Can't the explanation wait?" she whimpered. "I don't feel like talking now."

"It concerns that Yellowhair, I know that already," he said. "We can wait all right, but when we stop, I want to hear everything. And I mean everything."

When the forest began to settle in for night, Scott finally halted. Juan had gone ahead and found the stashed tents, setting them up with the usual hammocks tied to trees. Marisa couldn't imagine how he found the pack tucked up in that giant tree among all the other giant trees.

"I know this is crude," Scott said, although his voice didn't sound the least apologetic to Marisa. "I've walked for a day and a night without stopping to find your Yellowhair village, and I had to travel light."

The rain stopped and although everything smelled damp, it wasn't uncomfortable. They ate a cold meal that Jacob had had the women prepare, and when she looked up, Juan had disappeared.

She and Scott sat by a dying campfire at the edge of a small clearing. The fire light caressed the tanned planes of his face and danced through his dark hair. Maybe she shouldn't have gone off without his protection, but he hadn't said he'd take her. Turning her gaze away from the crackling fire, she remembered only hours before, the feel of his lips, the lean, hard strength of his arms holding her.

"Marisa, I've been worried about you. Don't ever do that again. Anything could have happened and from the looks of you, did. Want to tell me about it?"

She nodded. It was time.

He unwrapped his scarf gently, testing the ankle with his strong fingers. In spite of the pain, his touch felt soothing. She hated it when he stopped.

"It looks like a bad bruise. If you can stay off it a day or so, you'll be good as new."

"Thanks, Doc."

He grinned, self-deprecating for once. "I don't know much, but I've studied a little medicine. Sometimes problems come up in remote villages. The people think because I'm not one of them, I must know more, I guess."

Wasn't there anything the man didn't know? For once the question didn't nettle her and she accepted it as part of his charm.

"Wait here a minute. I'm going through the brush to the river. I want something warm on this foot."

"How do you know about a river? How will you get warm water?"

"Tsk. Tsk. You're full of questions, aren't you? Everywhere you look in the rain forest you'll find a river. The water is mostly lukewarm, and when it touches your skin, it will turn warmer." He grinned at her, his eyes warm and his teeth white against the tan of his face. "Is it okay if I go now?"

Don't be gone long, she wanted to say.

In a few minutes he returned, kneeling in front of her to wrap the wet scarf around her ankle. His fingers were strong and sure and may have lingered overlong against her skin but she felt glad for it. She watched his big, tanned hands move gracefully with no wasted movements. Did he know her shameless thoughts? She looked away, toward the trees, confused.

"How did you know where to look for us? If you knew so much, why didn't you bring me out here in the first place? Then we wouldn't have had all this trouble."

"Damn! You beat all. You should be thanking me for saving your bacon. Here, settle yourself down and prop your foot up on that log. Put your head in my lap. Go on, it's not so hard to let go, once you get the hang of it."

She did as he asked and felt a release of pressure in her foot immediately. At first it felt disturbing for her head to touch his thighs in such an intimate manner, but she soon became used to the sensation. Taking a deep breath, she started telling him about Sara's letter giving her and her father the treasure chest of money that belonged to the Elliott Bank. She told him everything, but didn't mention the diary. Trusting him all the way was difficult.

She didn't tell him about her fax to Thomas or the later fax canceling the first one. What would it serve to mention something he need never know? It was water under the bridge.

"You didn't trust me enough to tell me about the money?" His voice held a hard edge.

She struggled to sit up, to look him in the eyes, but his hands, like steel bands, held her in place. She relaxed and gave up for the moment, not wanting to move from the comfort of his warm body.

"Why should I have trusted you? You didn't trust me enough to take me to all your diggings. You've been talking ever since we met about searching for diamonds and gold, what was I to think? That you *weren't* a treasure hunter?"

He bent his head down until his gaze met hers. She wanted to smooth the frown from his forehead, kiss the anger from his long, sensuous mouth.

"It doesn't matter," he said. "You can't take a load of cash home from Brazil. They wouldn't allow it."

"Are you going to report me?"

"Hell no! But you'd never get away with it. It seems to me that you and your father are overreacting about this bank situation. What do you care if the citizens set aside a special day to remember the event? Did you ever consider the town's remembering your family name after a hundred years might be an honor? Probably three fourths of the people in Elliott wouldn't even know where the name came from otherwise."

She'd never thought of it that way. "That sounds reasonable, but you don't know my father. He thinks the practice is an indignity, an affront against him personally."

"Neither of you takes things very casually, do you? Can't you enjoy life without pay-backs? Nothing comes with a guarantee. If you analyze a cloud instead of letting your imagination loose, you end with dust motes in front of your eyes."

"You're a great one to talk! You don't think of the next minute in front of you. That's immature and selfish. Ever thought of that?"

He grinned. "Nope. If I died tomorrow, I would have only lacked one achievement in my life."

"What's that, pray tell?" She wriggled, struggling to sit up and regain a little dignity, at least.

With a laugh, he lifted her and drew her close, encompassing her in a bear hug that took her breath away. Then without giving her a chance to protest, he tilted her chin and kissed her long and hard.

She had no desire to protest. Her heart beat so rapidly, he must have heard it. The strange warmth emanating from the center of her body worked its way up and down until even her skin pulsed with a need for him.

He stopped kissing her and crushed her against his body. His deep voice rumbled in her ear through the fabric of his shirt.

"You have a great capacity to love. I felt that from the moment we met. Yet you're so controlled, it's pathetic."

She pushed away from him. "Pathetic? Is that what you think? Why? Because I don't fall head over heels for the first bush pilot I meet? What do you do? Keep score on your airplane steering wheel?"

"That's ridiculous." He disentangled himself, stood and paced up and down the little clearing. "If you're referring to Elaina, we are strictly business. I told you that in the beginning. There's a little matter I've been wanting to set you straight on, but I can't yet. There's something I've got to know first."

"See! You demand my trust, but you don't trust me!" She leaped to her feet, forgetting her ankle. When the wave of pain struck, she collapsed in a heap, holding her knees up to her chest against the anguish.

In one long stride, he was at her side and had her scooped up in his arms. "Shh. Let me put you in the tent. That's enough talk for tonight. You need to rest." He carried her to the tent and bending down inside, deposited her gently on the bedroll he'd spread earlier.

"There. I'll go get some more water for that ankle again. Wait here."

She smiled in spite of her pain. Wait here? Where did he think she would go?

When she woke, she found herself snuggled in his arms, his chin resting on the top of her head. She could tell by his heavy, even breathing he was asleep. She lay very still, afraid of waking him. The thought of him removing his warm body from hers was not something she wanted to think about just now.

He had called her cold and unfeeling. He thought her out for security and nothing else mattered. He also had something else important he was holding back. What?

The ache in her heart was equal to that of her ankle. Was he right? Was her life so structured, everything must always make complete sense and logic? What was wrong with that? She was her father's daughter, all right. Where was the sense in loving someone unworthy? Someone who would not repay her love with consideration, respect, and yes, commitment. What was wrong with wanting guarantees from life?

When she awoke the second time, Scott was making coffee over the campfire. She lay awake watching him, the lean strength of him, the stubborn angle to his jaw, the straight nose, and the light crinkling of laugh lines around his eyes. If he ever got over his mistrust of women, he would make someone a good catch, even if he was content to be a bush pilot and amateur archaeologist. She supposed there were worse aims in life. Nevertheless, he wouldn't be anyone she could take home to meet her father.

"Hi. You're awake."

He must have sensed her watching. She stretched, but didn't move her bad leg. The ankle still throbbed, but not as miserably.

"Juan and the men should be here any time now. How about some coffee?"

While she drank the strong, fragrant brew, he examined her ankle. Pressing here and there, his hands felt gentle and comforting.

"It doesn't hurt as much as yesterday. Bet I could walk to Kayapo if we didn't hurry."

He brushed the hair away from her cheek and kissed her lightly on her nose. "Such beautiful hair." He removed the rubber band holding the single braid tight and pulled his fingers gently through it, releasing her now-wavy hair in a spread around her shoulders. "I think of you, riding in the car, the wind blowing through and the sun turning this to gold. Too bad you keep it tied back."

His mixed compliment made her feel good. She kept the part she liked and discarded the rest.

"I've been thinking. I can see you're on the level about this ancestor thing, and even though you didn't tell me about the money, I don't blame you there, either. A lot of Brazilians with American ancestors have settled in Belem, that's a town near the coast. I want to take you there before you leave."

"Leave?" The word sent chills down her spine. She didn't want to go home. Not yet. "I can't leave until I find Sara. I must go back to the village." She almost said after she read the diary, but caught herself in time.

He looked at her speculatively. His eyes seemed to bore into her soul. "Juan says it's dangerous for you there. He says the patriarch warned you."

"Ah, Juan is sweet, but he is terrified of that big old house. They all are. For no reason. Still, I've left unfinished business there and must return."

"That's crazy! Sara doesn't exist or she's dead."

"I showed you her letters. They came sporadically for years and then stopped. I tell you, she didn't mention any illness or dying."

"I guess that last would be hard to do," he said dryly. They laughed and the tension broke. "Okay, when did she tell you about that fabulous treasure she was leaving you? I take it the stately mansion didn't turn out so well."

It gave her pause for a moment. It was as if he guessed about the diary, but that couldn't be. "Her last few letters mentioned a trunk. She never wrote of it as money, but called it a treasure. I know she meant the chest of money Jacob took from the bank."

"What did the old man, Jacob, say about it or couldn't you trust him with the secret either?" His jibe made her flush, but she decided not to take the bait.

"I didn't ask him about the treasure in so many words, and he didn't mention it in so many words. Still, he knew about it. He warned me not to mention it and let me know he wanted no part of it, for himself nor for his people. Something like that would ruin their lives. Or so he thinks."

"He's right there. Every fortune hunter from here to Paraguay would descend on them like a flock of vultures. That's exactly the problem with the Indians. They get pushed back farther and farther into the Amazon, and soon they'll have nowhere to go. That will be the end of them." His expression was somber, his mouth set in a harsh line of disapproval.

"That's why I need to take the money away. That's why I have to go back to get it."

"This tall, blond fellow, was he after you or the treasure? Juan couldn't be sure, but he didn't like him."

"It wouldn't surprise me if he was interested in both me and the treasure," she said lightly, knowing better. Sounded as if Scott and Juan had a long talk while she slept.

"You never said where this treasure is. Why didn't you bring some back with you, or did you?" His glance stabbed into her backpack.

"No. I couldn't find it. That'll take time." Now was the time to tell him about the diary.

"I'm not taking you back there again," he stated flatly.

She shrugged, as if it didn't matter. "If you force me to leave now, I'll find a pilot who will bring me back. It'll be easier since I know about the landing at the village and how to get inside the jungle."

"Oh sure, and you aren't forgetting your admirer, are you? He'll be waiting for you."

That idea of confronting Manolo again, alone, definitely troubled her. "I've been taking care of myself for years."

Scott raised a dark eyebrow. "Oh? By living at home with Papa and teaching school? Sounds like a rough life."

"What do you know about my life?" she retorted.

"You have to admit, you were glad to see me back there."

"Very well, Mr. Perfect. I was glad to see you. However, that Viking type wasn't half bad, now that I think on it. With a little smoothing of rough edges—"

She never got to finish the sentence. In an instant he stood in front of her, pulled her to her feet, and lifted her high in the air as if she had been a child.

"So, he's a hunk? Is that what you're trying to say, you rascal?"

He held her suspended above him. She grasped his shoulders as he lowered her seductively close, moving her slowly down the length of his body.

It was then she knew how much he had worried about her. The thought made her light-headed. She took a deep breath, willing herself calm.

"What am I going to do with you, Marisa?" He shook his head, clearly puzzled. "I've never known anyone like you. You're forcing me to change my mind about women."

She reached to push the lock of hair gently back from his forehead.

He grabbed her hand before she could withdraw it and put his lips to her palm, kissing it softly. Then he brushed his lips over each finger separately and trailed a string of hot kisses up her arm, pausing at the quickening pulse in the soft crook inside her elbow before continuing slowly up her arm.

When he reached her throat with his questing lips, she tried to push away. But now he was beyond gentle shoves. His hands roamed over her back as he pressed kisses against the softly throbbing pulse at the base of her neck.

Her body began to tingle all over. She wanted so badly to let go, to return his lovemaking. She twined her fingers in his thick hair and tried to pull him even closer.

"Marisa, my sweet, I want you so." His hoarse whisper penetrated her desire, splitting her passionate need into shards of awareness. He wanted her. Was that enough? She had abstained this long, waiting for marriage. Was she going to surrender her innermost self to a fly-by-night pilot she didn't even know? To have him toss her away like discarded laundry when he tired of her, as he was apparently so willing to do with Elaina?

She pushed away, hard.

"What the hell?" he demanded, visibly trying to regain his control. "What's wrong?"

She willed the tears to stay back so he wouldn't see them. "I apologize, but for a moment I forgot the commitments back home. And I don't want to be anyone's temporary girlfriend," she added.

"Is that what you think when I make love to you? What do you mean by commitments? Are you talking about Thomas? You seldom mention him."

She shook her head, unable to speak against the hurt in his voice.

"Why is security so important to women?"

"Is that what you think women need? How do you define this security you think we all need?"

"Money, of course. Women have to know there's a steady income available."

"Now hold up a minute, Mr. Macho," she said. "That's just plain stupid. You can't lump everyone together because your wife—"

"Ex-wife, and that happened years ago. It has no bearing on what I think now."

"No, of course it doesn't. You assume every female on earth is looking for easy pickings in a husband. You've been away from civilization too long. We're emancipated back home. We even vote and get elected for political office now."

Scott looked startled at her angry sarcasm for a minute and then he grinned. Was he laughing *at* her or with her? She never could tell.

He took a deep breath. "You made your point. Still, you've got reservations about me as a person, because I'm a bush pilot and that's hardly fair. Tell the truth," he added.

She flushed. "It's true, in part. Not altogether because of the pilot thing, but your easy friendships, your lack of ambition. I don't know. Nothing in your life seems real, with any substance. But hey, that's okay for you. It's your life."

He shrugged, without even the decency to look chagrined. He must love his way of living, but she didn't. Security was important, why be afraid to admit it?

"You're beginning to like Brazil, aren't you?" he asked.

She smiled across the campfire, glad their contentious mood seemed to have lifted. "Yes, I guess I am." The answer surprised even her. "This has to be the most exciting place in the world. Sometimes I still can't believe I'm here in the jungle, along the Amazon."

"I know. I still get that feeling, too, after all these years. It isn't something you take for granted. I'd have to admit that's what attracted me to you in the first place. Besides your looks, of course. You mix a little girl's eagerness with a cool composure of a schoolteacher. Makes you hard to figure, but I'm enjoying the effort."

Her crazy heart did flip-flops at his spare words of praise and the look he gave her under those thick dark lashes.

"Since we're being direct," she said. "You surely are a puzzle. You're satisfied being a pilot and taking dangerous risks. You're always available to an eccentric millionaire and yet capable of important responsibilities like helping with Radam and caring what the future generation does about the land and saving the antiquities for the people."

"What if I told you it's my opinion that money can only buy so much in this world? I know, it's a big, fat cliché, but it's my philosophy in a nutshell. Is it so hard to understand that security comes from inside, not from outside?"

"Maybe so," she admitted reluctantly. He made her sound like a status-seeking gold digger. "I understand your point of view, and you have mine wrong. I'm not looking for a husband with a bank account, I'm going to marry someone with self-worth, someone who doesn't look at work like it's a four-letter word."

"Well, it is, Teach, it is." They laughed and the tension briefly lessened. "What it boils down to is that I don't fit into your preconceived notion of what a man should be doing with his life. Is that a fair assumption?"

She flushed again.

"Aha! Are all the men you know in Virginia so settled down, nose-to-the-grindstone types?"

"I'm hardly an expert on the matter," she retorted. "But yes, most every male over the age of twenty is probably involved in getting the most out of his life, knowing what he wants and what it takes to get there."

"That's really so important to you?" He sounded mocking, but his clear gray eyes had taken on a look of seriousness as if the answer was important.

She reflected a moment, looking up at the sky, at the top of the gigantic overhead branches. "I'm not so sure anymore," she admitted. "I've always thought it was important. My father is the proverbial absent-minded professor without a practical bone in his body. If I hadn't managed our funds over the years and planned ahead, no one would have. I suppose that may be why I hold a lot of respect for achievers of this world."

"I can understand that. Still, you must see that the world doesn't fit conveniently into a mold because you prefer it that way. It doesn't make your values right and everyone else's wrong, does it?"

He sounded so sensible, it irritated her. "Of course not," she replied with annoyance plain in her voice. Why must he always make her sound so self-seeking and materialistic? It wasn't fair. She only wanted out of life the same things expected by everyone she ever knew.

The firelight played across their faces. "You're so beautiful, here in the light," he murmured. "Like a butterfly, fragile and golden." The words broke from his lips. She stared at him, startled. Obviously he hadn't meant to speak so plainly, with such a longing in his eyes.

A loud bird sound split the quiet morning air and Scott grinned, cupping his hands around his mouth to answer back.

In less than a half hour Juan burst through the woods with several men following. Everyone began speaking at once. They looked at her, their hands moving with excited gestures, their Portuguese so loud the nearby monkeys squalled with anger, trying to outdo them. The jungle was in bedlam. She put her hands over her ears, laughing, and the men laughed with her.

The trip back was not easy, lying in a stretcher, bouncing around as the men hiked through the forest. She would have preferred to walk, but Scott was apparently taking no chances she would not be ready to travel when they got back to the village.

She supposed he wanted her out of Brazil as soon as possible, thinking her a nuisance.

While they walked through the jungle, she wondered what she was doing here, trusting her life to this unpredictable man. At times he let out a low whistle, sometimes answered, sometimes not.

Often he passed her stretcher on a widening of the trail and walked in front a while, looking back frequently as if to assure she still followed.

He could be so sensitive, as he was with the villagers and Juan. He was also protective and full of authority. All the things she might have admired in a stranger, but she wasn't sure if she admired those traits in anyone closer.

What was she thinking, anyone closer? Scott would never be closer. She knew it wasn't a question of Elaina. She believed him when he said they were only friends.

Yet it wasn't hard to know what he wanted. The desire in his eyes showed plainly at times, and while flattering, it wasn't enough. Was it?

Could she settle for giving up that special part of herself to someone who, like a bee, would move on to the next flower without thinking about the last?

Had she pegged him wrong? She didn't think so. It was a tempting idea to give in to him, to find out what he wanted from her. She watched his broad shoulders and muscled tan legs in the cutoff shorts disappear in the bend of the trail. Very tempting indeed.

CHAPTER 19

When the three arrived in Kayapo, everyone turned out to greet them. Angelina's mother, aunts, and family looked importantly solemn as they directed the men to deposit her in their hut. Marisa felt embarrassed by all the attention. Scott was nowhere in sight, and she missed him already.

He returned in time to supervise the binding of a new wrap on her ankle, although Angelina's mother had taken over the chore and wouldn't let anyone else touch her, not even Scott. She'd be quite a handful as a mother-in-law. Marisa didn't envy Juan in his courtship of with Angelina.

Marisa would have liked to tell the women about Saffron, but couldn't break the language barrier. Juan might have helped, but he stayed within Scott's shadow, probably trying to atone for taking her into the jungle without his permission. She smiled, knowing Scott wasn't really angry with the boy. He treated Juan like a younger brother, a very admirable quality.

"I'm going to bring the plane back. I'll take Juan, leave him in his own village. Don't go off and leave me this time." The mock severity of his expression made her smile.

"I thought there wasn't any place to land near here. Isn't that why we hiked through that jungle for ages?"

He grinned that lopsided smile that made her want to hug and scold him at the same time. "Not exactly. I needed to see how serious you were about finding those relatives. I also was curious how you'd do in the jungle first time out."

"How did I do?" What other surprises did he have for her? She wasn't upset with his ruse. It had helped to break her in for her journey with Juan to see the Yellowhairs.

"Not half bad." He smiled at her snort of exasperation. "Hey, I'm kidding. You did good."

"Will you be long?" It had taken them days to hike here from Juan's village.

He leaned over and kissed the top of her head. "Nope. A day is all. Don't look so annoyed. I didn't want to rush your first trip out, so it took us a little longer."

He spoke to the women, who nodded in unison, and then turned back to her. "I instructed them to walk with you around the compound. Leave the wrapping on loose and practice walking but have someone close by, so you won't injure it again."

"Yes sir, certainly sir, any more instructions, sir?"

He looked flustered for an instant, which he quickly overcame. "I guess I come off pretty bossy. Sorry, it's one of my more endearing faults."

She couldn't have agreed with him more but wouldn't have said so for anything.

He reached for her backpack, but she put a hand out to stop him.

"I'll just toss it in the plane so we don't forget it when we leave again. You shouldn't need it for a day."

She'd planned to read the diary while he was gone, but could think of no reason to give him that he couldn't take it with him. It would have to wait.

Juan walked up to her and shyly touched the tip of her braid lying over the front of her shoulder. It seemed to be a special greeting with people out here, because Angelina's mother and aunts had done it too.

"We will meet again, very soon, *Senhorita*."

"Of course we will." Who would take her back to find Sara if Scott refused? "You look sad. Are you missing Angelina already?"

His eyes dark and brooding, Juan glanced at the girl standing in the doorway of the little hut. "I want to marry her. My mother say damn fine idea. Her mother say no. I need steady job first." He waved a hand toward the village. "No work here."

She took his thin, hard hand in hers. "I know. It may look hopeless right now, but can't Scott help you?"

"He did plenty already." Juan gently pulled his hand away and returned to Scott's side, turning once to wave.

Marisa watched them go, Juan trailing behind. A baby cried fretfully in the background along with all the sounds of the jungle she was beginning to accept and barely hear anymore.

"Be ready when I get back, Marisa. And don't go on any adventures alone this time," Scott called out, his voice swallowed by the gray fog sifting up from the forest floor.

How could anything be so wrong if it felt as good as his arms around her and his lips against hers? Yet, he did not need her beyond his immediate desire. Imagine going home to tell her father she had fallen in love with a bush pilot. A man with no more ambition than to dig in the earth for treasures he couldn't even keep and hang onto a wealthy businessman for support in a luxurious life style? Where would she fit in?

She tried to tell herself this sudden feeling in the pit of her stomach when she saw him was only a newly awakened passion on her part, a mad desire to flit too close to a flame, but she knew better. It was more serious than that. She had fallen in love with Scott Dunbar, as much as she would ever love anyone in her life.

That night she slept poorly, tossing and turning, a feat not easily accomplished in a hammock. It would be so good to get outside, to stand in the cool, damp night, but she didn't want to waken the women sleeping in their hammocks close by. Toward morning she dozed.

"Go 'way!" she cried out as someone shook her shoulder. She opened her eyes a crack. Angelina stood near, still shaking her.

The young girl spoke softly, as if certain that by now Marisa could understand. She pointed toward the center of the compound. The meaning was unmistakable. Scott was back and waiting. She hadn't even heard the racket of the plane landing.

Before Marisa emerged from the hut, she gave Angelina one of her favorite blouses and a small gold bracelet for her mother and hugged them both. They seemed so overwhelmed by the simple gifts, she had to turn away and head for the door before she burst into tears.

Scott stood by the dying campfire in the center of the village. Recognizing his silhouette head and shoulders above the other men was easy.

"Good morning." He sounded exceedingly chipper. . "How's the ankle?"

"Good as new." And it was the truth.

Back in Virginia she hadn't been a gracious early morning riser. She noticed that had gradually changed since they'd arrived in the jungle. One had no choice but to arise early. To face the new day with anything less than grateful courtesy would be unthinkable. She smiled at her capricious thoughts.

"Love that smile," he teased.

"Thanks. Good morning to you."

"We'll head for Belem. I've got diggings near there I'd like to check out. Then back to Brasilia."

Brasilia, good and bad news. She still had to figure a way to get back here soon to find Sara, but meanwhile she needed a long, hot bath and a rest in a real bed.

They waved to the watching people while Angelina stood a little to the side. Perhaps she and Juan would never marry if Scott didn't find something for Juan to do to make a living.

The landing strip had been hacked out of the jungle as if in an afterthought. She had looked at the landing before, at Campo Largo, as a difficult place. Scott took off with an ease Marisa found fascinating. He appeared so...cool, the youngsters in her class would have said, sitting there behind the wheel and all those instruments, wearing his worn leather jacket with his newly washed, long silk scarf thrown casually around his neck.

"All you're missing are the goggles," she shouted as they settled into the sky.

He smiled in response but didn't reply. Unless he was pointing out a scene below, he liked silence in the cockpit. She understood that. If you could once get beyond the noise of the plane, everything below was so beautiful, words got in the way.

"Wouldn't it be something to float over this in a hot air balloon or a glider?" she asked.

"I've thought of that many times. What a spectacular panorama it would be."

When they stopped talking, it gave her time to think about Virginia, her new job at the paper, and how much she missed her father with his long dissertations at the dinner table on everything from politics to philosophy to music.

She knew Janice was taking care of him. Perhaps now they would settle into a more permanent relationship without a third party underfoot. That would be good for both of them.

"Where did you say we were going?" she asked.

"Heading for Belem. I've come across American descendants there, and my diggings aren't far. Do two things at once."

"How far is it? Do you have fuel?"

"My, you *are* a worrier," he said.

He grinned, and she fully expected to see a tooth sparkle like in those exaggerated movies of super heroes.

"I've installed an extra gas tank on Muscatel, if that makes you feel any better. Had to. There's not another half-way decent stop between the Matos and the coast. Of course with Muscatel, you don't worry overmuch about that. The old girl's got wings with lateral control that'll pull out of a stall at twenty-six knots. That translates to thirty miles per hour. I can stop on a dime and give you nine cents change."

Juan had told her about the extra fuel tank, but she'd needed to hear it from Scott.

The day passed quicker than she thought it would. When she tired of looking down at the green canopy of trees, she dozed.

"Ah, I see you woke up," he said. "Didn't have a good night's sleep without me there?"

"Don't flatter yourself," she countered lightly.

"How about reaching in the back and hauling out some grub. Mrs. O'Reilly made sandwiches."

They sipped on fruit juice and ate, neither feeling much like talking. Then she dozed off and on again. It seemed like no time before he jostled her shoulder.

"Wake up, Marisa. There's something you have to see."

She opened her eyes and looked down. As far as she could see was water, turned by the setting sun into a shimmering blanket of rose dust. "Oh! It's beautiful!"

"It's the mouth of the Amazon. The River Sea, they call it. Fasten your belt. We're about to land."

"Wait! I don't see any place to land down there." She closed her eyes for the descent. She trusted Scott's expertise, but even after several landings, it wasn't something she enjoyed—with the scenery rushing forward toward them at such an alarming rate of speed. Especially when the spot he picked to land on looked no bigger than a manhole cover at the start of the descent.

"I didn't see a town," she managed between clenched teeth.

He laughed. "No, we didn't get to Belem, it's only a skip and a hop away, but the digs came first, and there's something I wanted to show you."

The thought of spending more time alone with him in the jungle sent a message of delight down one-half of her body and a feeling of anxiety up the other half. She had begun to realize she couldn't trust her own responses around him, much less cope with his. Especially without the buffer of Juan between them.

He set the plane down in what he must have considered a clearing. After they tied it down, he set up camp near a lagoon. The sound of a waterfall echoed somewhere back in the jungle. The clearing looked eerie in the light of the coming nightfall.

He built a fire and they ate fruit and drank the fruit drink. "By this time tomorrow I'll have some fresh fish, which should taste pretty good."

"You bet it will." She liked fruit but hungered for something a little more substantial. "But how will you fish? I don't see anything moving in this lagoon."

"Have to get out a ways. I've got a collapsible canoe with a little motor stashed in the back of the plane. You've never gone fishing before, have you?"

"That's a wild guess on your part." She smiled. "But no, I haven't. I can't see my father doing any such thing."

"Do you always do just as your father?"

"Mostly, I suppose. He did raise me, and we were all we had for years."

"Two against the world?"

He didn't sound mocking, and she nodded.

"I understand that. Yet, you've got a hidden resource of enthusiasm you haven't tapped yet. I can tell it's there, waiting to pop out of you."

She laughed at the notion. "And you plan to get it out in the open?"

He bent close and his body-warmth transferred through the tee shirt he wore. His heart beat against her cheek.

"Come on, let's go. We don't have much time."

He looked upward continually, as if waiting to see something. The tree tops loomed overhead in the small clearing. A patch of blue sky lay over them like a cap.

"Are you expecting something or someone to drop in on us from up there?" she finally asked him.

He shook his head. "No, checking the moon. Look. There it goes up into the sky. What I want to show you happens just before dawn."

"We're going fishing at night? Isn't that dangerous?" She thought of the huge fish back in the jungle lagoon and the countless crocodiles she'd watched from the air. "Won't someone come into camp and steal stuff? How about Muscatel, will she be okay?"

He laughed and swooped her up in the air, holding her suspended for a second before setting her down again.

"Questions, questions, questions, that's all I get from you, woman!" He turned a mock frown on her, his eyes unreadable in the shadows. "No one lives around here. That's how I found the archaeological site. I don't want to scare you, but the Indians in this area think this lagoon is haunted."

"Haunted?" She was frightened of a lot of things, storms, weird people sometimes, but not of ghosts. She had proved that by rummaging through the big house of the Yellowhairs.

"I'll tell you a story about the lagoon later, but first the boat." He pulled the pieces of the craft out of the plane and began putting it together while she watched him.

It didn't take long for him to get it together and attach the little motor. It looked oddly fragile, outdated and dumpy, like a little old bag lady from the city.

He looked up at the sky again. "Come on, we've a ways to go." The urgency in his voice moved her forward without asking any more questions.

Scott pulled the boat a few hundred yards through the grass to the lagoon. Marisa looked ahead, down the stream, but saw nothing but a tunnel of trees and dark water. It didn't look too inviting.

She hesitated. "I don't know about this."

"Trust me. You'll be eternally grateful."

He stood close to her and tilted her chin so he could look down at her face. His tone was light and almost bantering, but his gray eyes, with their fringe of black lashes, were serious, as if it meant something to him that she go.

Deciding in an instant, she reached to touch her lips to his. "Okay. I'm in. Let's do it."

Making a loud whoop, he lifted her and deposited her in the front of the little boat. He stepped in the back and started the motor. As small as it was, it didn't make much noise and few birds and creatures bothered stirring from their night resting places as the boat passed down the twisting little river.

They traveled so long, she thought they were going to go on forever. The jungle closed in tightly around them. The trees sucked up the sounds, and the damp air hung in layers of gauzy mist. Marisa spent her time watching Scott, wondering what his thoughts were. Both of them were silent. The jungle suppressed any notion for conversation.

Finally, he said, "Here we are, the mouth of the Amazon."

She looked around and saw nothing but water on two sides and in front of her. Behind her, the jungle receded rapidly as he continued out into the sea.

He put his fingers in the water and touched them to his mouth. "This is still sweet water, amazingly. Doesn't get salty for a long way out." The moon dipped low in the horizon and he seemed anxious to make more time. He pushed the little motor, his expression eager. Suddenly, he turned off the motor and let down the anchor.

"Nope, not right."

He pulled up the anchor and started the motor again. They went a little further out to sea and he stopped again. This time the anchor went down a long time before the thick rope stopped uncoiling.

"Why do you have such a long anchor in such a little boat?" she asked.

"Because I've been waiting to come here for a long time. But it had to be perfect. You're very special, and I wanted you to share it with me."

He was being very mysterious, but she lost track of that when she looked at the moon, a huge, butter-yellow balloon in the distance, perched on the edge of the horizon. Any moment it was going to sizzle out in the water. She could see why some cultures in the past had thought the world was flat.

Suddenly she heard a terrible roaring sound, like a hundred small planes coming their way. "Oh, my God! What's that?"

He stood up carefully and moved to sit next to her, putting his arm around her shoulders and pulling her close. "Shh. Don't be scared, and for God's sake, don't move. I'm right here with you. Trust me."

She screamed in fright when she saw the giant flat wave coming at them, spanning the entire width of the horizon. She heard the huge trees crashing on the shoreline as it hit, a ten-foot wall of water crashing into the forest, just as the moon sank out of sight.

She clung to Scott, her heart thudding in her chest. His heart was beating hard, too. She heard his intake of breath as the crest of the giant wave slid under their boat. It lifted them up, gently, and was gone, melding into the great Amazon behind them, blending with the forest as it lost its momentum.

Swallowing, trying to catch her breath, she wondered if she was still alive. The exhilaration of knowing they lived through that upheaval made her senses whirl and her pulse race. Anger, at the chance he had taken, mixed with a sudden desire for him that left her shaken, more so than the fear of death. Passion flooded the center of her being with liquid fire. It was as if the world had suddenly had a giant orgasm and she was in the center of it.

He turned her toward him, his lips descending on hers. His tongue searched her mouth. She kissed him back, withholding nothing. His hard thighs pressed against hers. She held him to her, needing him with a blinding passion that had erupted with the giant wave.

When they broke for a breath, she leaned away to look at him. It was dark, the moon had gone, but she could feel that dawn was not far away.

"What the hell was *that?*"

He laughed and held her close again for a minute, as if not wanting to be separated even by a little air.

"That, my love, was the *Pororoco*, the Big Roar. Ever since I came to Brazil I wanted to witness it, but never so much as with you."

"Thanks a lot." Her words were dry, her tone not amused. "You could have gotten us killed."

"Ah, no Marisa. Never in a million years. All we had to do was anchor in a deep spot. I knew the water would rush right under us. It's called a tidal bore and only happens when the tides are unusually high with a full moon ready to set. I knew this was the time if it ever was going to happen, so that's why I had to get here in such a hurry. We almost missed it."

"What a pity," she said.

He kissed her. "Don't tell me you didn't get a thrill out of that."

She had been frightened, but those enchanted moments would last a lifetime, never to come her way again.

"Where does all that extra water go?" she asked. "Aren't you afraid our camp and your plane will be gone?"

"So many questions—all that water goes back up the Amazon, four or five hundred miles. It's more a case of the Amazon reversing itself to some unknown timing of the moon. This new water will be sweet too, not a bit salty. And our camp is safe. I found the only high knoll in the area, that's why the artifacts lasted through the century."

Marisa leaned against him, needing to feel him close to her. "I thought we were doomed," she admitted.

"Ah, love, I wouldn't let anything happen to you. I had to show you that life is so much more when you don't plan everything out and just take the joy from it. You have to savor life as it comes without guarantees."

"You planned this escapade," she accused. His calling her love shot a thrill up and down her midsection.

"Yes, but the important thing is, you didn't. Yet, you enjoyed it, lived through it, and your worst nightmare turned into something very different. Go on, admit it." He kissed her eyelids, the tip of her nose. Then she surrendered her lips again to his invading mouth and tongue.

The excitement stayed with them all the way back to camp.

CHAPTER 20

By daybreak, Marisa and Scott were on their way back to camp. The way they had come had been filled with debris from the forest. Huge fallen trees lay about blocking the entrance to the river. He took an offshoot of the Amazon, and they wound their way up the little tributary until she recognized the campsite. When he helped her out of the boat, she felt stiff from sitting so long.

"Now, let's relax, maybe get some shuteye for a few hours."

"I thought you wanted to check out your treasures?"

He smiled, shamefaced as any young boy. "No, I removed them from here, afraid the high tide would eventually get them. I heard it might be time for the *Pororoca* and had to share it with you."

"You went over a thousand miles just to include me?" The lump in her throat made it hard to swallow. She didn't know how to respond, he'd overwhelmed her so.

His rugged profile was tinged with the dust falling from the overhead trees, and his thick, dark hair was mussed and coated with a fine layer of the stuff.

She must look a mess herself after helping to set up camp, tie down the plane, and then sitting out there on the boat for hours.

"Is there a place to wash first?" she asked. "I feel so tired and grubby, I'd love a bath and then I'd sleep like a baby."

"That's a good idea. That lagoon is perfectly safe. No crocs for miles or fish either. Something about the water, that's why the natives think it's haunted."

"Maybe it's poisoned."

"Always the optimist. No, it's brown, as is all Brazil's water, but it's potable." He took her hand and led her toward the forest-enclosed pool. They stood watching the swarms of colorful butterflies floating like thistledown over the area. The sound of the waterfall in the background made her feel lethargic and a deep sense of well-being filled her with contentment.

"Actually, the natives think Saci lives here. By the way, you've got dirt streaks on your pretty nose."

She laughed. "I was thinking the same about you. Anyway, don't change the subject. Who is Saci and why should anyone fear him or her?"

He grinned, an endearing, slow-moving parting of his lips, a quick flick of tongue against his teeth that made her heart beat faster.

"He's Brazil's national hero, and what you might call a gremlin, all rolled into one little person. All Brazilians have seen him at least once in their lives. You can ask any of them and they'll swear to it."

She spread a blanket at the edge of the pool and pulled him down beside her. Brazilians loved a good story, she'd noticed.

"Most folks swear he's a tiny black man who jumps rapidly around on one leg. He wears a red nightcap with a tassel on the end." His expression was one of mock solemnity as he continued his story.

"He lives in the jungle but he's been seen in all the cities of Brazil. Housewives blame him for their burnt beans. Husbands swear he's the cause of their drinking that extra bottle of *batida*. Children always tell their parents it was old Saci who made their school grades so poor."

"My goodness, he sounds like a real trouble-maker."

"Oh no! Never say that. Saci may be listening. I hasten to add that he has many good qualities, too." He looked around behind him as if expecting the little man to pop into their midst.

"I'm listening." She had never seen this facet of his personality before and she smiled at his boy-like enthusiasm.

"Well, then, Saci hates pomposity and lets the air out of windbags with delight. He has a sense of humor that endears him to Brazilians, even while his tricks irritate them. He protects miners and treasure seekers if their conscience is clean but if not, they might wind up with a lump of coal for all their work."

Have you ever received that lump of coal? she wondered.

They began to remove their boots.

"I suppose you intend to keep your clothes on so you can wash everything at the same time, being so practical and all," he said dryly.

"That's an excellent idea. Something your friend Saci would approve of," she countered. "Actually, I didn't think to pack a bathing suit."

He grinned. The laugh lines around his eyes bespoke his humor, though she didn't always see much of it. Mostly because they rubbed each other the wrong way. Why was that?

"What's wrong with your underthings? I've probably seen more bare skin on the beaches in Rio."

"I'll bet you have."

"I'm taking off my shirt. If that won't offend you." His voice held a hint of mockery, but his eyes asked a serious question. "Turn around unless..."

"Do what you usually do," she said, uncomfortable with his idea that she was so prim and proper.

When he turned away to hang his shirt on a limb, she sneaked a look at the play of muscles across his tanned back. From dallying on the beaches in Rio, she thought uncharitably.

"Okay. I'm in the water now," he said needlessly as she heard the big splash. "I'll turn my back, that is unless you plan to come in and wash your clothes too."

She felt propelled by the ridicule in his voice so as soon as she saw the back of his head in the dark water, she slipped out of her trousers and blouse and, clad only in her bra and bikini panties, she touched a toe to the water. Then, watching his back, made an impulsive decision and stripped off everything.

After the long, sweaty day, she wanted to feel the silky water against her skin. She hurriedly leaped into the pool of warm water, which was deeper than she had imagined, but smelled clean and earthy.

"Are you sure there aren't any crocodiles?"

"A little late to be asking, don't you think?" He swam closer. "No. That sound you hear is the waterfall. It discourages crocs from swimming downstream and the series of rapids above helps, but don't assume you can swim in any old river in Brazil."

"I know. You told me." She splashed him playfully. "You're a stick-in-the-mud."

"What did you call me?" He spoke in mock anger and dove under the water to tug on her ankle. She went under and popped to the surface again, sputtering and laughing. She splashed him with the plane of her hand to get even.

She treaded water to get away from him, and passed by a low place in the barrier to the river. As if in answer to her next question, he spoke.

"We can go into the river, it's much cooler water, but keep out of the middle. The current is so strong it would sweep you right away."

"This is fine with me." Marisa longed to float on her back, but of course, didn't dare with no clothes on. The water felt like velvet against her skin and knowing Scott was so close, and naked too, sent shivers of fire all over her body. She knew her face must be as red as a beet. Suddenly shy, she pretended to regard the other shore with interest.

"Look! A big fish!" he yelled.

Alarmed, she swam toward him, having no intention of sharing her space with anything larger than a minnow. He reached out to pull her close.

"No fair!" She suddenly realized what he'd done. Her heart hammered against her ribs at his nearness. He slid his hands over her body, and her skin absorbed the warmth of them. The water made only a whisper of a barrier between them. He bent to claim her lips, his mouth closing over hers, his tongue moved, searching her moist warmth.

Scott thrust his thigh between hers, and she wrapped her legs shamelessly around it, staying afloat in the deep water. Dipping his head beneath the water, he took one hardened nipple gently between his teeth. His mouth felt hot with the contrast of the water against the rest of her body. His fingers slowly traced a line down her center until she began to tremble.

His head came up, his eyes dark and unfathomable as the water surrounding them. He pulled her closer, lifting her up out of the water until he touched his lips to her breast, kissing each one with a maddening thoroughness.

She arched her back only a trifle, but he felt it immediately and let her down until they could look into each other's eyes. She leaned forward, tracing her lips across his cheek, tasting the faint mustiness of the pond water on his skin. Her tongue teased his jaw, her fingernails carving little dents into his back. When she moved her palms across his shoulder blades, caressing the taut muscles, they tightened beneath her hands.

She leaned into him, feeling him against her flank, and suddenly doubt fled, replaced with the sweet aching desire coursing through her body. Every inch of her being wanted him. She pushed herself downward, forcing her throbbing core against his muscular thigh.

Scott drew a sharp breath and groaned, hands pausing a moment in their wondrous explorations, as if shocked by her bold caress. "Oh, God, Marisa, I want you so." He buried his face against her throat.

Tracing a finger down the forbidden length of him, she felt his shudder and the leap of his heartbeat. She moved her palms slowly up and down his rib cage and across his shoulders.

Every part of her quivered with intensity, with the anticipation of the moment. It was as if they existed alone in the world.

All the years of waiting, of keeping the center part of herself intact. No man had ever touched that part until now.

Scott slipped down into the water closer to her and kissed her wide eyes closed, moving his mouth across her cheeks until he found her lips.

She writhed beneath his roving hands as his tongue penetrated between her teeth in a kiss of such passion she felt swept into a whirlpool, going around and around in the velvet water.

He lifted her out of the pond and carried her to the blanket at the edge of the river. The thick grass beneath them released a sweet smell of crushed vegetation as he gently lowered her. Stretching out at her side, he leaned on his elbow to look at her.

"I imagined you just like this, Marisa, so beautiful, so passionate, so giving."

His eyes, his voice, told her she was all that and more to him. She reached her hand to his lips, her fingers lightly playing over them. Uncertainty intruded as her cooling body lay defenseless to his marauding eyes and hands.

He nibbled her throat and body, leaving a trail of fiery kisses over her breasts, and savored each rosy orb with lingering slowness. Then he buried his face between them, holding them together so that they pressed into his cheeks.

She felt the prickly rasp of his skin, the shadow of new bristle on his jawline against her delicate, most intimate places as he moved down her body.

She twined her fingers in his thick dark hair, trying to pull him back up, but not wanting to at the same time. When he came to the parting of her thighs, he gently spread her legs. His plundering mouth made her arch her back in reflex and he put his hands beneath her buttocks to raise her up. The fanning breath on her most secret place, the moist warmth of his tongue, sent electric shocks through her body. The exquisite feeling of need enveloped her so that she moaned and writhed. Hot spasms lashed over her when the magic his mouth and tongue worked on her body finally gave her release.

He moved back upward and again took her nipple in his mouth, working his tongue around it, with loving care. Before she could move her legs, he gently reached down to massage the bud where his mouth had just left and reached a finger into her warm silky entrance. When it met resistance in spite of her passion, he froze and rolled off her. He was breathing hard and she waited until he could talk. Why did he remove himself from her, leaving her bereft and needing him close again?

"Scott?"

He pulled her swiftly across his body so that she lay on top of him, her face close to his. She felt the warmth of his still heavy breathing and the movement of his chest beneath her breasts.

"I'm sorry I started this. I didn't realize you had never...I mean, I didn't know no one had ever..."

"I love you," she interrupted. "Why did you stop? I needed you to...finish what you started," she blurted out, amazed at her brazenness. If he didn't return her love, it would hurt—worse than anything she could imagine. But it didn't change her feelings. For the first time she realized she didn't need any guarantees in order to give her love away.

He suddenly reversed their positions and rolled over on top of her, holding his weight up with his elbows resting on the ground. He looked into her eyes and the gray of them was like a fog enveloping her soul. She still tingled at the apex of her thighs and knew what should have come next. Why didn't it? For the first time in her life, she was ready to open herself and give without promises or pledges.

She turned her head and looked up at the thick rim of trees and vines overhead circling the still pond. The sun barely penetrated, only gossamer bright chains of light filtered through here and there, falling over their resting place like golden sheets of rain.

She thrust her hands up into his hair and trailed her fingers back over his ears, tracing his face from his forehead, to his nose, down to encompass his mouth with her searching.

He groaned and took her hands, holding them in his. "Sweetheart, don't. I can't make love to a—"

When he didn't finish, she claimed his lips and let her own tongue explore his mouth until he pushed her away, groaning. They lay entwined, the moisture gradually evaporating from their damp bodies, leaving crisp little brushes of sensation behind as the skin dried.

"A virgin?" she finished. "Is that so terrible? I know it's unusual, but I just never..."

He smiled, and his eyes held such tenderness that it took her breath away. She ran her hand over his wide, bronzed chest, caressing his hardened nipples and felt his tremor.

"I've never felt anything like what I'm feeling with you," he admitted. "It's like a bolt of lightning jolted through my mind and body and now I'm damned confused."

"Is that bad?" she asked, smiling back at him.

He touched his fingers to her face, his thumbs rubbed gently on her swollen lips. She was fully aware of his hardness between them, resting against her thighs. A shiver of desire, of incomplete arousal washed over her and she caught her breath with the enormity of her need for him.

"Don't you want me?" She took away his hand from her face and kissed each finger.

"Ah, god, don't do that." His voice caught in his throat, coming out hoarse. "You know I want you, but somehow this re-arranges everything I've believed in for so long. It's—it's like a betrayal. My thoughts and emotions no longer belong to me."

"Can't you just leave your mind out of this and make love to me?" She knew her voice held a tinge of exasperation, but she couldn't help it. Weren't men supposed to think with their..."

He interrupted her thoughts and it was just as well.

"Ever since you ran off alone with just Juan to protect you, since the Yellow Hair confronted you and could have done God knows what to you, and when you limped through a forest with a sprained ankle without bothering to tell me, and sat in the midst of a tidal bore without screaming your head off, my mind has been boggled. It's like a deck of cards that have been shuffled higgely-piggely and then thrown down on the floor. I can't grasp it." He claimed her lips and nibbled gently on the bottom one.

She answered with a brush of her tongue against his.

He sat up on the blanket and pulled her onto his lap. She could still feel the length of his hardness beneath her buttocks. Nothing had diminished there. Out of spite, she wriggled. He groaned and held her tighter so she couldn't move.

"Minx!" he growled. When he caught his breath, a deep sigh erupted from the middle of him. She felt his heart beating against her.

"I realize that I don't ever want to let you go. I want you to stay in Brazil. With me."

"How could I do that? We haven't known each other very long, I—" Did he want her to be his mistress? She was almost ready to say yes to anything at that moment.

Marisa snuggled close in his arms, her face against his chest. For a moment she was content to feel his deep voice rumbling in her ear, not hearing the words, enjoying the calming sensation it brought. Odd how being near him gave her a sense of strength and constancy, although she had tried to deny it from the first because it didn't fit in with her preconceived ideas.

"I thought you stopped making love to me because of my not knowing—"

"No. No sweetheart. It's just that you condemned me for wanting a one-night stand, as you put it. I don't want that. I'm thinking I need to have you with me for the rest of my life."

She pushed away and sat up, looking down at him.

He winced. "Uh, oh. Is it still that bush pilot image you have of me that's troubling you?"

She laughed and tousled his already mussed hair. "No, not any more. Back there on the water, waiting to be drowned by that giant wave, I could see that things like that don't really matter in the long haul. What matters is having someone to love you and someone you can love. Without reservations."

"Ah, there's my girl. You've made me the happiest man in all of Brazil, maybe the world. Now that's said, there's something that has bothered me, something I've got to confess. I despise deception and hate liars more than anything, and I'm probably guilty of both. It started innocently enough I didn't think, I mean, I didn't suppose we'd ever get serious."

"Is it Elaina?" She put a finger to his lips to shush him.

He took her hand to kiss her palm. "No, nothing like that. What I said about her and me, that was true. Nothing there, never was. No, this isn't serious, at least I hope not."

"Well, come on, spit it out."

"It's about the boss. There isn't one. I own the condo and the planes and—"

She twisted away from him and struggled to stand, arms crossed over her breasts, suddenly ashamed. "I don't believe you! I said it made no difference what you did, let it go."

"I'm telling you the truth, damn it! I did make most of my money in gold and diamonds, but unlike the other miners, I invested it in Brasilia and Sao Paulo."

Stunned, Marisa felt as if someone had struck her. Was he teasing? No, she could see the truth in his earnest expression. Her mouth tightened. At first she'd suspected he was the boss, but then when he'd had plenty of time to come clean with the deception and didn't, she began to take him at his word. He was playing the fool with her and it made her mad.

"You must have found this little country bumpkin quite amusing. Elaina shared your joke, I'm sure. I remember now she seemed shocked at first when you introduced us, posturing as a hired hand." She made a grab for her clothes and began putting on her blouse, fingers trembling.

He let her talk until she had finished, at the same time he drew on his khaki cut offs and pulled his tee shirt over his head.

"Wait a minute here. It's not like I'm confessing to being a serial killer. You straight away assumed I worked for someone and I admit, it did amuse me for a while. Honestly? It felt good having someone accept me for me rather than what my money can buy."

"Of all the conceited dolts, you take the cake, Mr. Dunbar. I don't give a hoot about your money."

"That's my point. You thought I was a spin-in-the-wind kind of guy and yet you said you love me. That is present tense, isn't it?" His lips turned up in an engaging grin, but his eyes looked concerned, as if he wasn't as sure of her now.

"You rant and rave about truth and honesty and how some terrible newspaper woman made a fool out of you and then you do it to me. How everyone must have laughed at me, the naive outsider, being made a complete fool of."

"Now just a damn minute." His expression was puzzled and hurt. "It wasn't like that at all. No one made fun of you. Part of it was your fault, for making assumptions at face value. I never thought I'd see the day when I had to apologize for having money."

She tried to calm her indignation long enough to think back on the day she met him. The way he stood in the hanger, broad shouldered with tan legs in the cutoff shorts. She remembered him turning to face her and those incredible gray eyes that were so incongruous in that chiseled tan face.

"Maybe you're right. It was partly my fault. But you had no reason to continue the farce. Because you were burnt in your marriage is no reason never to trust anyone again."

He held the palm of her hand to his cheek. "I know that, my love. I surely know that now. But once I had started, I needed to know if you loved me for myself. Besides, you weren't honest with me, either. Did you forget that so soon? When were you going to tell me about the treasure?"

Oh, sweet petunia, the treasure and the diary. And the commitment to write the article about him. She had forgotten about all of that. But she had changed her mind, that counted for honesty. Temporary insanity, what else? She hadn't given the diary another thought since leaving Kayapo. It might even prove illegible, useless for clues to the money's whereabouts. As far as the fax to Thomas, she had cleared that up, hadn't she? No need to dig into all that.

He stopped her next sentence with a kiss. If she thought the kisses they had exchanged before were heated, his lips now pressed against hers with a demanding urgency that surprised her. His tongue probed the tender recesses of her mouth. She felt the lean hardness of his body against the length of hers.

"You're not backing out of staying in Brazil are you?" His whisper teased her ear and sent shivers of delight up and down her spine. "I won't let you go, you know."

He moved his mouth away to kiss her on each eyelid and the tip of her nose. Then he pulled her down to the blanket and wrapped his strong arms around her, her back to his chest, his chin resting on the top of her head while they stared into the dying coals of the campfire.

"I'll make you happy, Marisa. I promise I will."

She knew that. What else the future with him might hold, she wouldn't worry about it now.

He hugged her tighter. His heart pounded against her back. "Ah." He cleared his throat, "There's another little matter."

What now? She waited, hardly daring to breathe.

"I work, unofficially, for the government, the Brazilian government."

"What?

"It's FUNAI, an agency established to protect Indian rights. As I said, it's strictly unofficial. In my travels through the jungle I keep my eyes open for problems or maybe even solutions."

"Problems? Solutions?"

"It could be disagreements between the Indians and the local whites over farmland, or mining claims infringing on Indian land. The government staff can't be everywhere at once. People like me, concerned about the natives, can be very helpful, or so they assure me. Once or twice I came upon excellent areas for a reserve and made suggestions."

Was there anything else he should have told her? She was afraid to ask. She felt her eyelids droop and, through a haze, felt Scott lift her gently into a hammock and wrap her with a light blanket. She absorbed his gentle kiss on her lips, so delicate she might have imagined it.

That was all she remembered as she fell into a deep sleep.

CHAPTER 21

Marisa awakened to Scott's soft kiss. She opened her eyes and saw him kneeling at her side, a cup of steaming coffee in hand.

"Good morning, love. Sleep well?" He pushed the hair back from in front of her shoulders.

"Um. You brought me coffee in bed, or should I say hammock. Is that a promise of things to come?"

"Definitely. I intend to spoil you rotten."

She smiled and slid out of the tricky swing. It was getting to be second nature now. Many times at first she thought the hammock would win, some night twisting her around and around until it wrapped her up like a cocoon.

Scott sat on a campstool, watching her sip the coffee. "I never thought I'd see anyone wearing pajamas in the jungle," he commented. "When did you put them on?"

She blushed and pretended to pout. "Don't you dare make fun of me. What did you expect, a long, black negligee? I must have fallen asleep while we talked. Guess you put me to bed. Then I awoke sometime during the day and put on my pjs. You were snoring like a hippopotamus."

"Was not! How do you know they snore?"

"No. You weren't snoring, and I don't know about them."

He had looked so little-boy-like, lying in his bedroll last night. She recalled the need to kiss his lips, touch his thick black lashes against his cheek. She'd wanted to kiss him so badly last night when he was unaware of her.

"Do I smell fish grilling over that fire?" She pointed to the glowing coals a little off to the side of the camp. He had speared the fish on a slim branch and the moisture dripped off as they cooked, sending a delicious smell skyward.

"I thought you said fish didn't live in this particular body of water," she accused.

"I lied." He grinned that wonderful grin and she forgave him immediately.

When the fillets were done to his satisfaction, he pulled them off onto a broad leaf and split the flaky white meat open with a knife, sprinkling them with the juice of something resembling an orange.

"How come you always insist on my sleeping in a hammock and you don't mind the sleeping bag on the ground?" she said around bites of the tender fish.

"Well, if you must know, I'm not afraid of creepy-crawlers any more. Live and let live is my motto. I didn't think you held the same opinion of them."

She shivered. "You're so right. Thanks." She glanced around the clearing, seeing it as if for the first time. It looked different somehow. Everything looks different to a woman in love, she supposed.

After breakfast, they washed their sticky hands in a pot near the fire.

She began to brush out her hair and braid it.

"Mind if I do that for you?" His casual expression looked forced—as if he thought she would probably refuse.

"I'd love it. If you can braid, you're hired forever."

"I'm counting on it." He kissed the top of her head and then brushed her hair with firm, gentle strokes. When he finished, he braided it in one thick, precise braid and reached for the coated rubber band she held up to him.

"Excellent! Where did you learn to do that?"

He laughed. "What a suspicious tone to your voice, my sweet. Truth is, I had a horse when I was a teenager. I always groomed and braided her mane and tail. She was a Palomino too, only more ordinary coloring. You've got sunlight steaks in your hair, beautiful in a braid."

She kissed the hand that held the brush. "Thank you."

"I can't believe you said yes to me last night. Or this morning, rather. Was I dreaming?"

She shook her head. *I can't believe you asked me*, she wanted to say. The look of love he turned on her might have melted the ropes of the hammock. She stood up, easily disentangling herself.

"Hey, you're getting the hang of that pretty good," he commented.

He took the cup from her hand and pulled her close. They stood toe to toe, in a silent, still dance for a long moment. Then he drew back to look at her, kissing the tip of her nose.

His hands rested on her shoulders. She felt their warmth through her pajama top and the memories of his touch on her bare skin intruded.

"I might have caught you in a weak moment last night," he declared. "But you said you'd stay with me. And to my surprise, you didn't lay down any conditions. Not like the feisty school ma'arm I'm used to talking to. I've lain awake all night thinking—in spite of your suggesting that I snore—and you have erased my last doubt."

She sighed, hoping he wasn't going to complicate matters with a lot of talking. "When do we start? Being a couple, I mean."

"Is tomorrow too soon?"

He chuckled at the confusion she couldn't hide. She smiled back, loving the rich sound of his laughter.

"Nut!" She ruffled her fingers through his hair. It felt crisp and curly and thick.

"Come, sit here and let's talk about it." He pulled her forward to the sleeping bag and they sat close together. "Do you want formal or casual?"

"What are you talking about?" It was hard to concentrate when he blew gently in her ear.

"I never thought I'd hear this come from my mouth—again. But I'm not asking for a shack-up arrangement. I want to marry you."

He tipped up her dropped jaw with a finger.

"Oh!" She felt as if the air had been knocked out of her. "You mean I finally meet all your requirements for a wife?"

"Good! I'm glad to have the old Marisa back again, teeth bared and ready to fight. You were being too compliant there for a while. Had me nervous."

"What made you change your mind about your bachelor status?"

"When I saw you the first time in the hanger, that started it. Your unselfconscious beauty, your total commitment to what you want to do, your feelings for the children, that all made me want to be with you and want a family of my own."

"When?"

"Like I said, is tomorrow too soon?"

A wedding was supposed to be one of the most treasured times of a woman's life, but all she could think of was getting it over with so she could be with him always. "It doesn't matter. This is your adopted country. I've no one here. My father could never come." It would take him some time to get used to the idea anyway. And then there was Thomas.

"Ah, that is a pity, but soon you'll have all the friends and family you'll need. How many kids constitute a real family do you suppose? Four? Five? How about six? That's a nice, round number."

Marisa snuggled closer to him. "Come on, now. I know the women of Brazil are proud of their fertility, but have a little mercy on me. I'd be so busy with babies, I'd never get to be with you. We can wait on that a while, can't we? I thought you weren't big on families. 'Seems like they cause a lot of problems.' Wasn't that how you put it?"

He looked disconcerted for a moment. "I know I probably said that. I also probably meant it at the time, or thought I did. But somehow being with you makes me think of my mom and sis and even my father in a more, well, loving way. Does that sound corny?"

She shook her head. "Sounds wonderful to me. That brings up something else. Will you take me with you on your trips?" She caressed the hard planes of his cheeks, moving her fingers over the rigid jaw line that she admired so much.

"Of course. Why would you ask? I want you with me all the time."

"I don't want to be an ornament in your life. I want to share everything."

"Sweetheart, don't give it a thought. When the kids do come, we'll have housekeepers and nannies, whatever you need to help. Meanwhile it may take several years to get this serious business of honeymooning down to a science so we can move on to other things."

She loved listening to the rich timbre of his voice. It had a different quality when he first woke up, causing an almost indecent urge in her to hurry the marriage. She wanted to hear that early morning voice every day for the rest of her life.

"I still think that was rotten of you to lead me on in thinking you weren't a substantial citizen. Are you sure we can get along? You make fun of every value I hold dear."

"I never did tell you I worked for this rich guy. You figured that out yourself in that funny little way you have of sorting people into categories. Don't ever forget that. So don't start getting mad at me all over again. Lying disgusts me. " He kissed her earlobe and nuzzled into her neck.

She had to laugh at herself. He was right.

"I had a joke at the cool, collected *senhorita's* expense," he continued. "It was something I had to prove to both of us. Fortunately for us, it worked. I'll always cherish the fact that you accepted me as is, warts and all."

"Warts? Let's see what I'm getting myself into." She made a grab for his shirt and began unbuttoning it. Then her fingers stopped in midair, shocked at her audacity.

"You're priceless. Earthy and innocent. I love you, Marisa. I love you so damn much."

She kissed him and he responded by holding her in his arms as they looked out over the clearing at the butterflies and listened to the bird calls echo back and forth.

"You never did answer me. Do you want something formal back in Brasilia?"

"Or what? Give me a choice."

"There's a special place, a little town called Diamantina. I got my start in prospecting there, made my first glory hole not far out of town. I know you'll love it.

It's the most incredibly romantic, old fashioned town you could ever imagine."

She felt contentment, yet Sara and the Yellowhairs intruded on her happiness—with Saffron's golden eyes and sweet voice, and the promise to return to the Yellowhair village. She was letting both the girl and her own father down without so much as a twinge of conscience. What kind of person was she? Yet, she hated to rain on Scott's parade.

She would tell him more about the village and her promise later, after reading the diary or discarding it as useless. Then she would tell him about that, too. It was time her father learned to live with the idea of never paying back that debt he had assumed for the whole Elliott tribe.

When she arrived in Diamantina, she could call her father. Better yet, perhaps she would wait until they returned to Brasilia and started their marriage for real. Time enough to do it then.

Scott's voice brought her back from her troubled thoughts.

"We slept all morning. Now, we should get back to Campo Largo. That's on our way to Diamantina, and I'd like Juan to be our best man. What do you say to that?"

"Fine. Excellent idea."

☼ ☼ ☼

They didn't talk on the journey back to Campo Largo. Marisa looked out of the window most of the time when she wasn't sneaking glances at Scott's profile. As soon as they landed, the entire village turned out to greet them.

Scott made the announcement of their upcoming wedding, standing on the wing of the plane. She loved the way he looked up there. The long white scarf blowing around his shoulders, the worn leather jacket, and the tight chino trousers, made him seem like a Hollywood legend.

He jumped down and motioned to her. They stood close together and she leaned into the crook of his arm. As he talked, everyone broke into laughter and loud applause. Several of the women ran and hugged her. The men embraced Scott.

When the tumult died down, Marisa took him aside. "What did you tell them that had them all in stitches?" she asked suspiciously.

He grinned. "I said that we found the *Pororoco*, sat on top of it and for that we decided there was nothing left to do but get married."

"You are a crazy man!" She punched him lightly on his arm. He grabbed her fist and raised it to his lips.

"Come on, they want to make a feast for us."

During the next hours Marisa saw a more excited, happy conglomeration of humanity, than she had ever seen before in her life.

"There is no time to roast the ceremonial pig in the ground, *Senhorita*," Romeo O'Reilly told her. "But we will have a delicious goat."

She tried to keep from wrinkling her nose. As far as she knew, eating goat meat had not been on her list of must-do-in-her-lifetime things.

Scott saw the look and correctly interpreted it. "Don't sell it short, dear heart. Goat's meat and Old Clothes are a delicacy only spread out for their most beloved."

"Old Clothes? Now I know you're teasing. Goats may eat old clothes, but the idea of people eating both the goat and the old clothes, well you can forget it. I won't even pretend to be polite. Some wedding feast," she said in mock indignation. "Goat meat and old clothes."

Scott tweaked her nose then went off to join the men drinking *batida*.

But she was wrong, as she had been wrong about so many other things lately. The goat meat was roasted crispy-golden, with crackly skin, while the inside was tender and juicy. The Old Clothes turned out to be a colorful dish of shredded beef jerky, fried with onions and served with mashed black beans. Everything tasted delicious.

She was sure she would never sleep a wink on such a heavy meal, but as soon as her head hit the hammock, she was out.

They took off before daybreak the next morning. Juan was in the back, sitting on a blanket spread out on the floor, since Scott had removed the seats to carry the boat.

Marisa loved to watch Scott at the plane controls. He was so self-assured, yet casual. She looked out her window at the rich countryside below. So many colors, so much contrast to this place. He swung low over the high mountain slopes and pointed to what seemed to be a huge green lawn but instead was the tree tops of the rain forest.

"That's the mighty Parana River, we'll come back soon to see the giant falls. It's magnificent."

They touched down at a small airport just outside the town of Diamantina. A ripple of anxiety struck Marisa. She had no idea where it came from, so she brushed it aside. This was to be the most important day of her life. Nothing of her old habit of worrying should be allowed to intrude today she told herself sternly.

CHAPTER 22

The only rental cars available were the vintage cars of the city dwellers, renting them out to help pay for the fuel they used. Scott chose a nineteen fifty-eight Chevy Belair, shiny and clean, the very thing for a honeymoon trip, Marisa thought with amusement.

They drove through the mining town and he pointed out the places of interest along the way to the hotel. The atmosphere was colonial with romantic old buildings, huge trees and profuse banks of flowers everywhere. He pulled up at a quaint little hotel. To her surprise he ordered separate rooms.

"Don't look so disappointed, love, let's do it right."

She hit him lightly on the shoulder with her fist. "Did I look disappointed?"

"I expect every woman looks forward to her wedding day, and I want to take time for this to be special. When we look back fifty years from now, you'll have to remember what a gentleman I've been."

"Oh to be sure, I will. I will." She didn't think her body could contain the love she felt for him at that moment.

"We'll go shopping next. We need clothes. Can't very well go around dressed like Tarzan and Jane. This is a very conservative little town."

Behave, Marisa scolded herself. She wanted Scott so badly it was almost a physical pain to stand close to him. Did he feel it too? One glance into his eyes and she knew the answer. He was doing all this for her, to give her something she would always remember. Tears came to her eyes at his thoughtfulness, and she turned away before anyone could notice.

"I guess I'd better call my father and break the news," she said. "Maybe you'd like to talk to him?"

"Sure. After that I'll go next door and get settled in, call the condo and see if everything's okay."

When no one answered at the house, she called a neighbor who told her Janice and her father had gone to a teaching seminar in South Carolina for the weekend.

Why that old faker! He would hardly budge out of the house to go anywhere with her. She felt relieved, though. It wasn't so much like she was abandoning him if he had Janice. He wouldn't have to live alone—if he just gave Janice a chance to care for him.

Marisa decided she'd try to call him again later.

As for Thomas, she'd have to call him later, too, when she had more privacy. It wasn't going to be easy, but she couldn't imagine how she thought they would have been happy together. Well, she guessed they might have been—if she hadn't found out life could be different

It would have been impossible to tell her father about the diary, anyway, with Scott sitting next to her on the couch. What a pity, she had kept that bit of information from him. She couldn't very well tell him about it now, not without risking a deep rift in their new relationship.

While he and Juan unloaded the artifacts from the trunk of the rented car and stashed them in the hotel safe, she took a shower and freshened up.

When Scott rejoined her, she was standing in the parlor, gazing out the picture window at the street scene below. He came up behind and wrapped her in his arms, nuzzling the side of her cheek.

"Quaint old town. I can't wait to show it to you. But that may have to come later. I called home and Elaina tells me there's been a labor strike at our new condo in Sao Paulo. My partner there should be able to handle it, but he claims it's urgent."

"Oh." Disappointment flooded her. She tried to stem back her tears as she knew he must be as disappointed as she was.

"I won't take Muscatel. I can go and get back quicker in a jet. A friend of mine here will loan me his. Want to come with me? We could marry in Brasilia. Or would you rather stay here and relax until I get back? It's safe, perfectly safe. "

She touched his arm. He looked so concerned for her feelings, and here he was in the midst of some awful labor strike. "I'll wait here, my love," she said. She wasn't used to the endearments shared between them. It would be hard to imagine speaking to Thomas in such a way.

Scott turned her around and kissed her long and thoroughly. When they came up for air, his expression was so tender, so full of love, she felt weak-kneed, wobbly.

"I hate to leave you here still single. I don't want to take a chance of some swashbuckling Brazilian sweeping you off your feet in my absence, or some tall, handsome Yellowhair following you here."

She laughed. "Don't be ridiculous." But she didn't think it was ridiculous. She thrilled to the idea of his wanting them to be together from now on. "When will you go?"

"I called my friend. He can fly me to Brasilia, but I'd have to leave in a few hours. He'll drop me off at Brasilia. Then he has to fly to a meeting early the next morning a couple of hundred miles away." He took her hand and held it to his lips.

"Should we go back to the rooms then so you can get ready?"

He shook his head and laughed ruefully. "Frankly, I don't trust myself. You've waited this long for a proper courtship and wedding. That comes with a special first night, don't you think?"

She wasn't so sure, remembering the way he had brought her to ecstasy with promises of more.

"I want us to have a wedding you'll always remember and a proper honeymoon. Before I go, though, I'll take you shopping, strange as that sounds, and have you pick out your wedding dress so I'll remember you in it while I'm away."

☼ ☼ ☼

Marisa was amazed the shops they visited were very elegant, very expensive, and very cosmopolitan. Scott chose several day dresses for her. His taste was perfect but the colors, the styles, a bit bolder than she was used to.

Come on, girl, no more of this safe, conservative outlook. You're starting a new life.

He nodded to the salesperson when Marisa touched a deceptively simple georgette crepe in a deep rose color.

They brought out one in her size, and she stared at it a moment, not realizing that he had been watching her so closely.

"Try it on, sweetheart," he urged. "That's perfect for you."

When she came out of the dressing room, she felt a sudden shyness at the look of open admiration and desire in his eyes. The dress had a gently draped neckline with a bodice that clung to her every curve. The skirt flared out softly into creamy folds, falling past her hips and thighs.

"Perfect. Like you, demure and sexy at the same time."

She blushed. "I can't accept it. It's far too extravagant."

He turned to the salesclerk. "Will you excuse us while we have our first lover's quarrel?" The clerk giggled and walked away to a discreet distance. "Let's get this over once and for all. I know we'll have many subjects to disagree on during our life together, and I love that in you. But you're a different person than when you first came to Brazil. Surely you see that, don't you?"

"Didn't you like me the way I was?" she challenged.

He laughed. "Touché. Yes, of course I did, and that sweet little brown wren is still there. We don't want to get rid of her completely. But I want this lovely, free hummingbird that you've become to live too. You were looking at that dove gray dress with the wide white collar," he accused. "Weren't you?"

"Well, yes," she had to admit it. "I thought it suited me."

He shook his head vigorously and brought her hand to his lips, causing a funny feeling deep within her body. "I don't agree. It suited the person you always thought yourself to be. But I know deep down there is a wild woman buried somewhere. I mean to bring her to the surface."

"You might be sorry if you do," she warned.

He grinned mischievously. "I'll take my chances. Would the rose dress suit you as a wedding outfit, or do you prefer the traditional white?"

The color of her dress was of little importance. She thought the rose dress beautiful, more lovely than any dress had a right to be.

He touched her chin, tilting it up with a finger. "I love you so much Marisa," he whispered.

She got lost in the depth of his eyes, and they stared at each other for a long moment.

"Enough!" he pronounced. "I'll take you back to the room, so you can settle in. In the meantime, I'll round up Juan. He can stay in the adjoining room. He won't like it. His father has friends here and Juan usually stays with them when we're in town. But he'll get over it. Then I'll have to leave. I promise, I'll be back as soon as possible."

"Can we marry as soon as you come back? Isn't there a waiting period or something like that?"

Scott grinned. "Usually. Eventually, we'll have to wade through paperwork—since we're both Americans, and I know the officials here, they will smooth things out. When I told them our circumstances, they said the protocol could come later."

In her room, Marisa hummed as she combed her hair. In the mirror, she had trouble relating to the woman who stood looking back at her. Tall and slender, she could accept that. But with the smooth tan from days on the trail and the longer hair which she pinned into a soft French twist, slightly curling around her face from the high humidity, it was as if a stranger looked back from her. It made her very, very happy.

She heard Scott's firm knock on the door.

"Ah, lovely, my sweet. You are a most gorgeous creature." He grabbed her shoulders and pulled her into his body for a kiss that would have sent her reeling if he hadn't been holding her so tightly. She opened her mouth slightly to allow him full access and his tongue sent shivers of desire trickling downward, beginning the throbbing exquisite torture he had started when he first made love to her. He released her, reluctantly she thought, and stepped back. "You see why I can't linger here?

She struggled to stop the trembling that threatened to buckle her legs. It was still so incomprehensible to her how she could have gone all the years of her life without knowing the delight that loving someone could bring.

"I think you should try to call your father again. We have time before I leave." He brushed past her without touching her and stood aside, waiting for her answer.

She looked in his eyes and saw the raw hunger there, marveling that she could cause such an emotion in another. She also saw the tension in his body, and understood his restraint, loving him all the more for it.

Scott's idea was sweet, but did she want her father to know about her marriage before it happened? What if he rained on her parade? Would it matter so much at this point? Old habits died hard, and she feared it would matter to her.

However, at Scott's insistence she made the call. Her father had returned from the conference. At first he sounded puzzled and for the first time in her life, she read uncertainty and hesitation in his voice.

"Are you all right, Dad? Would you like to talk to Scott?"

Scott and her father spoke briefly then she hung up the phone. Marisa didn't blame Scott for the look of puzzlement and concern on his face. Apparently her father hadn't been too civil. She winced when she remembered some of his barely sheathed barbs that he hid behind his "civilized behavior."

"Sit, please." She motioned toward the sofa. "I apologize if he was rude to you. He gave us his blessing. Sort of."

Scott shrugged. "It was a shock to him, I'm sure."

"I've never known him to be so discombobulated. He sounded lost. His long-time companion didn't return from the conference with him because he wouldn't commit to marrying her. He even admitted that decision had been a mistake. He'd like to do it over but he can't find her. Oh, my love, he'll be all alone if I stay here."

Scott ran his fingers over her knuckles in an absentminded way, as if gathering his thoughts. His touch sent a warming shiver throughout her body. She waited.

"I told you my outlook on family had changed since getting to know you. But sometimes a person has to make a choice."

His words brought tears to her eyes. She wanted her father to be happy and safe, but wanted to stay with Scott.

"Right now, you're all your father has. That's true enough. But mightn't you say he's lived his life as he chose? And now it's your turn? Sweetheart, as much as I love you, as much as you mean to me, it would kill my soul to leave Brazil. That is the one thing I don't think I could do, even for you."

"I wouldn't want you to. I promise you that." She managed to hold her tears in—barely. "I've a feeling my father will find Janice again and tell her what she wants to hear. She wouldn't have left completely. She cares too much for him. They fit together."

"As we will in time." Scott's eyes held such love that it was hard to look at him and feel guilty about her father at the same time.

"You can fly back to Virginia when you want to, sweetheart. But not until I know you are mine, and I can bear to let you out of my sight."

She had her back to him when he strode across the room, pulling her roughly close, crushing her against him so that her soft curves melted into his hard, lean body. She felt his uneven breathing against her cheek as his strong arms encircled her. Almost against her will, a sigh of pleasure escaped her when his hands cupped her breasts through the fabric of her dress, his thumbs brushing against her nipples. Her legs refused to hold her and she sagged against him in complete surrender.

He nestled his chin down on her shoulder and whispered, "That's so you don't forget me, love." He turned her around and as if sensing her weakness, he picked her up in his arms and set her gently on the edge of the bed.

"Oh God, Marisa, I need you so much. I want to make love to you. Right now." His voice was husky, intense.

In another moment she would have shed her clothing gladly and let him sweep her into his arms and onto the bed. As if he sensed her surrender, he pulled away, reluctance in his eyes. He rubbed his fingers over her chin with incredible gentleness.

"We waited this long, my sweet. I'll be back before you know it for our honeymoon and then home to Brasilia. We'll figure out what to do about your father, I promise."

She swallowed hard, holding tightly to her fragile control. In her wildest dreams, she'd never imagined she'd feel this much desire and love for another human being. It was physically painful for her and she knew it had to be for him too.

He reached into his jacket pocket and drew out a ring box. Opening it, he picked out the ring inside and held it out to her. "This is my promise to you. Keep the ring close to you until I return."

Stretching out her palm she accepted the wide, gold band. "It's beautiful, Scott," she said, brushing her fingers over the delicately raised leaves of antique rosy gold and reading the tiny words he'd had the jeweler inscribe on the inside.

"*Ontem, hoje y amanha,*" he said. "Portuguese for yesterday, today, and tomorrow. That's how long we'll be together."

She bent his head down, and pressed her lips to his, tears streaming down her cheeks. "Is the ring from your family?" It wasn't important to her, but she needed to back off from her emotions a little, and so did he.

"It's from a dig and all perfectly legal. It isn't so valuable, antiquity-wise, so the government gave it to me as my share. I put it in a pocket in Muscatel and remembered it today. It may need to be sized, but I asked the jeweler to inscribe it anyway."

Marisa thought of the times she mistrusted Scott and the times he hadn't trusted her, either. As if he read her thoughts, he said, "From this day forward, we'll never have any misunderstandings between us that can't be talked out. I can't tell you how important it is to me that we can so fully trust each other."

She tried to swallow with a dry throat and almost choked. Would he consider the unmentioned diary as mistrusting him? She couldn't destroy the moment between them and tell him now. Not when he was almost ready to leave. Chances were the journal didn't amount to any big deal.

The subject of trust made her uncomfortable. "I love this ring, Scott, it's perfect."

"You're perfect. And after we're married, you can go home to visit when you want to. I might even go back with you from time to time. We'll get the papers fixed as soon as we get back to Brasilia."

"This *is* my home now, Scott." It boggled her mind, trying to imagine Scott Dunbar setting foot in Elliott.

He glanced at his watch. "Juan's waiting downstairs in the lobby. I called my partner again, and he sounded worried. I know he wouldn't bother me at a time like this if it wasn't urgent. We can't afford to lose the contract on that apartment complex, and labor misunderstandings can get out of hand, spreading like wild fire. The men like and trust me, so I hope I can cool things down." He kissed her hungrily. "I'll always remember how you look this moment, if I live to be a hundred."

She took his hand, feeling the hardness of it. She brought it to her lips and kissed each knuckle with tender care and then, opening his hand, rubbed her cheek against the hard plane of his palm. She knew he'd had his choice of many beautiful women and had probably never set his desires aside to please anyone before. This, more than anything he could say, told her he loved her.

"Marisa, do you have any idea of how much I love you right this minute? *Ontem, hoje y amanha*—'yesterday, today and tomorrow.' That's us. I never wanted a family before, but now I want a family. You're my family."

They walked out to the front of the hotel. The sky had darkened with the threat of rain. "Shouldn't you wait for the storm to pass? I'll worry about you up there with the lightening and wind."

"I thought I lived a charmed life before, but now nothing can interfere with my good luck."

She hoped not, but something told her their life could become more complicated than they could ever imagine. She pushed the worrying thoughts away as he climbed into a taxi. Through her blurred tears, she watched him disappear down the street.

CHAPTER 23

Marisa blinked back her tears as Juan took her hand.

"He will be back soon. I have seen the love in his eyes for you. If you need me, *Senhorita*, I will be in my room."

"If I'm going to be in the family, you must call me Marisa. Soon you and Angelina will join us as part of our family, too. You know that, don't you?

Juan looked pleased for a moment and then a worried little frown wrinkled his forehead. "I will not be allowed to marry with Angelina until I have a steady job."

Marisa decided she would talk to Scott about that later. He seemed to think it would displace Juan to bring him into to the Brazilian work force. But what other alternative did the young man have? No one wanted him to work as a miner or a rubber worker. All the schooling in the world wouldn't help him if he couldn't find a decent job somewhere.

"I could go to Rio or Sao Paula," he said, "But I do not think I want Angelina to live in the city. And when our children come I do not wish them to live in Rio or Sao Paulo."

"I know. I'll talk to Dom Scott, and we can work something out." She patted him on the shoulder and the smile he gave her back lit up his face.

"Go on now, please. Visit your friends. You may not get a chance again soon."

"Oh no! Dom Scott said not to leave you. You might need something."

There was no use arguing with him, so they said good night and went to their rooms. The diary had been calling her all day. It had been in her backpack so long, waiting for her.

The hours passed while she entered inside the minds of the writers. There were more than one. Apparently, a young woman from Virginia, one of the originals, had started it and each succeeding generation of women after that took it up. Marisa could imagine how elated her father would be to get it. She rifled toward the end, wanting to know if Sara had written anything.

She couldn't find any reference to Sara at all, but the last writer's handwriting proved to be easier to decipher than the earlier, old-fashioned script. Marisa sat up abruptly on the bed. She knew where the treasure was buried! It told her right here in the last pages of the book.

I am dying and so unhappy to leave my son. Even though our people will care for him as well as I, it will be different. Jacob has left me for that better land above and I go to join him soon. I have decided not to confide in young Jacob as to the money chest buried beneath the back porch of the big house.

Poor lad, without a mother or father he does not need the terrible burden of deciding, as did one person from each of our generations, if the money should be used. Since our arrival in Brazil in the winter of 1864, we have always resolved that the money was ill-gotten and would bring only

*misfortune. It was not a risk any of us were
willing to take. After I go, no one will know. I
have protected our people as did those before me.*

Tears came to Marisa's eyes as she finished reading
the last line of the diary. Such pioneering spirit, such a
love of life and family poured through the pages. El Viejo
must be the "young Jacob" and the last writer, his mother.
That meant the old man really didn't know where the
treasure was or even if there was one, although surely
some legend must have passed down through succeeding
generations.

Who was Sara? It was obvious Sara wasn't the person
writing this. That meant Sara was someone who didn't
want herself known. Chills crawled up her skin like
moving through icy cobwebs.

*Someone wanted me here but didn't want me to know who he
or she was.* That someone beguiled her into coming to
Brazil, hoping she'd find the treasure. Whoever wanted
the treasure that badly wasn't about to share it. She
thought back to Manolo. He was the only one unafraid of
entering the big house. Did he have something to do with
Sara and her letters? Had he killed Sara?

It would be hard to wait for Scott's return. She
needed him to go with her to the village of Yellowhairs,
not only for the money, but to see Saffron again as she
had promised.

She drank a soda from the hotel refrigerator and
decided it was time to bite the bullet and talk to Thomas.
She wasn't sure what time it was in Virginia but she
figured it must be sometime in the middle of the night or
close to morning. What she had to tell him was important
enough to both of them that an inconvenience of time
shouldn't matter. She didn't want to wait another minute
to get it all out.

She didn't know what she'd say to Thomas until he answered, but when she heard his voice, she didn't hesitate. She told him she'd fallen in love with someone in Brazil and planned to stay here.

"What? Are you drunk? Is this Marisa Elliott?"

He knew who it was. She recognized the typical stalling technique he used until he could collect his thoughts in a logical manner.

She pictured him sitting on the edge of the bed in his silk pajamas, scratching his head. "I'm sorry to have to break it to you like this, Thomas, but there's no other way."

"I don't understand. I thought we had a bond. Good Lord, we've known each other since grade school, and it was always going to be us together."

Hearing him sound irritated instead of hurt helped her own emotional outlook. Hurt would have been much harder to overcome. "I know. But things change. We change. I met a man who..." How could she tell him about Scott?

"Have you told your father?"

"Yes. He gave us his blessing." She didn't feel guilty exaggerating a little. "I'm going to call him again later, when I'm sure he's awake."

"Can't you come home? Talk about it with me? Don't I deserve that much?"

"You do. Of course you do, but that can't happen right now. And anyway, talking wouldn't change anything. He had to leave for several days in an emergency, but we'll be married as soon as he flies back here."

Thomas ran out of steam and his voice faltered. Already, he had given up. No outpouring of love, no pleading. He didn't have any fight in him. Which was very sad, Marisa thought. Maybe that had always been the basic difference between them. Over the years, her father had managed to overshadow her at every turn in her life. Yet she was willing to fight for what she believed in.

"I'm hanging up now, Thomas. I wish you a good life and hope someday you'll forgive me." She waited to hear if he had more to say, but it was silent on his end, so she gently replaced the receiver.

Now to call her father again. That conversation didn't last long. He was no longer shocked or hesitant. He'd had time to prepare. No, he didn't approve. He wanted her to come home instantly and forget about their relatives. He demanded she pack, get on the next plane, and stop the foolishness.

In the end, she interrupted his tirade to say, "Goodnight, Dad. I'll talk to you later when you calm down, but nothing will change."

After she hung up, she sat looking at the diary and wondering what would her future be like if she hadn't come looking for Sara?

☼ ☼ ☼

When the telephone rang several nights later, Marisa picked it up quickly, knowing Scott would be on the other end of the wire. When she heard his voice, her pulse quickened. The warm feeling in the pit of her stomach began spreading through her body as she pictured him talking, the serious look in his gray eyes. Suddenly his words penetrated her fantasy.

"How could you lie to me? How could you, Marisa? I believed in you!"

"What? What are you talking about?"

It was as if she stood in a shower of ice water. She would surely wake up any second now, from this crazy nightmare. Scott's voice was cold, his words clipped and angry.

"When I got to Brasilia, Elaina showed me a letter. It was addressed to you and had been opened accidentally."

Marisa waited, wondering how "accidental" it had been.

"A letter from your boss. This Thomas person. You remember, the newspaper you work for? I'll bet you never were a schoolteacher. Everything was a fabrication."

"No! There's been a mistake. I am—was—a teacher. What is the letter about?" Thomas hadn't said anything about sending a letter to her. Surely he'd received her fax saying there would be no story. Oh, why hadn't she confided in Scott while she had the chance?

"It's a contract for the series of articles you proposed on archaeological finds in the Amazon and an additional advance with the receipt for your first. I'd be willing to bet all that stuff on your ancestors is just so much hooey too."

"Oh, Scott, I'm sorry." Tears welled up in her eyes and she brushed them away, needing all her concentration to make him understand. "It's true, before I knew your circumstances, I had planned to do an article about you, the Brasilia Museum, and your finds. But when I learned what doing that would mean to you, I cancelled it. Look in my apartment. There should be a copy of the fax on top of the dresser where I left it."

"That's all been cleaned out and packed up. The maid didn't find any papers, or she would have told me. Elaina went with her to check. But Elaina did tell me she found a map on your bed the night of the party at the yacht club. Why would you have a map of the Amazon area?"

"I told you. That's where Sara lived last. It wasn't an up-to-date map. It would have been useless. Sara sent it years ago in one of her letters."

Elaina. The woman had hated and resented her presence from the beginning. Elaina opened that envelope from Thomas on purpose and if there was no copy of the fax in the room, she had to have taken it. But accusing her would only compound the problem. Scott would put any accusations down to spiteful jealousy on Marisa's part.

"Scott! Please listen. The Yellowhairs *are* my ancestors. My father *did* send me down here to find the missing bank money. I can prove it to you if you let me. You can't turn love off and on like a light switch. Can you? I thought you loved me." Marisa looked at the diary on the nightstand. How would she explain having the book for so long and not trusting him enough to show it to him?

He must have sensed hesitation in her voice for he sounded grim and unforgiving. "I can't stand being lied to. I was taken for a fool once in my life. Who said lightning never strikes twice?"

"What do you want to do?" Her spirit was crushed. She felt as if her soul had been ripped apart and lay bleeding on the floor beneath her feet. Oh, God, she loved him so much at this moment, the moment when she was losing him forever.

"I'm sending your luggage on to Diamantina. I've paid for the room for a week. If you have to wait longer for a plane back to The States, charge it to me and of course anything else you need."

"Scott, please. At least come here and talk to me in person. I know I can explain. It's so hard on the phone." Her voice cracked with desperation as utter despair washed over her. She didn't care if he heard her pain and sorrow.

"Ah, Marisa." His voice broke and then he coughed and turned it to ice again. "That's what I can't do. There's no need. I don't want to see you. I set you free."

I don't want to be free from you—not ever. She couldn't say the words. Her pleas had already fallen on deaf ears. A wretched despair settled over her, numbing her mind.

"Goodbye Marisa," Scott whispered hoarsely, and the line went dead.

She threw herself on the bed as the sobs nearly tore her apart. Her first anguished thoughts were how unjust his accusations were. After her sobs died away, she could see how he might have come to his conclusions. Both she and Scott had made a game of deception from the first. But while his game was harmless, she knew his way of life could have been endangered if she had gone through with her idea about the articles. And she had no proof that her intention had changed.

She hugged the diary to her bosom. She wasn't going to accept his decision. She'd given up her life's work because circumstances had overwhelmed her, and drifted into a relationship with Thomas to please everyone. But she wouldn't do it again. She wouldn't give up without a fight. The thought of spending the rest of her life back in Virginia without Scott Dunbar was a bleak prospect, one she refused to accept.

She splashed water on her face in the bathroom and went out in the hall to knock on Juan's door.

"*Senhorita*, is something wrong?" He hurriedly stepped out in the hallway and shut the door behind him, as if remembering discretion even in the face of a possible emergency.

"Juan, I have to get back to the Matos and the Yellowhairs."

He looked troubled, and although she regretted that, she persisted. "It's a matter of life and death, Juan. I must go."

"We go when Dom Scott comes. He said so."

She could tell he was sensitive to the urgency in her voice and uncomfortable with her tear-swollen face. In spite of his discomfort, she knew he could be very stubborn when he needed to be. Since he had disobeyed Scott once, he might not do it again. Should she tell him everything?

She decided she'd told enough half-truths since her arrival in Brazil. If she'd learned nothing else in the past weeks, it was that truth, however painful, was the better than lies or equivocations.

"Juan, I can't stand out here in the hallway and talk to you. Either I'll come into your room, or you into mine. Which is it?"

He hesitated only a minute before he nodded toward hers. As soon as she motioned him to a seat, she brought him the diary, even while she knew he couldn't read the tight old-fashioned script.

"I discovered this at the Yellowhairs' village, in the big house." As impatient as she was to get on with what she had to do, she knew she had to explain everything in detail so Juan could make a decision.

She told him about the stolen bank money, how her father had lived with the mockery of the Bank Holiday every year. She showed him the letters from Sara promising 'a treasure' and giving them the big house if only they would come down to claim it. Marisa couldn't be certain how well Juan could read, but he looked impressed by it all and was no doubt puzzled as to where her story was leading.

She went on to tell him about her temporary job with the newspaper and how Scott could have been damaged by her articles if she'd written them. She stressed that she'd canceled the articles when she found out how they might have hurt Scott.

"He doesn't believe me, Juan. He doesn't believe I wasn't going to write those articles about his diggings along the Amazon. He thinks I made up everything about my ancestors just to get here. He doesn't want to marry me."

Juan looked dazed by all the information she suddenly poured into his ear and bewildered by the tears slipping down her cheeks, tears she could not seem to stop. He pointed to the diary on the bed. "How could he not believe?"

She bowed her head, ashamed of her answer. "That's the problem, Juan. I didn't show Scott the book. I wanted to read it first."

When Juan didn't answer, she continued. "I can't lose Scott, not without fighting for him. I know he loves me. You know he does. If I could get that money, he'll have to believe I came here for that and not for anything else."

"But Marisa." His calling her by her first name told her how distressed he was. "I cannot fly into the Matos. It is not a possibility."

"Didn't Scott say he would get your pilot's license when you landed the plane in Kayapo? Don't you want to marry Angelina and begin your family? I'm sure you will do just fine." She wasn't a bit sure but unwilling to let him know of her doubts.

"I do wish to marry Angelina. I think maybe she could find someone else when I am away so much."

Marisa wanted to hug and shake him at the same time. Of course Angelina wouldn't marry anyone else. There was no time to spare. She must go now, before

Scott did something foolish. Before Elaina could take advantage of the situation she'd created.

She held onto Juan's arm, willing herself to be calm. From her experience as a teacher, she knew the boy was not one to be pushed, but rather encouraged into an action if he wasn't sure which course to take. An icy thought cut through her impatience. What if she was endangering both their lives? She had no excuse for playing God with Juan's young life. Scott had mentioned he could land the plane in Kayapo. The clearing in the Yellowhair village was much too small with trees ringing it closely, all the way around.

"I would like to do this for you." He looked at her with trust.

"I have faith in you. Scott will be angry for a bit, but when he discovers you are not fearful of landing in the jungle anymore, and that I truly came to find the money for my father and not for any devious plan to ruin his life, he will forgive us both. He loves us." With all her heart she hoped she hadn't just lied to him.

Juan looked down at his shoes. She removed her hand from his arm and sat quietly, waiting. She could do no more. If she forced him to go against his instincts, he would never trust her again. She would have to find another way to the Yellowhairs if he wouldn't take her.

Silence filled the room except for the gentle ticking of the little travel alarm Scott bought her before he left. Scott—practical and yet a dreamer. A romantic soul, blending children's coloring books and tidal waves, and teaching her how to enjoy life. She wouldn't let him go. She couldn't.

Juan lifted his chin to look at her, his dark brown eyes serious. "You are right. We both have something to prove, and if Dom Scott is angry, we will face his anger.

Having Muscatel here is a sign, a sign that we have a blessing."

She swallowed. A blessing? She didn't feel as if anyone blessed her right now, but she was glad he felt that way.

CHAPTER 24

At the airport, it felt as if she had moved backward in time, and was just arriving in Brazil. Her new clothing lay bundled in the hotel, safe, along with the artifacts Scott had forgotten to take with him. Marisa looked at the ring on her finger. Caressing the smooth edges and the raised leaves brought a keen sense of Scott to her mind. Would she be able to win him back? She *had* to.

Juan had to show his papers at the little out-of-the-way airport where Scott had landed Muscatel. He was only allowed to take certain flights that Scott had arranged for him to earn his pilot's license. Marisa held her breath while the official talked to Juan and then waved him on.

In the airplane, she laid her head back against the seat, trying to imagine Scott sitting next to her at the controls. He'd only been gone a short while, but half of her heart and soul had disappeared with him. But she wasn't going to lose him.

She surprised herself more every day. Where was the mousy, dull person who had catered to her father's every frown and was afraid to take the bus into the closest big city? The only time she'd ever argued with her father was when she changed teaching directions from academic to special education. That was another thing, she should never have let him intimidate her with his belief that it was her fault Kenny died. She knew she was good at her job, had, in fact, accomplished some near-miracles for her children.

When Juan started the plane, her heartbeats revved up to match the roar of the engine and her throat constricted so she could barely breathe. What if he didn't make it? What if he wasn't ready to fly solo?

Then she remembered what Scott said about the plane, how it could recover from almost anything in the sky and land on a dime if necessary. The memory didn't help much. She reached in the back, pulled out Scott's long, white scarf, and draped it over Juan's thin shoulders and around his neck in a carefree gesture she didn't really feel.

"Oh, but I cannot wear Dom Scott's talisman," he protested.

"Nonsense. He would want you to share his good luck. You will earn it when you land the plane at the village. Won't Angelina be proud of you?"

He leaned back, his thin shoulders squared, his eyes closed. He was either saying a prayer, envisioning Angelina rushing out to greet them, or both. She silently said a prayer of her own. .

When they were airborne, she pushed her worries to the background and began doing some serious thinking.

Sara had feared Manolo. He had to have been the one who knew about the treasure and wanted it for himself. But why would Sara be so irrational as to expect that such distant relatives would find the money when no one in the Yellowhair village could locate it?

Manolo had been the only one to show any interest in her. She figured he must not know how to read, even if he'd found the diary first. She felt foolish when she remembered thinking him smitten with her charms. Even old Jacob warned her that probably wasn't so.

When the last writer who corresponded sporadically with her father died, Manolo must have discovered Sara writing to them. The man was good, she had to admit. A lot of planning had gone into his plot. He might have been the one to take the letters to a village to be mailed for Sara. He was the only Yellowhair who had ever made such flagrant outside contacts. The others in the Yellowhair village wouldn't have gone.

To take her speculation further, she knew her fall down the stairs had been no accident. Manolo must have suspected she'd discovered something important in the old house. He wanted her to stay, to find the treasure, so he could take it from her.

Damn her father and his obsession! What she needed was to get a fistful of the money to show Scott, to prove her motives. Manolo could have the rest. Would Manolo be willing to allow her and Juan to leave unharmed afterward? It was a chance she had to take.

It wasn't far to Kayapo, Angelina's village. Juan explained he couldn't land in the center of the Yellowhairs' village. The clearing was too small, probably even for Scott. Marisa felt guilty when she sneaked a look at Juan's drawn expression, at the worry line between his eyes. He was scared, and so should she be too if she had a lick of sense. But if Scott had taught him, then Juan could land the plane. She was more worried about returning to the village to confront Manolo.

Juan began to bank the plane, slowing down for the landing. She closed her eyes and leaned her head back, trying to relax.

"You can do it, Juan. Scott taught you, and he's the best."

He licked his dry lips and nodded. "Yes. Yes, I believe it," he whispered.

When he tilted the plane too much and corrected too fast, he jerked the wings so hard she feared they might rip off. She closed her eyes again and prayed as he zeroed down on the tiny meadow. After a few neck-jolting bumps, they landed, mere inches from the huge trees at the edge of the clearing.

"I do not know how we are going to leave, we may stay here forever. I will not fly this plane out again. I swear by all that is holy!" Juan crossed himself and muttered a prayer under his breath, just to be sure, she assumed, that he'd covered all the bases. She understood the terror beneath his attempt at composure.

"You did it!" She unlocked her seat belt to turn and give him a high-five. "Don't you see? You've proven you can do it. Scott said this is one of the hardest spots to land."

His eyes still held panic, and he sat very still as if frozen. The high-five he'd given her must have been a simple reflex. Well, leaving was a hurdle she'd cross later. She had to get Juan to take her back to Scott in Brasilia or this would be for nothing.

By now the villagers had rushed out to greet them. When they saw Juan behind the controls, they went wild, all of them yelling and screaming at once, pounding each other on the back, dogs barking and children screeching. It was bedlam.

She leaned over and planted a kiss on the side of Juan's cheek. "I knew you could do it. Scott will be so proud of you."

"Juanito?" Angelina, usually so self-effacing and shy, rushed up to the side of the plane, and looked anxiously through the opened door.

He leaped down and hugged the girl. Many hands reached up to help Marisa before he could turn back to her. Words sang through the air, words she couldn't understand, but she knew they were asking what had happened to Scott. She hoped Juan didn't tell them the whole story. She didn't want their pitying looks.

When they settled inside Angelina's home, her mother bustled around getting a meal together. Marisa was too excited to eat, but she drank the fragrant, strong coffee and tried to make out a little of the conversation. Apparently, there were a lot of questions from the family Juan was not answering to their satisfaction. Every so often they would turn to her with big smiles as if to include her.

"No, we don't want anyone to go with us," she told them emphatically after Juan asked the question from Angelina's father. No use putting someone else in jeopardy. Manolo would only feel more threatened if a crowd followed them in. She felt sorry for Jacob. He didn't want the money to interfere with their simple, quiet lives, but it looked as if he wasn't going to get his wish. Once she told Manolo where the money was, it was over, unless he took it all with him and left the village.

Marisa wanted to see Saffron one more time as she'd promised. That goodbye was something she didn't want to think about.

When they finally disentangled themselves from the villagers, Marisa took Juan and started hiking through the jungle toward the community of the Yellowhairs.

"This will be very dangerous, Juan," she said, though he appeared very aware of that. "Manolo wants the money. I can't be sure he'll share even the small amount I need to take back to Scott. The truth is, he may not want any witnesses left alive to tell about the treasure."

It made sense that Manolo wouldn't want anyone to know about it. He had to have invested a lot of time and effort in trying to locate the treasure.

Her best bet was to find old Jacob first thing and tell him. Not even Manolo would dare harm the old man.

The afternoon rain had made the forest floor damp and spongy beneath their boots, so she and Juan slept in hammocks strung between the trees that first night out. Late at night she'd heard roars and snarls of big cats near the Yellowhair village. "Are you sure we don't need a fire to keep the animals away?" she asked Juan.

He slid into his hammock and pulled the netting over his body as she had done. "No, the animals will not bother us. Maybe. They fear men. Many people kill them for food."

"What would you like to do with your life, Juan? You don't want to work in the rubber, and I don't blame you. That part of Brazil is nearly past."

He didn't speak for a few minutes, and she thought he must be considering his words. For a young man, Juan was very judicious in what he said, weighing each word before he spoke as if to make certain it came out right.

"Maybe you should study to be a lawyer. You'd make a good one."

He bolted up in his hammock, nearly turning it over in his excitement. "Oh, that is very wise of you to see that in me. It is my secret wish, but first I must earn my way. My people need much help. They do not own their land, but they have lived on the same property since my parents came there as children. Someone must fight for them, to save something for them and the people in other villages."

"What an excellent idea! Have you told Scott how you feel?"

"No. I cannot. He might tell me it is but the dream of a child. I could not bear to hear that."

"He would never say such a thing. He loves the jungle and the people. He'd help you. Think of how much time, effort, and money have gone into those coloring books he gives the children. Why would he not understand your desire?"

"He has done enough. He sent me to school, then secondary school. I must get my pilot's license and earn my right to go to the university."

Marisa yawned, and burrowed deeper in the hammock as a night bird flew overhead. She wanted to keep talking about Scott. She missed him so much. His rejection was a wound deep within her that might never heal.

☼ ☼ ☼

Marisa was awakened early by Juan, and they began the second day's journey. They moved along in silence, but the jungle produced enough noise to make up for any lack of speech on their part.

Later in the afternoon as they walked, Marisa suddenly had an "eureka" moment when the answer to what had been puzzling her came thundering into her brain. Before she had a chance to express the idea out loud, the bushes parted and her heart sank into her boots.

Two light haired men, walked out, barring the way. She studied their expressions, unable to decide if they remembered her. Since Manolo was not with them, perhaps they were not from El Viejo's village.

Juan spoke to them in Portuguese. For a heartbeat, Marisa feared they didn't understand—or didn't want to. They nodded for them to pass and then followed behind.

How had they known she and Juan were in the jungle? Had Manolo sent them? Their safety depended upon her seeing Jacob before Manolo caught her alone. She had to explain to the patriarch why she had returned. Even so, it was flimsy protection. Manolo could break the old man like a straw if he chose to.

When they entered the village, she didn't see Manolo, but she straightened her shoulders and tilted her chin in the air, just in case.

Saffron ran to greet them, talking so fast, she almost didn't take a breath. In spite of Marisa's worry, the chatter made her smile.

"Bring your grandfather here, child." She knelt and looked the little girl in the eyes. It was like a mirror image of her own.

Saffron began to sob, pressing into Marisa's thigh as if she wanted to be a part of her. "He is very sick. Manolo and he fought and..."

"Did Manolo hurt him?" They hurried toward the old man's cabin.

"Oh no." Saffron's high-pitched voice registered shock. "Even Manolo would not dare to touch El Viejo. They argued and my grandfather, he hurt here." Saffron hit her skinny chest with a small fist.

"I knew you would return," Jacob said as they entered the darkened cabin through the door left ajar by Saffron's hasty exit. The old man's voice was weak and thready.

Marisa knelt at his bedside, taking his fragile hand in hers. It was like holding a bird's claw. "I had to come back. You know why, don't you?"

He nodded and licked dry lips. Saffron hurried to wipe his mouth with a damp cloth.

By now all of the villagers had gathered outside, Marisa could hear their murmurs.

"Where is Manolo?" she asked.

"He ran away, thinking he had killed me. But he will return. You must go."

"I can't leave yet. I have to find the money. It's important that I take some of it back with me."

"You know where it is hidden. I was certain that Manolo thought so."

She pulled the diary from her backpack. "It is here, in this diary left by our ancestors. Perhaps your mother was the last to write."

Jacob reached for the book, his eyes showing a desire that didn't match his trembling hands. He couldn't grasp the book and his hands dropped to his side. His chest heaved.

"Don't worry. I'll read you parts of it."

In the dim light of the little cabin, she began to read. As she did, she looked up once and saw the villagers crowded close on the porch, listening through the door and windows. Even if they didn't understand all she read, they sensed something important was happening.

"Stop. Wait." Jacob commanded, his clawed hand pulling on her shirtsleeve. "I wish these words to be the last I hear. I need to say something to you before you read them. No, do not argue," he said when she opened her mouth. "Listen to me."

Marisa worried that Manolo would return any moment. Without Jacob's protection, she and Juan wouldn't stand a chance against him. But the plea in the old man's eyes pushed her concerns aside. He was dying. There was no help for that. His time had come. She had to listen to what he needed to say.

"Saffron. Take her with you. I have seen the look exchanged between you. You have been sent here to help her. She is not one of us, has never been."

The girl stood close to her grandfather's bed with her little hand clutching Marisa's pant leg.

"But I can't take her." Marisa paused, seeing the old man clinging so hard to a few more minutes of life.

"Manolo posed as this Sara person when he wrote to you in America." Jacob took a deep breath. "You know that. I can see it in your eyes. That is what puzzled me. Who was this Sara you talked about?"

Marisa nodded. The idea that Manolo knew how to read and write and had made up Sara was the conviction that had come to her while she and Juan had trekked through the jungle.

"Goodbye, child. You have been the light of my life." His eyes turned from Saffron and focused again on Marisa. "Now read," he commanded.

Once she started to read, she became caught up in the story unfolding on the page. She didn't know when the old man slipped away, but when she looked up to take a breath, his eyes had closed. His chest not moving.

Saffron, wise beyond her years, cried silently. Big tears fell out of her eyes as she laid her soft cheek against the old man's blue-veined hand.

Marisa reached for Saffron's hand. "Come outside, little one. You and your grandfather have said your goodbyes. He's not in that poor, frail body anymore." She had no idea what sort of religious training, if any, the people had. How to begin comforting the girl? All she had were with the usual platitudes people used at the time of death to cover their own unease.

Her worry wasn't necessary. Saffron leaned over the bed and kissed the dry, wrinkled cheek, holding her own against his. Then she took his gnarled hand and kissed the back of it and, with tears in her eyes, turned toward the door.

Marisa stepped outside, the crowd close now. "Juan, tell them Jacob is dead. Tell them his was a peaceful death." Most of them knew already. Half of the village had gathered on the porch. A group of women started what sounded like a hymn in Portuguese. The men who weren't out working in the fields gathered in a group, their hats in their hands. Several women walked forward, nodded shyly to her as they passed and went inside to take care of the body.

A heavy-set, middle-aged man stepped onto the porch and held out his hand. He spoke Portuguese and Juan translated.

"I am Sergio. Next in line. It is as El Viejo said. He talked to all of us after you left. The girl Saffron does not belong here. The old man has taught her your language and filled her head full of stories that we no longer care to hear and do not wish to share."

"But I cannot take her," Marisa protested. If she had to return to Virginia, how would she get the little girl out of Brazil? And Saffron belonged in Brazil.

"Ah, *senhorait—senhora.*" Sergio must have spotted the ring on her hand because he quickly changed from the *senhorita* he was about to call her. "You will find a way. Jacob knew you would, and he was never wrong. I must go now, talk to the people. They all loved him, but when our time comes, we have nothing to say about it." He shrugged his shoulders in a typical Brazilian gesture that Scott used sometimes. It tugged at her heart.

She twisted the ring on her finger. She'd worn it on her right hand, but still Sergio had caught some kind of signal from her. It made Scott's abandonment so heartbreaking. What if she did what her father wanted and what her logic told her was most sensible and just took the next plane home?

She took Saffron's hand and motioned for Juan to follow her to the big house. "We must hurry, Juan. When Manolo comes back, he won't want any witnesses to tell of his greed and treachery."

Sergio spoke to the villagers and an exclamation erupted from their throats as if all spoke at once.

"What's that about?" She asked Juan.

He looked uneasy. "This man say need to rid people of bad house. If they burn house with old man inside, the ashes of his goodness will purify this place."

If they did that, she'd never find the money. Marisa grabbed Juan's arm and pulled him toward the house.

Suddenly a hush fell over the crowd. Marisa felt the tension spark into the air. Had Manolo returned? She swallowed past the dryness in her throat, preparing to face him. She heard Juan's indrawn breath at the same time a hard hand gripped her shoulder, spinning her around.

"Marisa."

Was she dreaming? She rubbed her eyes and looked up into Scott's anxious face

He laughed at her expression and lifted her high in the air, bringing her down slowly, without letting her feet touch the ground, then he ravaged her mouth.

"Oh God, how I missed you, love." He kissed the palm of her hand, touching his lips to her ring. *Ontem, hoje y amanha.* "I need to see your face the last thing before I close my eyes at night, And when I awake, your sweet smile is the first thing I want to see in the morning. It can't be any other way. Can you forgive me?"

Forgive *him*? She hugged him, hard. Her throat was so tight she couldn't speak. She could only nod.

"But how did you find us, Dom Scott?" Juan asked.

"I'll talk to you about your little adventure later." Scott's frown didn't go all the way to his eyes and Marisa heard the relief in Juan's sigh. "By the way—and this isn't letting you off the hook—that was a terrific landing. Angelina's people told me all about it. Congratulations."

Juan looked as if he was going to float off the planet.

"But how did you find us?" she asked, repeating Juan's question.

"Easy. I thought about what you said, and after I cooled off, I knew you hadn't lied to me. You'd made a mistake, an error in judgment. God knows, I've made enough of those in my life. When you told me you tried to correct it, I should have believed you. I do believe you."

She clung to him, feeling their hearts beat together. "I came here to find the money. I wasn't going to give up on us. I needed proof to show you I was telling the truth."

"I know. That's how I realized where you were."

"But how did you fly in? There's surely no room for another plane at Kayapo."

"I had a friend drop me."

"Drop you?"

He grinned, that lopsided, mischievous grin. She couldn't help it. She pulled his head down and kissed him, loving the feel of his smile against her lips.

"Mmm. I like that," he said. "Anyway, I did some skydiving in my time, so I had him drop me off."

"Oh, I forgot. Where are my manners? This little girl is Saffron, the one I told you about."

Scott knelt and took her tiny hand in his. "I'm very pleased to meet such a lovely young lady." Then he said it again in Portuguese.

Saffron's swollen tear-filled eyes lit with pleasure. Her wide smile spoke volumes. Boldly, for her, she leaned over and kissed Scott on the cheek, then hid her face behind Marisa's leg.

Perfect, Saffron, Marisa wanted to tell her. "Scott, there might be a problem. Her grandfather wanted her to go with me. I know that's impossible, but..."

"Why is it impossible?" He put his hands on Marisa's shoulders and looked deep into her eyes. "I know you want to teach again. This would be a perfect beginning for us. I could find you a place in Brasilia, maybe even in the condo. There are vacant offices on the first floor. Start with her and then eventually we can find others like her, willing to learn."

Marisa loved him so much, she felt every bone in her body turn to jelly and hugged him for dear life, needing his strength to support her wobbly legs. "And Juan?"

He glanced at Juan, who cringed and stepped back a pace. Reaching out his long arm, Scott held Juan's shoulder in a vice-like grip that should have made the boy grimace, if he hadn't been far too proud. "We have a lot of talking to do, but I think he's ready for his pilot's license. From there, we'll see. After the university, who knows?"

"University?" Juan's eyes grew big in his thin face, and his lips tried to form words of gratitude, but nothing came out.

Scott shook him lightly and dropped his hand, as if to say, "Never mind, I understand."

Marisa moved away, the moment too poignant to prolong. "We don't have much time. Manolo will be back soon, and I have to find that treasure chest and keep it hidden until the house is burned. I've come too far to leave without at least seeing it."

They were walking toward the big house by then, and Scott stopped her with a hand on her shoulder.

"I've been meaning to talk to you about that. Did you ever consider maybe you and your father take this money thing a bit too seriously? I mean the Bank Holiday and all. It seems to me that the community is pulling together, enjoying a common bond and doing it with humor. They know their roots and are reveling in it. I don't think it's meant to be disrespectful or ridiculing."

Marisa thought back to Virginia and how that yearly event had colored her and her father's life all these years with a grim gray pall. It all seemed so insignificant, like a world apart. Her heart and soul were here now, in Brazil.

"You're probably right. My father has always had a tendency to narrow things down to suit his own ideas of propriety and convention. Now that I stand back and look at it, the people did show a deference to our ancestors. They combined it with their spoof of the missing money, but it was never mean or ugly. Why didn't I ever see it in the right perspective?"

"Does that mean we can leave the money alone?"

Marisa shook her head. "Nope, sorry. I have to see it. I have to."

"But what will that do to the village? You said the old man was afraid of the money."

"Maybe they won't have to see it. I'll open the trunk and leave it where it is. You probably heard Sergio tell the villagers they should have El Viejo's funeral pyre within the old house. If that happens before Manolo goes back in there, it will be the end of it. We can do it if we hurry."

"Okay, lead the way."

They made a little parade of four—Marisa, Scott, Saffron and Juan—marching toward the house. The villagers followed at a distance, curiosity plain on their faces. Marisa stood on the porch and counted the slats on the flooring and then knelt and looked up at Scott. "Tear these four out." The last letter in the diary made it clear where the earliest settlers had stashed the money box.

He knelt at her side, so close she felt the electricity between their bodies. "Are you sure? Seems a shame to tear into this fine old wood."

"I know, but it will go up in smoke before long. It's a darn shame one generation didn't outgrow the fear of the house."

"My grandfather and I, we did not fear the house," Saffron said, her fine, high-pitched voice toned down to a conspiratorial whisper. "I came here many times with him when the village slept. Manolo did not fear it either."

"Well, there you go," Marisa said. "There's the new generation." "Something could be done with this house. Use some rooms for a nursery, a clinic, a schoolroom. But the money has to be lost again, if we find it."

Juan and Scott bent to the task, obviously trying to do as little damage as possible to the flooring, while Saffron ran for more tools, and Marisa kept a lookout for the tall figure of Manolo. She couldn't see or hear anything of the villagers. Fear had taken over their curiosity, and they had gone home to peer out doors and windows.

The rear of the house pushed almost into the encroaching jungle, which muffled the sounds around them—except for the usual cries of monkeys and birds in the trees.

"That's it!" Scott exclaimed.

Marisa looked down into the open wound on the porch. "Look! There it is!" She saw a large object in the murky shadows of the porch. "Let's get it out! Hurry! Manolo could come any time."

"Come on." Scott's voice was scornful. "He's just one man. You make him sound like a superman."

"You've no idea of what lengths he's gone to in order to get this money," she said. "Besides, when he's here, the young men in the village join with him. Without him, they ease away and blend in with the others."

Scott and Juan jumped down into the dark under the porch. Marisa cringed, thinking of snakes and bugs. They hauled out the chest and stood looking at it on the broken porch.

"What's it covered with? Do you suppose the money is all mildewed and damp?" she wondered.

Scott and Juan began to work on the covering. "No, they did a good job. They wrapped this trunk in canvas, coated it with liquid latex from the rubber trees, and smoked the whole chest over coals. It could probably stay buried another hundred years without harm."

When they had peeled off the cover, they stood back and looked at Marisa.

"Go on. It's your baby," Scott said.

He looked adorable, with a smudge of earth across the hard plane of his cheek and his mussed hair. She wanted to hug him more than anything else. Would opening this trunk change their lives? Probably, it would change everyone's. For that she felt sorrow, but it was something she had to do.

Kneeling in front of it, she pried open the rusty clasp and lifted the cover.

"Oh! Look at all the money!" She sucked in her breath with excitement. "I bet it's all here. No one spent a dime of it."

Scott reached across her shoulder and picked up a bundle. "No wonder," he said dryly. "It's not worth a dime."

She examined the pack he handed her.

"Confederate money?" Her voice came out in a squeak of protest.

Scott and Marisa looked at each other a moment and began laughing. They held on to each other, tears streaming down their cheeks, sides hurting until they could laugh no more, before finally collapsing on the porch steps. Juan and Saffron, puzzled expressions on their faces, watched in silence.

Marisa threw a stack of the bills into the air. The money floated down on their heads like paper rain.

"Well, looks like that's it." Scott stood up and brushed off his trousers, pulling Marisa to her feet. "What do you want to do with your treasure?" he teased.

"Let's leave the trunk for Manolo," she answered. "He surely deserves it. I wish I could watch him try to spend it." She giggled. "If we can convince Sergio the house isn't haunted, maybe they won't have to burn it after all."

Scott lifted Saffron onto his shoulders and took Marisa's hand, bringing her wedding band to his lips.

"It's going to be a bigger crowd than I expected, but we have a wedding and a honeymoon to get on with, so let's go, guys. After that, we'll head for home."

Nested against his broad shoulder, feeling his heart beat against her side, Marisa closed her eyes for a moment of thanksgiving.

'*We'll head for home.*' Were any sweeter words ever spoken?

The End

ABOUT THE AUTHOR

Born in Phoenix, Arizona, Pinkie Paranya traveled all over the U.S., Alaska, and most of Mexico with her late husband. Ever since she can remember, writing has been her passion. After completing her fifteenth novel, trying to discover the genre she loved most, she still hasn't decided.

Paranya enjoys romances with their intrigue and uplifting happy endings, but she has also published two paranormal, psychological suspense novels, a cozy mystery, and an Early American Alaskan trilogy. To date, she has thirteen published novels.

Visit Pinkie's website at www.pinkieparanya.com

WATCH FOR PARANYA'S

NEW ROMANCE

LOVE LETTERS IN THE WIND

COMING

FEBRUARY 11, 2012